Dread and Buried

ANGIE FOX

Also by Angie Fox

THE SOUTHERN GHOST HUNTER SERIES

Southern Spirits

The Skeleton in the Closet

The Haunted Heist

Deader Homes & Gardens

Sweet Tea and Spirits

Murder on the Sugarland Express

Pecan Pies and Dead Guys

The Mint Julep Murders

The Ghost of Christmas Past

Southern Bred and Dead

The Haunted Homecoming

Give Up the Ghost

Dread and Buried

Death at the Drive-In

THE MONSTER MASH TRILOGY

The Monster MASH

The Transylvania Twist

Werewolves of London

THE ACCIDENTAL DEMON SLAYER SERIES

The Accidental Demon Slayer

The Dangerous Book for Demon Slayers

A Tale of Two Demon Slayers

The Last of the Demon Slayers

My Big Fat Demon Slayer Wedding

Beverly Hills Demon Slayer

Night of the Living Demon Slayer

What To Expect When Your Demon Slayer is Expecting

SHORT STORY COLLECTIONS:

A Little Night Magic: A collection of Southern Ghost Hunter and
Accidental Demon Slayer short stories

Dread
AND
Buried

The Southern
Ghost Hunter
Mysteries
Book 12

NEW YORK TIMES BESTSELLING AUTHOR
ANGIE FOX

This edition published by arrangement with Moose Island Books.

First Edition

ISBN: 978-1-957685-15-1

MIB
Moose Island Books

"Now and then we had a hope that if we lived and were good, God would permit us to be pirates."
—Mark Twain, Life on the Mississippi

Chapter One

I gripped the rough wooden bow of the old fishing boat as we crested another wave.

"I've got you," my boyfriend, Ellis, called over the roar of the motor. He hooked his arm around me, his chest brushing my back.

Fog swirled so thick it was difficult to see the endless ocean beyond the next swell. But I felt its power. We slapped hard against another whitecap, and I winced, the frigid spray dusting my skin.

At least it wasn't raining.

"It's pretty," I said, trying to be optimistic.

"So are you," Ellis said, giving me a little squeeze.

A saucy grin tickled my lips, and I felt lucky to be there with him, even if the ocean had appeared a lot calmer from the dock. I loosened my hold on the boat and leaned back against his chest. He wrapped his arms around me tight. Safe.

A crisp wind whipped my hair into a small tornado, and I was grateful I hadn't spent any extra time curling it that morning.

Ellis rested his chin on my shoulder. "Let's get you back into the pilothouse." He wound a hand into mine, glancing behind us to the grizzled sailor who manned the wheel.

"Not until we see the island," I said, resisting his tug. "It should be visible by now."

If not for the waves and fog and endless ocean.

We weren't traveling to the ends of the earth, even if it felt like it. I braced myself as the cold cut through my jacket.

Ellis drew closer, the corners of his eyes crinkling as he studied the horizon—as much of it as anyone could make out. "You might not see it until we get there. From what I read in the brochure, the place we're headed is not much more than a mile square and hidden behind the breakers. It tends to disappear and reappear in the mist."

I'd paid more attention to the parts of the brochure with glossy pictures of the mostly restored historic inn and lighthouse. Intimate and secluded, the cheerful photographs had made me look forward to seeing it all in person. At the same time... "I suppose that's why they call it Phantom Island."

A ghostly chuckle tickled my ear, sending a chill up my spine. "Sounds like my kind of place."

Glancing over my shoulder, I caught the faint outline of a square-jawed, hook-nosed ghost. I knew him well, seeing as he haunted my property back in Sugarland, Tennessee. At times, it felt like he'd taken to haunting me personally as well.

Frankie "The German" appeared in black and white, nearly transparent in the fog. He wore a 1920s-style pinstriped suit coat with matching cuffed trousers and a fat tie. He also stood close enough to drop the air temperature on my left side by about twenty degrees.

And here I thought it couldn't get any chillier.

Frankie liked to startle me. Today, I wouldn't give him the satisfaction. "You don't care about historic sites. You came to avoid your chores at home."

I'd been hoping to leave him back in Tennessee with his girl-friend. Molly was a polite, proper Victorian ghost who haunted the Sugarland Historical Society. She and her housemates had recently come up against a cleaning project they couldn't put off, and I don't mean cobwebs. The darker spirits in the cemetery at the back of the property were attracted to the house. Given enough time, they liked to creep inside the walls and hide in the corners, under the floorboards, and in any nook and cranny they could find.

Every so often, Molly and the girls got together to send them on their way. She'd invited Frankie, if only to spend more time with him. Unfortunately for her—and for me—Frankie the hardened gangster tended to get spooked by ominous spirits. Not that he'd ever admit it to his girl. Instead, he'd declared it necessary to follow Ellis and me on our weekend getaway.

I didn't mind.

Much.

As long as he didn't stir up trouble.

The ghost grinned at me as if he knew what I was thinking.

"Hey, don't worry," Ellis said, shrugging a broad shoulder. Luckily, my boyfriend was used to seeing me frown at invisible people. He was practical, smart. A deputy sheriff with an eye for detail and a talent for solving the toughest crimes. He was also a hottie. "Just because they call it Phantom Island doesn't mean it's haunted."

Frankie hitched a brow. "Spoiler alert: it's haunted," he stated, not flinching as a rogue spray of water crested the boat, plowing straight through his chest to slap me in the shoulder. He took my glare as an invitation to continue. "I mean, think of all the places that don't sound haunted but are. There's the library back home."

"Knew that one," I said. We'd solved the mystery of the phantom in the stacks and made friends with the Civil War ghosts playing their eternal game of poker.

"There's the First Bank of Sugarland," the ghost added, counting off on his fingers.

I braced myself as the ship lurched again. "Your gangster friend really needs to stop trying to dig a tunnel under the vault."

Ninety plus years was enough. "I mean, now that Suds is dead, he's not making any progress anyway."

"There's the pond out behind your house," Frankie said, resuming his count.

I gasped. "You could have mentioned that before now." My home was my pride and joy.

"Relax." The ghost waved me off. "It's only when I host skinny-dipping parties."

My mind refused to go there. "You know what? I don't want to know," I declared. "I'm on vacation."

"That's the spirit," Ellis said, wrapping an arm around me.

"I'm the spirit," Frankie countered.

He was also on me like a tick until we succeeded in freeing him from our little entanglement. I hadn't meant to end his wild, crazy gangster ghost lifestyle by trapping him on my quiet little acre of property. I'd merely grabbed a dusty old vase from the attic, hoping it would look nice on the mantel in my parlor. The neglected relic only needed a quick rinse with the hose outside and a fat red rose blossom from the garden to brighten it up. But it turned out the vase was actually an urn, and I was way too efficient at cleaning. As soon as I'd rinsed the ash out over my flowers and watered it in good, Frankie appeared, fit to be tied, saying I'd grounded him onto my property.

It had put quite a crimp in his hard-living, dishonest lifestyle, but I tried to make things better. He could leave the property with me if I carried his urn with the little smidges of him left in there. I'd even duct taped it shut for our foray to the coast. It currently resided in the hemp bag slung over my shoulder, bumping against my side as the boat crested the waves.

"If you want to pretend there's no ghosts on that island, I'm not stopping you." Frankie shoved his hands into the pockets of his trousers. "Just keep telling yourself how much ghosts hate old hotels on isolated islands, ones with a coast so rocky and pocked with shipwrecks you have to build a lighthouse."

"You've got yourself a deal." I'd pretend.

"Holy smokes," Frankie said, rushing to the rail, forcing me to step sideways. The ghost hovered a little too close for comfort, but of course, he didn't notice. "Is that a pirate ship in the distance?" he demanded, giddy as a goat in clover.

He pointed the way, but I didn't see a thing.

Frankie was the only ghost I could see on my own. He also had the unique—and probably forbidden—power to show me the ghostly realm. When I was tuned in to his energy, I could experience the ghostly side almost as vividly as he could.

There was usually a price to pay in the form of favors for the scheming gangster. Not to mention the danger. When I was tuned in to that world, it became as real as my own. Ghostly knives could slice me; ghostly bullets could kill me. I'd nearly drowned when an angry spirit held me underwater in a haunted bathtub. Even more terrifying, I'd been on my own. No one in my world could save me.

On the other hand, tuning in to the other side had helped me start my own ghost-hunting business and solve a fair number of crimes. Justice had been served because of me. Call me crazy, but it had been worth the risk.

Plus, some of the things I'd seen were downright incredible.

"Show me the pirate ship," I said, itching for a glimpse.

"And waste my energy on this trip?" Frankie snorted. "No thank you. I'm on vacation." He loosened his tie. "I plan to have some fun."

"You haven't had energy problems in a long time." Not since he'd gotten together with Molly. "Just a peek," I pressed. I'd never seen a real skull and crossbones flapping in the breeze, not to mention a crew of swashbuckling outlaws straight out of the history books.

This could be my chance.

"I just want to see a bit of history." It was one of my favorite parts of ghost hunting, next to meeting some of the spirits themselves.

Frankie sighed. "I can't wait for you to be dead for a hundred years so you can have someone say to you, 'Oh, look at your life. It's so historical!'" He edged his jacket out of the way and planted his hands on his hips. "It gets annoying. Ghosts never do that to each other because it's rude."

"Even you said it was neat," I pointed out. "And I'm not getting gushy on them. I want to observe from a distance."

The gangster began muttering under his breath.

Then I felt the prickle of his energy wash over me like thousands of tiny cold needles piercing my skin, digging down through muscle and into bone. The ghostly power settled into my body. It dug down to my very core.

I gritted my teeth, braced myself, and focused on the swirling ocean and not the shocking invasion of the dead.

I inhaled sharply when a ghost ship swirled into view directly ahead.

"It's beautiful!" I gasped. A grand ship straight out of the history books, with billowing white sails. It crested the waves, proud and strong.

I saw a captain on the deck, barking orders to a man who saluted and scurried up a net ladder toward the highest point on the ship, a crow's nest with a... "Uh-oh."

Frankie saw it at the same time. "Dang it." He deflated. "It's a British Royal Navy frigate." The Union Jack rippled from the top of the highest mast. He shook his head in disgust as if he expected me to share the sentiment. "Whenever you get a good business going, you always get the fuzz poking around."

"Of course, you'd be pro-pirate," I observed. Frankie had dedicated his afterlife to breaking the law. He honestly enjoyed it. I didn't see the draw of booze running, armored car heists, or any of the rest, but he kept hoping I'd take a shine to it one day.

The gangster ran a hand across his jaw. "I've never met a pirate," he admitted, "but I admire their business model."

Naturally. "I thought you were turning over a new leaf." On our most recent adventure, the gangster had learned he needed to distance himself from his criminal past if he hoped to free himself from the bits of him that remained tied to my property.

"There's nothing wrong with getting to know the locals this weekend," he reasoned, "as long as they're fun." He grinned. "Or gamblers or drinkers. With any luck, all three."

"Frankie looking for trouble again?" Ellis asked wryly.

"And then some." If the gangster had his way, it would be all trouble all the time.

"Maybe this'll distract him." Ellis pointed to where a light cut through the fog ahead.

The dark outline of an island emerged from the mist, the glow of a lighthouse barely penetrating the fog.

"With my luck, it will only encourage him." Especially if Frankie was right about the island being haunted.

"Now that you've seen it, let's head inside," my boyfriend prodded as another wave splashed over the bow.

I knew why he wanted to get me off the deck, and I didn't appreciate it. "Five more minutes." With any luck, I could stretch it to ten.

"You have to face them sooner or later," Ellis pointed out.

"Later," I decided.

"Hey, nice beach," Frankie said, fixated on our weekend destination.

I tried to follow, but the view was hazy. "I can barely see it through the fog."

"Exactly. A misty shore. Great for lurking around undetected," he said, as if he were an expert in creeping, prowling, and generally slinking about.

Come to think of it, he was.

At least one of us would have a guaranteed good time. I cringed as Ellis waved to the couple standing behind the old sailor in the pilothouse.

My sister—bless her—had been giving me space. I glanced over my shoulder, the wind tangling my hair into horse knots. Melody's blonde hair, attractively tousled, cascaded down her shoulders. She wore an orange flowered sundress with a cream sweater and her usual bright, unsuspecting smile, which she currently directed toward the jerk who stood next to her.

Alec Duranja was an uptight, judgmental pain in my behind who liked to sabotage my ghost hunts, accuse me of tampering with police investigations, and argue with me for fun. And during our town's recent homecoming celebration, while I'd been working hard to solve a murder case, he'd gotten locked overnight in the library with my sister. Now they were dating.

Maybe the library wasn't simply haunted—maybe it was cursed.

A soft, misting rain began to fall.

Lovely. We were going from wind-blown, to sea-sprayed, to straight-up wet.

Melody waved me toward the sanctuary of the pilothouse. Duranja pretended not to notice me at all.

"You promised to play nice," Ellis reminded me.

"Oh, I have been," I said sweetly, returning my gaze to the sea. "I haven't said one bad thing to Duranja since we've been on this boat." Mainly because I'd been outside on the bow while he took shelter from the elements in the pilothouse.

Unfortunately, Ellis had a point. Now that my sister was romantically involved with my nemesis, she wanted us to get along—as if it wouldn't be easier for her to break up with him and date some other guy.

Naturally, Melody hadn't seen it that way. Instead, she'd taken up my case with her new love. But even she hadn't been able to convince him I was on the up and up.

For the time being, she'd made him promise he'd treat me with the respect and courtesy I was due as a member of her family —despite the fact I liked to talk to thin air. Oh, and as long as I didn't break the law during my ghost-hunting adventures, which I hadn't...much. Darned if Duranja didn't always seem to catch me when I did.

Melody told me she'd keep at it.

I didn't hold out much hope. Not that I wanted to add a stuck-up killjoy to my circle of friends.

I scraped the hair out of my face. Ellis had been standing up for my intelligence, my sincerity, and the reality of my ghost-hunting skills for years now. He'd also solicited my help on a few murder cases for the Sugarland PD. But Duranja simply refused to believe I was anything more than a kook who had everyone fooled.

It hurt.

There was no sense pretending otherwise.

And so I'd given it time. I figured Melody would eventually see past the little picnics he brought to her work, and all the crazy adventure dates they went on—I would have gone skydiving with her if she'd asked. Not to mention the silly inside jokes they had that made no sense at all. I hadn't realized Duranja knew how to joke.

They'd only been dating for a couple of months, and so far, I'd been excellent at avoiding the two of them together.

But my luck was running out.

My sister could be as determined as I was, especially when she believed she was doing the right thing. And for now, that meant showing me just how wonderful her new boyfriend could be.

To celebrate her thirtieth birthday, Melody had requested a double date, one that lasted all weekend.

She was lucky I loved her.

I was also counting on Duranja dodging me as much as I'd be avoiding him. He'd suggested separate cars in order to fit all our luggage. I'd complied by packing everything I owned in two bulging suitcases that took up an entire trunk. He'd suggested I coordinate with Melody first. I'd complied by erasing his number from my phone.

So technically, we'd gotten along great so far.

Besides, I was there for my sister, not her date. Melody and I had grown up in a cozy house down a long dirt road, and often, it had been just the two of us. Over the years, we'd created our own special birthday memories and traditions. In fact—I couldn't help but smile as my hand brushed the lovingly wrapped bundle tucked next to Frankie's urn—I'd made a gift for her that harkened back to the old days, one we could enjoy together. She was the only one who'd truly understand it. I couldn't wait to show it to her.

I squared my shoulders. I could do this. I could survive a double-date weekend with Duranja and my sister. I'd stick to safe topics, like the weather and the mist. I'd plan special time with my sister to celebrate like we did when we were kids. Duranja could pepper Melody with all the weird jokes he wanted while I snuck off for romantic interludes with Ellis. I wouldn't give Duranja the chance to criticize my ghost hunting or provoke me because I absolutely would not get involved in any ghostly drama.

So what if the island was haunted? I deserved a vacation, too. From now on, I'd resist the urge to ogle any historical ghosts and make sure Frankie kept his power to himself. With any luck, Frankie wouldn't try to hijack any of the British fleet or hunt down any pirates. Or... Never mind. There was no reason this couldn't be a perfectly pleasant time.

The boat slowed as we steered past jagged rocks, green with algae clinging to their edges.

Our boat signaled with a piercing horn, and the engine shuddered as it shifted into slow gear. I felt in my gut the measured footsteps stalking me from behind. It was *him*.

"At last." Duranja's clipped voice made it sound like an order. "Do you realize how late we are?"

I pasted on a smile and spun to face him. I'd be nice for my sister. For her birthday. Even if it killed me.

Which it might.

"Melody said it was fine," I reminded him, although I sincerely wished it hadn't been my fault.

Bless my sister, she'd been as sweet as pie when I'd gotten us off on the wrong foot that morning. I'd called her as soon as I realized on the way out of town that while I'd dropped my pet skunk

Lucy at my best friend's house for the weekend, I'd failed to leave her favorite banana toy she slept with every night. My adopted skunk would be anxious enough with me out of town, and though I despised delaying the trip, I ran home lickety-split to make things right.

From his thunderous expression, I could tell Duranja didn't care one way or another for the emotional needs of a skunk.

No wonder he always managed to set my teeth on edge.

"This is your sister's birthday," he said, as if I hadn't been celebrating with her every year since the day she was born.

"Which is why we're *all* getting along," Ellis inserted.

Duranja needed the reminder, not me. If I smiled any harder, my face would crack.

The late afternoon sun broke through the clouds and reflected onto the water as we pulled in. I'd focus on that and the bright white hotel up the way. The boat lurched as the engine thunked off, and a deckhand tied the vessel to the dock. Two porters climbed on board and started grabbing luggage.

The square-jawed menace leaned in a little too close for comfort. "Your sister picked this hotel for its unique weekend itinerary," he hissed, "and we're late for the predinner reception because you had to climb under your porch for a stuffed banana."

Not just any banana.

I notched my chin up. "Lauralee never would have found it on her own, and Lucy is going to miss me terribly. She'll need a lovey from home." Sure, Lauralee's two oldest sons had already baked my skunk her favorite cinnamon crumble treat, and her youngest had tied bows in my skunk's fur and built her a blanket fort. But that was all the more reason to make certain Lucy had a reminder I missed her as well.

"Hey, sweetie," Melody said, slightly out of breath as she caught up to her annoying date. She carried a pair of wrapped gifts done up in yellow paper with glittery pink bows. "I just had to pull these out of the luggage before they deliver it to our rooms."

I glanced to Duranja, surprised he'd be romantic enough to give my sister an early present. But he was looking at me as if he expected me to take credit.

"I'll explain in a second," Melody said, handing a flat, wrapped box to me and one to Duranja.

"What is this?" he asked before I could. I'd been distracted by Ellis's sly smile. Whatever this was, he was in on it.

I was just about to ask him to explain when a gunshot echoed across the shore.

No lie—I jumped.

A portly bearded pirate strolled down the dock toward us, an antique pistol in each hand, his silver tooth gleaming in the light of the dying sun.

"Is he real?" I asked, glancing around for Frankie. Now would be a good time to turn my power off.

"He's something," Frankie's voice sounded in my ear.

"I have a surprise," Melody gushed, clasping her hands together. She grinned, exchanging another glance with Ellis. "There's more to this double date than I let on."

"Like pirates?" I asked, hoping for a simple explanation.

Duranja stared at me.

Oh no. "You don't see the pirate?" I asked.

Duranja's jaw dropped. "Of course I see the pirate. He shot his gun. He's got the boots and the outfit and everything save a parrot on his shoulder. What else could he be?"

"A ghost," Ellis reasoned, prompting an eye roll from Duranja.

"It's a treasure hunt," Melody gushed. "We'll get to explore the island. Together."

Duranja's gift thudded to the deck.

"Sorry," he said, hastily retrieving it.

"We're a team, you see," Melody explained as her boyfriend attempted to revive a crushed pink bow. "I was afraid you wouldn't go if you knew we were all on the same team, but it'll be fun."

"And the presents?" I asked, hoping to get a clue.

"You can open them at dinner," Melody instructed. "They're to help you get along."

"Oh, so like a watch Verity can use to be on time?" Duranja prodded.

"How about a saddle for your high horse?" I mused.

Handcuffs so we could leave him on the dock?

A furrow formed between my sister's brows. "Do you have it out of your systems now?" she asked, determinedly chipper.

Duranja took her hand while I gave her a stiff nod.

"Good," she said, turning her attention to the pirate, who stood on the dock, guns holstered, thumbs resting under a wide leather belt.

"Aye, then." He nodded down at us. "Your fully immersive adventure begins now."

"Fully immersive?" I asked.

"I'm not dressing like a pirate," Duranja balked.

Ellis merely squeezed my hand. "Welcome to Phantom Island."

Chapter Two

I turned to Ellis. "You're in on this."

He didn't bother to deny it. "Melody deserves a great birthday. Besides, I can never say no to a damsel in distress."

"I'm in distress right now," I pointed out, about to be stuck on a haunted island for the double date of my nightmares. Worse, I didn't see any way to weasel out of it.

The only thing that stopped me from trying was that Melody looked amazingly happy. She stood a short distance away with her nose pressed way too close to Duranja's. He'd lost the smirk and was whispering something that made her eyes light up. She let out a giggle.

"If you need a break later, we can sneak to the mainland for pizza and a beer," Ellis murmured in my ear.

"Just warning you, I might need more than one beer." I said it plain.

The boat captain, standing nearby, snorted. "There's no escape unless you want to climb back on board with me right now," he said, adjusting his cap. "This is the only boat contracted to serve the island. I'm taking the dock crew to the mainland with me, and we won't be back until Monday morning."

"We can order delivery," Ellis assured me, as if that were the issue.

"Good luck finding a place willing to sail out this far and past those rocks after dark," the boat captain mused. "Providing you manage to get Wi-Fi," he added, helping sling the last suitcase onto the luggage cart. "It's spotty out here."

"Great," I said as he ordered his crew to prepare for the departure of our only way off the island. I didn't relish the thought of being marooned with Duranja, even if Ellis promised to keep me warm at night.

While I fretted, the pirate actor climbed up on an artfully stacked grouping of what appeared to be old rum barrels. He straightened the eye patch that had gone crooked near his red-veined nose, and hooked his thumbs under the double leather belts slung across his ample middle. "There's no escape, mateys," he announced, boots planted wide as he grinned down at us. "I'm Rebel Bill Brown, captain of *Fortune's Revenge,* and you'll be my guests for the weekend."

I gritted my teeth.

Melody winked at me.

The actor made a show of drawing off his beat-up tricorn hat, revealing wavy gray hair and a generous bald spot. "Now, I know you're here for me gold..."

"Yessss!" Frankie's voice sounded in my ear. "Please tell me this guy is for real."

"He's not real," I muttered.

"So you say," my ghost countered.

"So I know." I could see the safety pins holding his blousy white sleeves closed.

Even if there were a few coins left buried in the sand somewhere, the gangster ghost didn't need to be stealing from pirates. Or ticking them off.

Seeing as the phantom British fleet still patrolled, I'd bet the pirate actor's boots there were a few dead scallywags lurking about. And it wasn't as if Frankie could keep any ill-gotten gains, anyway. Ghosts could only permanently keep what they'd died with. It never stopped my gangster from stealing, though. He'd declared practice made perfect, and I supposed if that was the goal, he could definitely use more practice.

The pirate cackled. "The gold is buried here on this island."

"See?" Frankie prodded, as if my entire job in life was to hold him back.

"Kept safe by a crew of cutthroats and killers," the actor taunted.

"I'll get them drunk on rum," Frankie reasoned.

The actor tossed his head, the beads in his long hair clacking together. "I'll help you find it for a price," he teased. He jumped off the barrels, his hard landing shaking the boards under our feet and sending a shock up my spine. "Come on up to the old hotel, and I'll tell you a tale. A legend I had to live to believe."

"Go for it," Frankie smirked. "I'm after the real thing." With that, the gangster shrank down into a glowing orb. He zipped off the dock and down the south coast of the island.

"Hold up—" I began. But he'd already disappeared into the fog.

Curse him six ways to Sunday. I scanned the beach for any sign of Frankie. The last thing I needed was for him to get on the wrong side of a bunch of pirate ghosts and expect me to save his skin. I was determined to do my best to relax and enjoy my sister's birthday this weekend, not to mention my alone time with Ellis. Was it too much to ask that Frankie keep himself from getting keelhauled by pirates for the next forty-eight hours?

Ellis nudged me. "Don't tell me he's going to take on the real Rebel Bill Brown's crew."

Of course Ellis sensed there was a problem. I wasn't great at hiding my emotions. And, naturally, Frankie was at the heart of it.

"I won't tell you, and then we won't have to worry about it," I said, trying to mask my concern with a bit of good cheer.

"Okay, well, how bad could it get?" Ellis mused.

I didn't want to dwell on that. Let Ellis look on the bright side. I knew better than to ask how bad things could get.

The kicker was, my ghost was right about one thing; the truth was always more fascinating than the legends. And whatever ghosts he was trying to tangle with probably had more to tell than the actor with the safety-pinned sleeves.

The pirate lit an old-fashioned black lantern. "This way, mateys," he said, stepping off the dock. "If you dare." He raised his lantern and gestured to a rocky path leading up the hill toward the lights of the historic hotel.

Melody grinned at me.

I held back. "What about our things?" I asked, tempted to at least grab the overnight bag with my essentials. It felt strange to abandon everything at the dock.

"Leave them," the actor ordered. "There's no one around who could take them. The other guests arrived hours ago and are already at the hotel. We're all alone."

That wasn't as comforting as I'd hoped.

"It'll be fine," Ellis assured me.

"It will," I decided.

Ellis was right. This was our fun getaway weekend.

My boyfriend might be a hardened officer, but I had to give him credit—he never went looking for trouble.

It usually found him all on its own.

A strange energy prickled at the back of my neck as I followed the others down the dock and toward the sandy beach. Then I saw why. Blending into the sea mist, I spied the ghost of a man. He sat on one of the thick dock pilings, shucking oysters into a bucket and tossing the shells into the waves.

He wore a hoop in his ear and a battered leather vest over a white linen shirt that had seen better days. His mouth formed a thin line as he worked.

My goodness, I'd been hoping to see a pirate up close.

Our host stopped to give final instructions to the deck crew. Melody and Duranja took the opportunity to giggle about something, and I couldn't drag my attention from the spirit.

Ellis followed my gaze, though he'd never be able to see the specter. "You might have a minute. Not a Sugarland just saying 'hi' minute," he specified, "a real minute."

Cute. "Are you saying I chat too much with strangers?"

"I'd never dare," he said, kissing me on the cheek and leaving me to it.

No matter what, I couldn't pass up the chance to at least say hello to a real pirate. I approached him casually. He worked at a steady pace, his mind on the task at hand, his linen shirt fluttering in the breeze coming in off the waves.

"Hi," I said, stopping several feet away from him. His jaw flexed as he gazed out over the water. "I'm Verity Long." I clasped my hands in front of me. "We're looking forward to seeing your island."

"This island is cursed," he ground out. "Best turn back ere the despair takes you too."

"Oh." I tried not to appear as shocked as I felt. And before I could ask him who cursed the place, or even who he was, he disappeared.

"Wait," I insisted as his oyster bucket began to fade away. "Hello? Sir?"

I heard his voice directly behind me. "Sadness lingers here."

I turned and caught no trace of him. "Who are you?"

He gave no response. I saw only swirling mist, and try as I might, I could only hear the murmurs of my group and the far-off cry of seagulls.

I chewed my lip. It wasn't as if I could turn back, as he'd so kindly suggested. I had a weekend celebration to attend, and the boat was basically leaving us here.

As for the curse—

"Verity." Ellis motioned to me. The group was ready to go.

Reluctantly, I hurried to join them. Curses were never good. I knew from hard experience. But I would at least have liked a bit more information. The island was cursed *how*? Shipwrecks? Bad luck? Bad Wi-Fi?

We already knew that last part.

"Frankie?" I called under my breath as I stepped off the dock and down onto the soft sand. The gangster rarely came when summoned, but I was hoping he hadn't made it far. "Frankie," I hissed.

Now would be a good time to stop seeing ghosts. Pirate curses might be a tad above my pay grade. And besides, it was Melody's birthday. I needed to focus on her.

"This had better be important," Frankie's disembodied voice said in my ear.

It was. "You mind taking your power back?"

"Turn it on; turn it off," he groused. "I'm not your undead lackey."

But I felt his energy lift and breathed a sigh of relief as much of the mist cleared. "Thanks, buddy."

The gangster gave no response. Chances were, he was already gone.

"What'd you see?" Ellis whispered, taking my hand.

"I'll tell you later," I promised.

Water lapped against the dock. Waves rolled over the rocks and washed up on the sandy beach. It felt like the calm before the storm.

Pirate Rebel Bill Brown led us up a gritty path made from crushed seashells. Spindly grass encroached on both sides as we slanted uphill. The path steepened, and our guide's breath became more labored as he trudged ahead of the group.

"The reception started a few minutes ago," he said, dropping his act. "You didn't miss anything." He swiped the sweat from his upper lip. "Well, you did miss the Q&A about the island, and I probably told one or two guests more than I should have about the pirate gold," he admitted sheepishly, "but you didn't miss anything else."

"Then you need to tell us, too," Duranja said, making it more of an order than a request.

"So is there actual pirate gold on this island?" I asked, hoping

Frankie wasn't around to hear the answer.

The pirate turned and began walking backward. "You don't know?" he asked, shaking out the tangled gold chains at his neck.

"I wanted it to be a surprise," Melody told him. To us, she added, "It's a treasure hunt based on a real mystery dating back to the 1700s. Although, sorry to say, the real gold is long gone."

"We don't know that for sure," the pirate cut in.

"There's no proof it ever existed," Melody said, sweet but firm. "However, the prize for this weekend's treasure hunt is ten thousand dollars." She paused to let that one sink in. And I admit, I stumbled on my next step. "We can split it four ways."

That would be a heck of a birthday present.

Duranja and I exchanged a surprised glance. "How did you get us in on the hunt?" he asked.

The entry fee had to be steep, and Melody worked at the Sugarland library. Her big yearly bonus was one of the library director's famous homemade Nutella pies with potato chip crust and a gift certificate to Hugh Lowell's Christmas tree farm.

"The tickets were Mom and Carl's gift for my big day," she gushed. "I told them how much I wanted to do something fun and exciting with my favorite people."

"Wow," I managed. My mom and stepdad had really gone all out. I hadn't realized how much this weekend meant to Melody. I doubted it was even about the prize money for my sister. That was more to up the ante and to get us working together.

But I could sure use my share of the prize. My home was lovely and historic and had been in the family for generations. It also needed a new roof, and this would help cover it. Quite literally.

"You're brilliant, Melody," Duranja declared, with a fresh pep in his step. "I'm all for a little friendly competition," he said with a little too much relish, "and you've got the best team going."

I wouldn't debate him on that. Duranja was detail oriented to a fault, and Ellis was the most intuitive officer on the force. Together, they'd solved plenty of impossible cases. I had the advantage of being able to tap into the ghostly side to solve mysteries, and I had a feeling Frankie would be very interested in helping us win a cash prize.

"I'm glad you're excited." The actor grinned. "I want people to go crazy, to spread the word so everyone wants to come out and see the island."

"How'd you find out about it?" I asked Melody.

She flipped her hair off her shoulder. "You saved that postcard for me, the one you got about pirates off the Carolina coast."

"That's right," I said, remembering. She'd been doing a library display to support the elementary school unit on the original thirteen colonies.

"The pirate section was a hit with the kids, and I was able to read all about Rebel Bill Brown. Hopefully that will give us an advantage."

Our host tugged on his beard, pleased. "This hunt is already a sensation in the towns along the seaboard. The locals can't stop talking about it. In fact, you'll be competing against one of the top historians in the county. This guy literally owns the Coastal Islands history museum."

Duranja grabbed a vivid green stone from the side of the path. It almost looked like sea glass. "I think we passed that museum on the way here," he said, tossing his prize in the air and catching it. "It's the one in the powder blue clapboard house."

"You're very observant," our host said, eyeing the rock Duranja held. He raised his lantern and quickened the pace. "You'll also be competing against Zadie and Zara Williams. They won TV's *Treasure Race* a few years ago."

Melody lit up. "I watched that show. It's like *The Amazing Race*, only better."

"And more ruthless," Duranja said.

Our host inclined his head, not bothering to deny it. "The internet would go crazy if they won," he said absently. "There's one more couple competing. I think you'll find them very interesting," he added cryptically.

"Why? Is he a professional treasure hunter?" Ellis asked.

"Not fair," Duranja said when our host pressed his lips together.

"No. No professionals allowed," our host insisted. "We want amateurs. The more the better. It's more fun that way."

"Plus the professionals might expect a bigger prize," Melody said pragmatically, slipping her hand into Duranja's.

The actor grinned. "I was being sly because he is a famous mystery writer, and she's a former medical examiner."

"Famous?" Melody asked.

"What's his name?" I clamored.

"I'm more worried about a medical examiner with police training," Duranja cut in. "We can beat any hack mystery writer. Not to mention a historian and the *Treasure Race* twins. None of them have our investigative experience."

"True," I agreed, generously placing myself in the mix with the professional investigators. I had closed several cases. I'd pitted myself against killers, both dead and alive, and had come out on top. And I didn't have to do it by myself this time. "I mean, I assume the four of us will be working together."

"We will indeed," Melody said, her lips tilting upward.

Yes, she was getting her way. But I didn't care. There was something about a mystery that always put a spring in my step. And this one would be pure fun—no killers after us. No ghosts who needed my help. Just me and Ellis and Melody. I could ignore Duranja. No doubt about it, this would be a weekend to remember.

"Are you ready to uncover the secrets of Phantom Island?" the actor asked, slipping back into character as we approached a large clapboard inn. Sturdy, gray slate steps led up to a gorgeous old building with wraparound porches on both floors. A wooden sign next to a white-painted rock read *The Phantom Hotel, all welcome.*

"Ready as ever," I promised as he stepped toward the red wood doors.

"Then let the game begin," he declared.

Chapter Three

The pirate opened a pair of blood-red doors and led us into the historic hotel. It smelled of aged wood and warm fires. The lobby ran wider than it did long, with polished white oak floors and an antique chandelier above the door. Flickering bulbs under etched glass reminded me of gaslight.

A battered, hand-hewn canoe stood propped on display to our right. Straight ahead, a grand white staircase displayed elegantly curved spindles and lush red-carpeted risers.

A pair of twins gathered near the foot of the staircase, their heads bent together as if sharing a secret. Tall and athletic, they'd dressed for action in matching charcoal cargo pants paired with soft, black yoga sweaters. They communed in front of a check-in desk that appeared as old as the hotel itself. Brass keys hung in neat rows in a cubby behind it.

One of the twins grabbed a mint from a polished tray on the counter and flipped it into her mouth, watching me as she made a side comment to her sister. When the sister's gaze darted to me, I waved in a friendly manner.

"That must be Zadie and Zara," I said to Melody, heading over to make their acquaintance.

"Stop," Duranja ordered in my wake, as if I wasn't supposed to acknowledge the competition.

The twin on the left straightened as I approached. "I recognize you," she said, managing to sound both intrigued and distant at the same time. "You were on *Naked and Afraid*."

"Ha." I choked a little. She'd managed to both shock and surprise me, while kind of making me want to be whatever person she thought I was. "No. That would never be me," I said, smoothing my cheery striped nautical sweater over my white jeans. "Not naked." It was important to get that straight. "Afraid plenty of times," I added, only partly in jest. "My name is Verity, and I'm a ghost hunter."

"Zadie," said the one on the left, sizing me up.

"Zara," said the other.

"It's a pleasure." Most people either called me crazy or at least took pause when I told them what I did for a living. I was beyond hiding who I was or what I could do, but it felt good when they took it in stride. "Congrats on *Treasure Race*," I said in all sincerity. I'd never seen the show, but coming out on top of a big, international reality competition had to be tough.

Zadie's eyes narrowed. "We won it fair and square, and we're going to win this time as well."

I rolled with it. "Believing in yourself is—"

"We've learned this island better than you know your own backyard," Zara said. "Topography, tidal maps—"

"Every nook and cranny in this hotel," Zadie added.

"I read the brochure," I ventured. That didn't sound good, even to me. I suddenly felt woefully unprepared. "It appears our team will have to rely on our investigation skills," I said, reassuring myself. "Two of our members are police officers."

Zadie smirked. "We beat two hotshot teams of police detectives on tryouts for *Treasure Race*."

"It's a different skill set," Zara concluded.

I tried to mask my disappointment, but I could feel my face fall. "We'll see." I believed in us.

"The FBI agents almost made it to the televised round," Zara conceded, with an awkward wave of a hand. "It's true," she reminded her scoffing sister. "So, hey, best of luck to you," she added to me, as if I needed it.

"I hope we all do our best," I said, meaning every word. That's all any of us could expect, right? Besides, I wasn't so much interested in the smack talk and sizing each other up as I was getting to know my fellow players. As a first step, I had to ask, "How should I tell you apart?" Both had the same heart-shaped faces, high cheekbones, and flawless dark brown complexion. They wore their hair cut short in the exact same style and sported identical dragon earring cuffs, the eyes glittering with diamonds.

"You don't," Zadie said.

"It's part of our charm," Zara added.

Okay, well for now, Zadie had her sleeves rolled up. But later?

"Zadie is the pragmatist, and Zara is the charmer," declared a booming voice behind me.

The twins rolled their eyes and took the opportunity to escape while I turned to see a dashing man in his early forties with a thick head of perfectly styled auburn hair and a winning smile.

"Wow, you could be in a toothpaste ad," I said without thinking. Perhaps I needed a better filter. But honest-to-goodness, his teeth were so straight and white they almost didn't look real.

"I'll keep that in mind if my next novel flops," he declared with a jovial wink. He wore a dark blue button-down shirt, open at the collar, tucked into black dress pants. The look was both polished and understated, as if he were trying to blend. "I'm just glad to find one person on this island who isn't out for blood," he said, leaning against the counter the twins had vacated.

"I could be vicious," I countered. "You don't know."

"The dangly skunk earrings aren't exactly hardcore," he pointed out.

I toyed with a ceramic skunk. "They were a gift from my boyfriend." Ellis was sweet that way. "It doesn't mean I'm not daring."

"It *is* brave to wear wedge sandals to a treasure hunt," the author agreed. "Besides, I couldn't help but overhear your conversation with the twins."

"What's their deal?" I asked, seeing the twins had regrouped behind a dark leather couch at the far end of the lobby.

"Hyper competitive. Street wise. Would sell their mother for two Snapples and a tray of sushi." When I laughed, he dropped his bemused expression. "I'm not kidding. During a special season of *Treasure Race 'Family of Champions' Edition*, those two kicked their mother off the team in exchange for a 'dream team dinner' and a beverage treat of their choice. In the middle of the Mojave Desert."

"Brutal," I said. Both about the race and the decision.

"Rick Stone," he said, offering me his hand. "I'm here for the research."

"Verity Long." His grip was warm and firm. "I'm here for a birthday party," I said, gesturing to my sister and Duranja sequestered in a quiet spot behind the canoe, partially obscured by a window curtain. Melody had a hand on his chest, talking while Duranja glared at me as if I were doing something wrong.

Again.

"Some party," Rick said, following my gaze.

"That's the birthday girl and her date. My boyfriend, Ellis, is outside." I directed his attention past the front doors, away from the train wreck-to-be that was my sister's new relationship. "Next to the incredibly large ship anchor." It was a beast, with pointed metal ends. Mounted upright, it stood almost as tall as Ellis.

"The plaque says it comes from the pirate ship *Fortune's Revenge*, circa 1722. But I think they bought it on eBay," Rick stated.

"Then the shipping fee must have been brutal."

He laughed. "I like how you think."

I focused on Rick. "Pirate Bill said he gave you and the others some insights before my friends and I arrived. Did he say anything special about the anchor? Or anything else?"

"Not that I can recall," the author said cagily.

Nice play.

And he'd claimed he was here for the research.

Rick cocked his head at me. "I did hear you're with the police," he said, his tone casual. But there was an excited edge to it. He was curious about us.

"I consult," I told him, because I had. Maybe if he knew we were the real thing, he'd open up a bit. "Ellis and Duranja are both detectives in Sugarland, Tennessee," I said, indicating to the two men I'd come with.

Rick leaned back and rested his elbows on the countertop. "My wife is a medical examiner with the NYPD." He cocked his head. "You know, we might be able to help each other. At least until we leave the twins eating our dust. Want to get our two teams together over dinner tonight?"

"I like that idea." It would hopefully keep me from having to talk to Duranja.

Or open the colorful present I'd left on the counter of the check-in desk.

"It's a date, then." His gaze darted to the staircase. "Well, if Mindy ever makes it down."

"She taming her hair after that boat ride?" I asked. "I wouldn't blame her," I added, fully aware I probably had a rat's nest on top of my head.

"Seasick," he said, grimacing.

And I hadn't thought anyone could have a bumpier ride over than we had.

The pirate actor slapped Ellis on the back, chuckling as they strode to where I stood with the author. "We're getting ready to start," he informed us, the beads in his hair jangling. "Mr. Stone, why don't you go see if that wife of yours wants to come down?"

"I'll text her," Rick said, pulling a phone out of his back pocket.

"No service," our host reminded him.

"Ah. Right." The author stuffed his cell back into his pocket and headed for the stairs.

The actor straightened his tricorn hat. "Everyone else follow me to the library, where we will begin our adventure."

Ellis took my hand and squeezed, giving me a wink as we followed "Rebel Bill Brown" past the closed gift shop and toward a room off the lobby.

He leaned in close. "I learned something interesting from our actor friend."

"Tell me," I whispered.

"Later. When we're alone," he promised.

Duranja waited for us by the entrance to the library. "Give me a minute," he said, drawing me aside. When he had me to himself, he sighed like I'd been poking him with a stick. "Can you keep to our team and stop being so chatty with everyone?"

I could, but I didn't see the point in it. "We're here to have fun." I didn't do anything wrong. He should know. The man was from Sugarland, after all. Most folks there could make friends waiting for a sandwich at the deli. "I was just being friendly."

My answer made him jumpier than a June bug on a string. "This isn't a friendly competition," he hissed.

"Not with you around." I turned and sauntered into the library.

"What was that about?" Ellis asked, waiting for me.

"Absolutely nothing," I said honestly.

Ellis shot him a questioning look as we entered, but I was done with it.

Melody had made it in before us and was geeking out over an antique globe on a bearskin rug. The twins gathered next to a massive stone fireplace, watching her. Flames crackled in the hearth flanked by wingback chairs.

A pair of leather couches anchored the center of the room, with a large chest serving as a coffee table between them. Built-in wooden bookcases dominated the far wall, packed with volumes, save for one section that gaped empty.

Below it, books teetered at least knee high, stacked like Jenga blocks. A man wearing work boots and a denim shirt tucked into tan chinos stood with his back to us and his nose buried in yet another volume.

"Ah, if it isn't Professor Fielding—" the actor began.

"I prefer 'doctor,'" he said, not bothering to look up.

"Kevin," our host clucked, "let's be polite."

"Bill," the professor admonished, his finger keeping his place in a leather-bound volume as he turned, "I earned the right to be called doctor. I'm also in the middle of—" His irritation shifted to surprise when he noticed us all standing behind him. "Oh, hello."

He looked to be in his midsixties, with high cheekbones and wire-frame glasses.

"Dr. Fielding has been dying to study the island, but the island needs paying guests, not scientists poking around—"

"Preserving," the doctor corrected.

"So he had to buy a ticket like the rest of you," the actor said proudly.

"Isn't that charming?" the professor asked without a speck of humor, one finger still in the book.

"Welcome to the pregame cocktail party," our host gushed, ignoring the scholar's ill mood. "If you'll turn your attention this way." He directed us toward the large bay window overlooking the water. "We have both red and white wine, along with a pitcher of sweet tea, set out on the map table."

"My *maps* are on the map table," Dr. Fielding balked. He stuffed his glasses into his book to hold his place and planted the whole thing on the teetering stack next to him before stalking toward the small assemblage of bottles and glasses on a lovely antique wood table with long drawers set into the front.

"They're not your maps, and I put them in the drawers while you were out digging around under the apple tree," our host shot back, blocking the bustling professor from reclaiming the space. "You're not as sneaky as you think. Now have some cheese and crackers," he said, handing the man a plate.

"Did you return the maps to their original drawers?" the professor asked, sidestepping our host in an attempt to slide open the top drawer. In his haste, he accidentally knocked a tray of chocolate-covered strawberries, nearly sending them careening to the floor.

He didn't notice.

"This is a hotel, not a museum," the pirate insisted, going red in the cheeks as he inserted himself between Dr. Fielding and the welcome reception snacks. "My father ran it before me and his father before him—with flair and pizzazz. You are being terribly inhospitable. And might I remind you, you are a guest, not the conservator," he added, forcing a hollow chuckle.

The professor wasn't as easily embarrassed in front of a crowd. Still, he did have some manners. He rested his hands on his hips and nodded to himself more than anyone. "I'll go through the entire map drawer later and organize it," he promised the pretend pirate, who appeared as if he'd rather eat the maps than sort them.

"Goodie," he said to the professor. He clasped his hands and addressed the rest of us. "Feel free to grab a plate or a drink. Make yourselves comfortable while I tell you the story behind the treasure you seek. Pay careful attention, because after this, I'll send you in search of your first clue."

That perked up the twins by the fireplace. They made their way to the front of the group.

"You ready?" Ellis asked.

"Excited," I admitted. I liked a challenge.

Duranja nudged past me to pour a glass of white wine for Melody, who wrapped both her arms around one of mine.

"Isn't this the most romantic place ever?" she asked, squeezing my arm, all lit up inside.

"Are you going to pay attention to the mystery?" I countered.

"Sure. Of course," she promised, accepting a glass from Duranja. He'd poured an iced tea for himself.

Ellis had grabbed a pair of red wines and a plate for us to

share. I accepted it gracefully, not certain if I should partake. I wanted to stay sharp.

Then Duranja nuzzled my sister's ear, and I found myself downing a good portion of the glass.

Ellis leaned close. "Don't worry. This is going to be great."

"Right." I sure found the idea of a weekend mystery exciting. And considering I'd faced down dead hit men and poltergeists, I figured I could handle the twins and even a few dead pirates if it came to it. But this was my sister. And an entire forty-eight hours with Duranja.

"You didn't toss your wineglass at him," Ellis observed. "It's a start."

"I am the soul of propriety," I said, toasting my date with what remained in my glass.

The actor positioned himself in front of a pair of rusty iron keys mounted in a frame on the wall. Each one was easily as long as my hand. As I drew closer, I saw the black cloth behind them was actually a scrap of an old black flag with a white bone hand-stitched on it. "Is that part of a Jolly Roger?" I asked, instantly smitten.

"Part of an old pirate flag my grandfather found down in one of the caves in the 1930s," the actor said proudly. "His father built this place, and Gramps liked to dig up souvenirs to draw in the tourists."

The professor began choking on his wine.

At least he'd gotten a glass.

"Captain Bill is a direct ancestor," our host confided. "Take a look," he said, leading me to a framed black-and-white picture on the wall.

Fading ink on stained and weathered paper showed a portrait of a stern-looking gentleman with the same full lips and bushy beard as our host. The pirate had a sharper nose and a leaner physique. Pictured in the stiff illustration style of the day, he held aloft a sword and wore a menacing scowl while ships burned on the ocean behind him.

"You look just like him," I said, opting to be generous to our grinning host as he lifted his eyepatch to scratch underneath.

"I was named after Captain Bill," he said, adjusting his patch, yet still managing to leave it crooked. He backed up to let the rest of the group admire the etching of his ancestor. "Excuse me." He stepped away to greet a late arrival, a thin man in black jeans and a polo.

The man rested a professional camera on his shoulder while shaking hands with our host.

"This is Steve," the pirate announced. "He's here to take publicity photos for the weekend, so please, forget he's here."

Steve raised his hand in a wave and took a quick, casual shot aimed in our direction.

"I think I had my mouth open," Melody lamented.

"I guarantee my eyes were closed," Duranja added.

"Don't worry about it," Bill said. "We want good pictures as much as you want to look nice. Now"—he took his place at the head of the group, right next to the framed photo of his ancestor—"I'd like to tell you the story of pirate Bill Brown. Rebel Bill Brown, they call me." He chuckled, slipping into character as he edged closer to the drawing on the wall. "You see, I grew up in a wealthy family, in a respectable town, until I went rogue." He gave us a practiced wink.

I noticed Rick had returned. He leaned against the polished wood trim of the doorway without his wife.

"I came from Folly Bay," the actor said, his voice booming over the room. "The very town you departed from. I joined a pirate crew at the age of sixteen, captained my own ship by the age of twenty, and by the time I died at thirty-four, I'd captured scores of foreign ships and stolen more than seven hundred and fifty thousand dollars' worth of goods and gold." He waggled his brows. "That's thirty million dollars in your money today. None of it was ever recovered," he said, pausing to let that one sink in.

"You mean it's still hidden?" Zadie barely concealed her delight.

"Pillaged two centuries ago," the professor said.

Pirate Bill raised a finger. "You never know!"

"Experts have concluded—" the professor began.

"Experts, schmexperts." Bill dropped the act. "Were you there for the pillaging? No. Therefore, you don't know anything."

"I wasn't hanging around to meet Al Capone and open his vault, either," the professor reasoned. "The 'not knowing' is the only thing keeping this island in business," he added offhandedly. "And now a treasure hunt. Have you no respect for proper research methods? Don't you know what your schemes are doing to this historic site?"

"What I know is everybody loves pirates," the actor concluded. "And Captain Bill, I mean *I* was the best kind of pirate," he said, slipping back into character. "We used to use long wooden matches to light the cannons. Well, I liked to light them and tuck them into my hat." He brought his hands up to theatrically grip the tricorn hat he wore. "The lit matches stuck out on either side of my face and made me look like a wild man in battle. Scared them to death. One captain had a heart attack on the spot."

"There's no historical proof of the heart attack—" the professor inserted.

"Let's just say there were times I needed to disappear," our host continued over the historian's protest. "And Phantom Island was the perfect home base. No one dared follow me here."

"Why?" I asked, more to Melody than anyone.

"Shh..." she said, when the actor halted.

"I mean if everybody knew he was here..." We weren't *that* far off the coast. Plus, I had it on good authority the British fleet had patrolled these waters. I doubted they'd be too turned off by a few matches in a hat.

"Good question!" the pirate gushed. "I actually forgot this part." He clasped his hands. "Phantom Island got its name because of how it disappears in the mist. Pretty spooky, right?" He planted his hands on his hips. "Add in tales of tragic shipwrecks and the fact that it's basically a big, windy, foggy rock, and you've got a hideout everyone thinks is haunted. Not that it can't also be a great vacation destination," he corrected. His face fell as he realized he'd lost his pirate mojo. "Anyhow." He cleared his throat and adjusted his eyepatch. "Phantom Island was the perfect hiding spot," he said, sinking into his role once more. "No one knew this was my base for years. No one dared build more than a lighthouse until this hotel went up in 1902. Almost two centuries too late for me," he joked. "I would have liked staying in a nice room like yours," he said, pointing to Zadie.

The twins rolled their eyes.

"My only downfall was love," he said, sparing a wink for Melody and Duranja. "One day, while pillaging my old home-town, I was instantly smitten with my brother's fiancée. So I stole her, too," he said, smirking as Duranja automatically pulled Melody closer. "I kidnapped her to this island to be my pirate bride. In fact, I brought her ashore not far from where your boat docked today. I gifted her with treasure the likes of which you've never seen before—a king's ransom of bridal jewels and gold. Would you go for it?" he asked my sister.

"Hardly." She chuckled, making eyes at my nemesis.

"Catherine was reluctant as well. Then my brother found me. He ambushed me by the caves near the shore." He whipped out his costume sword with a flourish and nearly knocked the framed keys off the wall. "I fought my brother and stabbed him in the heart."

The professor gasped as the frame wobbled.

Our host grinned. "My bride-to-be witnessed the tragic encounter. She cursed me and my treasure. While I buried my brother, she dressed herself in her bridal gown and jewels and jumped to her death from the cliff at Pirate's Bay."

"That's terrible." Melody tsked.

Our host planted the tip of his sword on the antique hard-wood floor. "Legend says I buried her and her bridal treasure on this island and set sail the next day, hoping to leave her in peace and her curse behind me." He sheathed his sword and strode toward us. "But a mighty storm whipped up as I was leaving, smashing my ship against the rocks and sinking it with my full crew on board." He stopped in front of me. "None of us survived." He tilted his chin down. "On certain foggy nights, you can sit on the porch of this very hotel and watch our ghostly ship set sail."

I liked that. "Have you seen it?"

"Plenty of times," he insisted to the audible scoffs of Duranja and the professor.

"That's wonderful." He shouldn't listen to the naysayers. I knew all about what it was like to have your home and your stories treated like they didn't mean anything.

Pirate Bill winked at me. "Archaeologists discovered the wreck of the *Fortune's Revenge* in the 1920s, but found no trace of my treasure." He looked to Ellis. "No one has found any trace of me either, although some say I haunt the caves, guarding my gold."

"I thought your gold was in the ship," Duranja pointed out.

"You said you buried it on the beach," Rick added.

"It could be anywhere," Bill insisted.

"Or nowhere," Duranja muttered.

"But there's a chance we could find it," Zara said, getting to the heart of the matter.

"You never know..." the pirate teased.

"Not a chance," the professor interjected. "People have been searching for Captain Bill's gold since he sank. The real treasure is in the history of this place and the artifacts."

"The pirate's treasure was the main draw of this hotel when it was first built," Bill said. "My great-grandfather had a rule: you got to keep any loot you found. People came out here in droves. Some left with coins they'd dug up in the sand. Lots explored the caves, but nobody found the treasure. So if you ask me, it's probably still here."

The professor gritted his teeth. "The 1927 archaeological investigation cast serious doubts that this island is the legendary

Phantom Island at all. The story has always been a tourist ploy, and who knows how much local history has been destroyed in the process of marketing."

"Ha!" Our host rested a hand on the hilt of his sword. "The legend is real, and you are going to live it this weekend. You'll be following in Rebel Bill's footsteps to find a 24-karat gold medallion. It weighs five ounces and is worth ten thousand dollars."

Ellis let out a low whistle, and I didn't blame him. That would be neat to simply hold, much less spend.

"From history?" Zadie gasped.

"Better," the actor promised. "Newly minted and appraised last week."

"And it actually exists," Duranja observed.

Our host hooked his thumbs under his wide leather belt. "The treasure hunt will take you to the lip of the cave where the brothers faced off, to the cliff where the bride took her fatal leap, and to the secret entrance to the hidden harbor where the *Fortune's Revenge* set off on its deadly last journey. And if you're lucky, it will lead to where your treasure is buried."

"Your first task begins here in the hotel. Hidden in each of four rooms is a mini treasure box with a unique map scrap and an essential tool you'll need to find the treasure. Each team gets a room, and there is only one map piece and tool per team. You might have to work with your competition and bargain for tools and information if you're going to find the treasure first. If you don't find your box before the dinner bell, you'll forfeit what's inside, and it will go to the team who finds theirs first."

"What do we do when we find it?" Zadie demanded.

"How do we let everyone know we're first?" Zara asked on her sister's heels.

"Come with me," our host said cryptically. He led us out of the library and across the expansive lobby to an iron ship's bell hanging beside the entrance to a small dining room. "I'll be right here," he assured us. "First one to show me your prize and clang the bell wins first place." He plucked a ring of tiny keys from his front pocket and jangled them at us. "I'll also open your mini treasure chest for you."

He paused an extra second for the photographer to take a photo, then our host withdrew a piece of paper from his pocket and made a show of straightening it as he located his reading glasses. "It's twenty minutes to dinner, so there's not much time. You may begin searching your assigned rooms on my signal. Zara and Zadie, you're starting out in the dining room."

The twins broke from the group and stood in the entryway to their room, their bodies pulsing with the urge to move. "Your clue is: salted meat, pickled vegetables, and grog. Your treasure is under a painted log."

"What?" Zadie demanded.

"I'll repeat it again at the end after everyone is gone," our host offered. "Mr. Stone, I'm assuming you'll do this alone."

"Unfortunately," the writer conceded.

I hoped my new almost-friend wouldn't be without any clues to bargain with. I'd meant it when I said I'd like to work with him, at least in the beginning.

"You're in the bar, Mr. Stone. Take the hallway by the stairs and follow it to the rear of the building."

He nodded. "I saw it earlier. Neat place."

Our host warmed at the compliment. "Your clue is: rum, brandy, beer and wine. Your treasure is hidden with a vintage find."

"Got it," Rick said, nodding one too many times.

I leaned closer to Ellis. "Maybe we should help him after we find our mini treasure chest."

"Let's find ours before we worry about his," Ellis murmured.

Right.

"Dr. Fielding, you're in the library," our host said, as if it were expected. "A pirate is only as good as his tale. But this volume is beyond the pale."

The professor smirked.

"Oh, no fair," Zara shot out. "I mean, you put the research expert's clue in a book? He's probably already found it!"

"Not necessarily," our host cautioned.

"I would have," Duranja said behind me. As if he'd been a crack investigator back there.

"You were too busy ogling my sister," I said, earning a frown from him.

"I'd have gotten the entire lay of this place if we'd been on time," he scoffed.

"He does have a point." Melody cringed.

Hardly. "Why are you taking his side all of a sudden?"

"Because I'm right," Duranja concluded.

Our host turned to us. "Last but not least, you'll find what you seek in the hidden room under the stairs."

"Good," I said. At least it would be a small area.

"How do we get to the room?" Melody asked.

Our host grinned. "Your biggest task is finding the entrance. Here's a hint: you won't see it anywhere near the stairs."

Oh, Lordy.

"The hotel is huge," Duranja protested. "How are we supposed to find anything if that's all we have to go on?"

"It's not that big," our host admonished. "Although it would have been beneficial if you'd had a chance to explore earlier."

Duranja glared at me. This would be a fun dinner if we didn't find our clue.

Our host adjusted his list of clues. "Fog and strife, and pirates bold. Your treasure is dark and cold."

"That does not tell us where to go," Duranja said.

"Like a 'vintage find' does?" Rick asked. "They got a log," he said, looking at the twins, who smirked. "And he got a book," he said, motioning to the professor, who was paying more attention to the antique bell on the wall than to our discussion.

"I'd caution you about making any assumptions here on Phantom Island," our host said cryptically. "Besides, I told you in the confirmation email—later arrivals get the objectively harder quests. And since you were last..." he added to our group of four.

Duranja's glare bored into the side of my head.

"I didn't think it would be that much harder," Melody reasoned.

"We have no proof it will be," Ellis said, slipping his hand into mine. "Let's keep our heads up. When the game starts, we'll see what we find."

"But everyone else knows where to go," Duranja pointed out. "We're already at a huge disadvantage."

"Have a little faith in our team," I insisted.

"Isn't that why we're here?" Ellis cut him off before he could dig himself deeper.

Melody gave him a long look, and that ended the argument.

"Fifteen minutes left," the mock pirate instructed. "Good luck. Now...go!"

Chapter Four

We scattered. The dining room was only steps away, so the twins barely had to turn around and they were there. The professor hurried across the lobby toward the library. Rick must have been a sprinter in college because the author blew past us and down the hallway between the stairs and the check-in desk, presumably to where he'd located the bar earlier.

Ellis and Duranja charged ahead, which was fine by me because we had only fifteen minutes total and less time than that if we wanted to come in first.

Melody and I exchanged a wild-eyed look. "What place could reasonably lead to a hidden room under the stairs?" she demanded as we came to a halt in front of the old staircase.

Ellis had veered to the right side, Duranja to the left, like a well-oiled machine. They hadn't discussed a plan as far as I could tell. Ellis ran his hands expertly over the solid wood paneling on his side of the stairway. Duranja had to be doing the same on his.

"Let's check the back," I said.

Melody sped past Duranja down the left-side hallway. I took the right. Both led to a small foyer at the rear of the stairs. Only she beat me to it.

I found her running her fingers over a wood panel painted

with a crudely drawn map of the island. "This would be a great way to disguise a secret button or lever." She traced painted stones that made up the rocky shore near a black striped lighthouse. "Watch it. This whole thing will pop open and—boom! Secret room under the stairs."

"And our prize." It wouldn't take any time at all to run back to the pirate and ring the bell.

Ellis was right. *Who said this had to be the hardest quest?*

I took the other side of the map, running my fingers along the dock and the beach, up around a small grouping of caves, searching for any breaks, nooks, or crannies. Anything that could house a hidden map fragment, our team's clue.

Coming in first would be a great start to the weekend. We'd be awarded any clues or map shards that any other team didn't find in the next fifteen minutes. Duranja would be put in his place. And that might even make my first double-date dinner with the unlikely couple a little more palatable.

My fingernail caught on a thick dab of paint that made up the entrance to the hotel. Hope flared then fizzled when I realized it was just...paint.

"Be gentle," I said aloud to myself, moving on to the thick globs that made up the slate roof tiles. The painting had to have been on the wall for decades. It appeared to be 1940s era or older.

"Oh, sweetie. It's me," Melody replied, running her fingers along a stream that led to a cliff.

"I didn't mean—" I began. My sister had handled historic artifacts before. She knew what she was doing and had every right to take offense, but naturally, she hadn't. I opened my mouth to apologize when Ellis joined us.

"Got something?" he asked over my left shoulder.

"Nothing." I dropped my hands. "It's solid as far as I can tell."

"I'll look it over for you," Duranja said, inserting himself between my sister and me.

"I didn't ask for help," I informed him. "And I did a good job."

"Another set of eyes couldn't hurt," Melody reasoned.

Something about him had softened her brain.

I turned my back on Duranja and the painting.

"We don't have time to retrace our steps," Ellis determined. "Where next?" He scanned the small back lobby.

Where, indeed?

Not five feet across from the painted wall, a pair of doors led to the porch outside. To my right, I saw the bathrooms and an Employees Only door.

To my left stood the open entrance to a frou-frou wood-paneled bar. A mighty *thwomp* echoed from inside as Rick tossed an oriental carpet across the floor, his hair mussed and his shirt rumpled.

He had it worse, searching for his clue all alone. "You okay?" I called.

"Oh, yeah. I do this all the time," he quipped, dropping to his knees and running his fingers along the hardwood. "Hey." He glanced up at us. "You want some advice?"

"No," Duranja snapped.

"Yes," Ellis corrected.

"He makes things up for a *living*," Melody's dreamboat hissed.

"I like him," Ellis said.

"Your treasure is dark and cold." The author took a second to rest back on his heels, wiping the sweat from his brow. "I'd head to the basement."

"Smart," I said, earning a grin from Rick and a frown from Duranja.

"You know how to get down there?" Ellis cracked his knuckles with the urge to move.

The author gave a quick nod. "That Employees Only door leads to a storage room. It'll take you down to the cellar."

"It's a good thing somebody got here early." Duranja angled past us and flung open the storage room door.

"And that some of us know how to ask for advice," I added.

But Duranja wasn't listening because he'd already charged into a narrow room crowded with extra porch chairs, mops and buckets, and shelves full of cleaning supplies.

"I think I found it," he called, cracking open the door at the back.

We raced down a set of steep servants' stairs, Duranja in the lead.

He flicked on an overhead bulb at the bottom as we spilled into the basement, Melody behind Duranja, and Ellis keeping a hand on my waist, steadying me as I nearly ran into my sister.

"The stairway is right above...here." Ellis brushed past a century-old built-in icebox with wooden doors and steel latches. He stood under the approximate location of the hidden room we needed to reach, in a small cloud of dust we'd kicked up from the earthen cellar floor.

Thick wood beams stretched overhead, the raw floorboards visible above.

"How do we get up there?" Melody pressed.

"More like how do we get in there." Ellis dragged a hand through his hair.

"There's no opening," Duranja groaned. "Even if we could get past the support beams, it looks solid."

Dang. "Okay, think," I urged. There was no way to access the hidden room from the basement, at least none I could see. The section of cellar under the stairwell was tight, the walls made of rough white stone.

Gong-gong-gong!

The bell sounded from above.

My stomach dropped.

Ellis closed his eyes. "Someone just took first."

"Argh!" I doubled over. Some small, crazy part of me was sure we'd surprise everyone and snag a victory to start. Okay. It was fine. We didn't have time to freak out. "Let's hope that was Rick." And that he'd be an ally.

"I doubt it," Duranja scoffed. "His clue talked about rum, brandy, beer and wine. So he decided to look at the floor."

"You're so literal, and it's not like you've found our clue yet." I brushed past him to take Ellis's hand as we hightailed it toward the first floor. We didn't have a second to lose.

"If we can't get in from below, we should try from above," Ellis huffed out as we clambered up single file, ran past the bar, then scrambled up the plush red-carpeted main stairs.

I'd neglected to peek into the bar to check on Rick.

"Seven more minutes!" our host called from the far end of the lobby near the restaurant. "Three more teams still need to report!"

He sounded way too happy about that.

Ellis reached the landing first. The open space was lit by a large window overlooking the rear of the property and the sea beyond. Huge paintings in ornate frames showed a variety of scowling old men. Ellis began checking behind them while I inspected the built-in window seat with fluffy red and gold cushions on top.

"Ooo...Founders Landing," Melody said, making it to the top as I tossed a cushion on the floor.

Duranja joined Ellis on pictures.

"These are the portraits of the four owners the inn has had since its founding," Melody said, pausing to take it in. "Notice the four different types of spindles on the stairway. They correspond to the four seasons."

"Not helping," I said, running my fingers over the wood window seat, hoping to crack it open.

"I'm just telling you what I know, and it might help us think," my sister reasoned.

Gong-gong-gong!

"Not again!" I winced.

Another team had finished before us.

"If you hadn't had to find a banana for your skunk, it might be us ringing that bell," Duranja muttered, inspecting the last of the portraits.

"So a contest is more important than Lucy's happiness," I concluded.

"Don't answer that," Melody ordered Duranja.

"Nothing behind the paintings," Ellis determined just as I realized the bench was as solid as a brick.

"Okay nothing on the sides, below, or above." This was getting crazy.

"There's got to be a hidden entrance in the lobby," Duranja said, gripping his head in his hands.

"Like a secret passage or something?" Melody asked.

"Of course!" This old hotel might be full of them. "I'll ask Frankie."

"Shoot me now," Duranja said.

"Frankie might enjoy that," I told him.

"Frankie!" I called as the rest of my team clambered down the stairs ahead of me and spread out across the lobby. "We need you, Frank!"

"They have *five* people on their team?" I heard one of the twins balk.

I didn't bother correcting them. Or glancing their way.

No time to be subtle. We had to be missing something. We needed to think it through, but there was no time to think.

The gangster shimmered into view directly in front of me, and I nearly fell down the last three stairs avoiding him. "Frank!" I said, swerving into Duranja, who caught me and set me to rights fast as if I were on fire.

"Don't call me Frank," my gangster buddy gritted out as I wheezed a few quick breaths.

"Fog, and strife, and pirates bold. Our treasure is dark and cold!" I beseeched the gangster.

"What does that mean?" he asked, reaching into his jacket for a cigarette.

"I was hoping you'd know. Don't pretend you haven't been snooping around since we got here."

"It don't mean I'm into poetry," he said as if I'd asked him to read me a sonnet.

"It's not poetry, it's—" I noticed the pirate actor on the other side of the lobby. Staring. "Can you show us any secret passageways?" I pressed.

"I'm a ghost, not a Google map," Frankie said, shaking out his jacket.

Now he was just playing with me. "You've never seen a Google map in your life. Do you even know what that means?"

"No, but I like how it sounds," he said, planting a smoke in the corner of his mouth.

"Forget it." I waved him off. I didn't have time to explain. The rest of my team had moved on without me.

Then I noticed my audience in the lobby.

The twins stood open-mouthed next to our host. And there was Rick, a treasure box tucked under his arm, studiously inspecting the large ship's anchor nearby.

"She's nuts," Zadie said to Zara, who didn't argue.

"They took first," the author said before I could get my hopes up for him.

"Five more minutes!" our host announced.

"Or not," Zadie quipped. "We'd just as soon have your box, too."

"Don't count on it," I said with a bravado I didn't feel considering we were no closer to finding our treasure than we had been at the start of the hunt.

The pirate lifted a finger. "Fog, and strife, and pirates bold. Your treasure is dark and cold."

"Yeah, thanks for repeating our clue," I murmured, as if that were helpful.

"Am I allowed to...?" Rick asked, taking one step toward me, then another, glancing to the pirate as he broke out into a jog.

"Be my guest!" our host boomed. "Every pirate needs a solid crew."

Rick took me by the arm. "I think I might have seen something," he insisted, slightly winded. "You trust me?"

"No," Duranja said behind me. When had he shown up?

"Yes," I said as Rick took off, leading the way.

We rushed past where Ellis and Melody searched behind the check-in desk.

"Come on," Rick said, out of breath. "I think I saw something in the old bar."

"Stop following him," Duranja ordered. "He's wasting our time."

"Unless you've got a treasure box hidden in your drawers, you'd better pipe down," I said, following Rick into a classic bar done up in leather and wood. Gold wall sconces cast shadows as he hurried me past tables and chairs to an antique fireplace.

"Fog, and strife, and pirates bold," Rick said, pointing to the carvings on the mantel, excited as a kid at Christmas.

He was right.

Under the gray stone mantel, colorful painted tiles showed a foggy island, ship battles, and pirates brandishing swords, guns, and golden coins.

Ellis drew up next to me, blocking Duranja. "Your treasure is dark and cold."

Gong-gong-gong!

"That must be the professor," Rick said, the warning clear in his voice.

If we didn't find this clue right now, it would go to the twins.

We'd be left directionless and powerless against a team that had proven themselves over and over again.

We'd basically be done for the weekend. Left in the dust. I'd be forced to actually talk to Duranja.

I could not let that happen.

"The fireplace is cold," I said, the realization thudding hard in my chest.

The hearth lay clean of ash. The logs unburned.

"Every other fireplace in this bar has had a fire," Melody said on an exhale. "Look." She began pointing around the room, but I didn't have time.

"Okay, so it's in the fireplace," I said.

"We're not anywhere close to the stairwell," Duranja pointed out.

I dropped to my knees to see if there might be a hidden lever in the iron log holder.

Ellis and Melody attacked the mantel.

Duranja began trying to pry the entire fireplace from the wall. And right when I was about to tell him he was nuts, "I found a lever!" he announced, and the fireplace cracked open a fraction.

Ellis let out a yell. Melody shrieked.

The whole log holder ground back into the hearth like it was on tracks.

Duranja choked out a laugh and appeared as surprised as I was.

"You've got it!" I said, scrambling to my feet.

Don't ask me how I knew, I just *knew*. Because if this wasn't it, we were done, and I couldn't entertain that possibility. I jammed my fingers into the space below Duranja's.

"Get out of my way." Duranja shone his light inside, yanking a green rock from his pocket and digging the pointy end into the hole like a crowbar.

"I think I see something," Ellis announced, getting in our way. "Stop it, you guys," he ordered when neither of us moved.

Ellis shoved his way past Duranja and dug his foot into the opening at floor level. "Out of the way. I think I feel another lever," he urged, stomping down and tripping a mechanism. I gasped as the entire fireplace swung open from the wall.

"You're a genius!" I declared.

"I get things done," Ellis shot back, victorious from behind the fireplace.

"I think I love you!" I charged in ahead, digging past the urn in my bag for the Maglite I always carried.

"You *think*?" Ellis asked from behind the wall.

"Wait up!" Melody called.

Good thing I flicked my light on when I did because not two steps later, the floor opened up into an ancient set of crazy steep stairs.

"Go," Melody urged, taking hold of my shoulders for guidance.

"Watch it," I warned, barreling us both down the stairs and into the soft dirt of a narrow passageway.

"Under the stairs," Melody announced, as I swung my light around. "He didn't say *which* stairs!" She pointed up at a small alcove beneath the stairs we'd just come down. "Look!"

She was under there before I could get my light on her. "Got it!" Victorious, she held aloft a treasure box exactly like the one I'd seen the twins holding.

"That was unnecessarily hard," I declared.

"Get up here!" Duranja ordered.

"Less than a minute left," Ellis warned.

Melody tucked the box under her arm, and we took the stairs two at a time in a dead run to the finish.

"Go!" Duranja urged, holding the exit with Ellis as we burst into the bar and made tracks for the bell.

"Five!" came a chant from the foyer.

I ran flat out.

"Four!"

Melody and I almost collided as we cornered at the staircase.

"Three!" The twins chanted gleefully along with our host, who held a stopwatch, his cheeks ruddy and his eyes wild.

"They're gonna make it!" Rick declared, waving his hands, as if we didn't see the old bell hanging off the wall.

"Two!"

We weren't going to be fast enough.

Melody broke ahead. I dug down inside me for every ounce of speed I had.

"One!" the actor called.

Melody held the box aloft while I reached out and rang that sucker for all it was worth.

Gong-gong-gong!

Ellis and Duranja charged out into the lobby, whooping and hollering.

Gong-gong-gong!

"We did it!" I leapt into the air and hugged Melody. The professor clapped his hands over his ears.

Gong-gong-gong!

"We're number four!" Melody chanted.

"We're number four!" I hollered.

The photographer snapped pictures, and for a second, it felt like we had paparazzi.

"You can stop now!" the professor exclaimed. I could barely hear him over the bell. I tossed the rope and hugged Ellis.

Rebel Bill Brown threw his hands up in the air. "Victory!" he declared. "You have proven yourselves to be worthy treasure hunters."

"Damned straight," Ellis said, hugging me tighter.

"You got so lucky," Zara said.

"They got help," Zadie corrected.

"You play the game your way. I'll play it mine," Rick said, winking at Zadie.

"See here, treasure hunters," the pirate said, instantly commanding the attention of the group. "You may have your hard-won prizes, but I have the keys." He held the ring with two fingers, the silver keys dangling. "So now I'll ask you to join me for a special treat and for a peek inside those boxes."

Chapter Five

Melody turned over the dark wood box in her hands. It looked like a mini treasure chest, down to the curved lid, gold bindings and latches, and a large gold lock.

"Let me see," I prodded as our host led our group toward the dining room.

When she handed it over, I brought it up to my ear and shook it. "There's definitely something solid inside."

"All will be revealed after dinner," the pirate teased.

"It's your share of the treasure map, plus an object you'll need to find the medallion," Zadie said, eyeing the similar treasure chest her sister held.

"Yes, but I wonder what kind of objects they're talking about," I said, noticing their box appeared slightly larger, with bronze rivets instead of gold.

"Come now," the pirate said, parading us past the young waitress who stood inside. "We don't want you to worry about what's in store until you've had a hearty meal and a flagon of ale."

"What about a martini?" Rick asked, clapping a hand on Bill's shoulder. "This pirate likes gin."

"So did my father," Bill said jovially. "I think we can put something together for you."

"The real pirates would have drank both," the historian said, hardly paying attention to his own box as we bottlenecked at the entrance to the dining area. "Ale was served when in port and on shorter ship journeys. It would go bad over time. But they could sail with gin forever. Although not to make martinis."

"Because we're going for realism," Duranja said, letting his sarcastic flag fly.

"We should do our best." The professor nodded, Duranja's lack of wit passing right by him.

At least Dr. Fielding could find a Duranja-less table to enjoy his dinner. I had to spend an entire evening with him.

Trouble was brewing, and I was in the thick of it. Ellis wore a pasted-on smile just like Melody did. Those two were in cahoots. No doubt she'd recruited my kindhearted boyfriend to help smooth the way for Robocop and me to get along this weekend.

It wasn't going to work. Why, only tonight, Melody had taken Duranja's side over mine. Twice. She'd agreed that he'd have a mental map of this whole place if we'd been on time. She'd said she didn't blame me, but I had to wonder. And a mental map wouldn't have done much good when he didn't catch that the missing logs in the hearth meant we'd found a trick fireplace.

Then, when he'd wanted to reinspect my section of the wall painting, Melody had seriously considered it. That would have only wasted time. And she had to know I'd been as thorough with my search as she was.

No doubt about it, Duranja was trying to drive a wedge between Melody and me. My sister and I had always trusted each other implicitly. This was the sister I could call while I was in the thick of a mystery, hanging on by a thread, and she'd have my back, no questions asked. Ever since we were little, we'd had each other's backs. And I knew we always would.

I did.

But now Duranja thought he could take over the show? Bless his heart, but no.

Duranja would never understand me or my world, and he

didn't want to. In his eyes, I was already locked in a special box he liked to call "crazy," and he'd tossed the key. Every success I'd had since I began ghost hunting seemed to lower me in his eyes. If he stuck around too long, his opinion might eventually rub off on my sister.

Still, I'd do my best to put on a brave face this weekend and be my sweetest self to Duranja, no matter what he did. Melody deserved to have an amazing birthday, and I deserved a getaway. I wouldn't let her boyfriend ruin it.

I sighed and smoothed my sweater. Besides, I'd never been on a treasure hunt before—and for a real gold medallion. I couldn't wait to explore the island on the next round. Even if I had to do it with *him*.

Zara cozied up to our host. "Hey, Bill, you know...it wouldn't hurt to let us look our maps over during dinner."

"Or skip dinner altogether and get outside before the sun sets," Zadie said, eyeing the fading light through the front window of the restaurant.

Pirate Bill waved them off. "I can't allow that because your chest also contains the key to your next quest."

"I fail to see the problem," Zara interjected.

Pirate Bill merely smiled. "This is a *fun* weekend, remember? Rest up. Enjoy. The real adventure begins after dinner." Tabletop candles illuminated four heavy wood tables at all four corners of the large dining room, like islands in a sea of unused tables. Poor Bill hadn't drawn much of a crowd. The setting sun cast the sky in streaks of red and gold above the deep, dark water. "You'll find your team place card on your assigned table."

"Fine," Zara gritted out, stalking toward a table near the windows overlooking the dock and the water.

"Maybe we can pick it with a knife," her sister muttered by way of consolation.

"I didn't see anything in the rules against it," Zara agreed.

"We have rules?" I asked.

"There's a rule card up in your room, along with a welcome packet," our host said.

Shoot. We hadn't had a chance to get up there yet.

"They seem to know exactly where they belong," Ellis said, keeping an eye on the twins.

"So does the professor," I said. He too selected a table at the front, his closer to the exposed stone wall.

"Ah, yes," our host said. "The tables were assigned upon arrival. The best table went to the first complete team to arrive. The second best table to the second, and so on."

"Like the treasure box clues," Melody said, somewhat dejected.

"Most of the place cards have been out all day," our host explained.

"Which is why we're by the kitchen," Duranja gave me the side-eye as we made our way toward the back.

I pretended not to notice.

"Let it go, bro," Ellis muttered.

There was nothing to be done about it now. "We're doing great," I reminded them. We had our treasure box. We had our table.

"It's still a pretty view," Melody called as she craned her neck to see the sunset from our dark table near the wall.

A sconce made to look like a nautical lamp cast soft yellow light. "This is nice," I said, with genuine sincerity. "It's cozy. We have all weekend to see sunsets," I added, purposely sitting with my back to the view.

And while I'd only meant to put a positive spin on our situation, I somehow ended up seated across from my nemesis, with the pirate chest on the table between us.

Ellis slipped into the seat next to me. "I can't believe we finished the first task without a second to spare." He grinned, running a finger over the lock.

"Did you see Verity run?" Melody gushed. She planted her chin in her hands. "I haven't seen you take off like that since we found that baby pig in the woods after school and decided to dress it pretty."

"That baby wild boar looked great in my doll clothes. Well, until mamma boar busted through our tea party."

"If you hadn't dropped those Nilla Wafers, we'd still be running." Melody laughed, leaning back to let the waitress place a salad in front of her.

"You're still a troublemaker," Ellis teased, unfolding his napkin onto his lap.

"And fast enough on your feet," Duranja managed, probably wishing the boar had been a little faster. Melody grinned at him, and his expression lit up.

"I'm so glad everyone is having fun," she said with the kind of gusto usually reserved for cheerleaders and children's television show hosts.

"I am," Ellis said, and I could tell he meant it.

"Me, too," I added.

"I always have fun with you," Duranja told her, a little too gushy for my taste.

The waitress arrived at the other table in the back to deliver Rick's martini. "I'm going to get one of those," I said.

"That was Grandma's fancy going-out drink." Melody laughed.

Rick saw he had our attention and held up his glass in a mock toast.

"Thanks so much for your help back there," I said, raising my water glass to him.

"Okay, see? Right here." Duranja pointed at me. "This is your problem." He redirected his finger at Rick. "You talk to too many people. You give away too much information, and you think it's helpful."

"It was massively helpful," Ellis observed.

"I've got this." I waved off the chivalry. "Rick has been great. There's no reason not to trust him. Not a lot of people would have jumped in the way he did," I added, with a nod to the author.

"Who wants to look at the wine list?" Melody asked.

"Alec will do the honors." Ellis snatched it off the table and shoved it in Duranja's face before my sister's date could insult me again. "Pick out something red. Or white. Or both."

The leather wine menu didn't shield me from Duranja's wrath for long. He slammed the menu down. "Verity, you told everyone we are police detectives. You took advice from a competitor."

"—who helped us find our treasure box," I felt obliged to add.

Duranja thwomped his hand down on the table. "You're so naive. Rick didn't help us. He directed us to the wrong basement entrance. He delayed us. Then he took second place while we were down there chasing our tails."

At the next table, Rick choked on his gin.

"Keep your voice down," I hissed.

"No, don't worry about me. I'm good," Rick said, coughing into his napkin.

"Our clue said dark and damp," I said, loud enough for Rick to hear. "That was a really good suggestion to look in the basement." I gave a little wave to Rick, who winced and waved back. "Our clue *was* underground. It turned out to be the wrong set of stairs, but the box could have been there."

Duranja sat smugly across from me. "Funny how he only noticed the clues on the fireplace *after* he secured his own box and we weren't a threat anymore."

"Why do you always have to think the worst of people?" I sat back, arms folded.

I really wanted to know.

"Why do you always have to assume everyone wants to help you?" he countered as the waitress greeted us.

"Okay, we're done now," Melody interjected, as if she could wave us apart with the drink menu. "Let's order a bottle of the Carolina Red. And a martini for Verity."

"It's not over if Verity's going to keep on doing it," Duranja fumed as Melody handed the drinks menu back to the waitress.

"Being myself? Being friendly? Yes. I am going to keep doing that." There was no shame in it.

Melody leaned her elbows on the table. "Now, Alec. You have to admit we wouldn't have found the fireplace without Rick." She exchanged a glance with our neighbor. Rick sat sipping his martini, watching our train wreck of a table.

Duranja didn't care. "He didn't want the twins to get our box if we failed, but he didn't have our best interests in mind either. Funny how his advice had us coming in last."

"I suppose that's possible," Melody admitted under her breath.

"Truly?" I asked. She wouldn't have said that if Duranja hadn't been sitting there.

"But Verity also has a point," Ellis said, voice low. "Rick is the person to ally with if we want to beat the twins. He's got a quick mind, and on that last task, he recognized a clue we didn't."

"We can beat the twins on our own," Duranja said, at full volume.

"I don't know if you noticed, but they are on fire," Rick said from the other table.

So much for being subtle.

"He's right," I said, more for Rick than Duranja.

I hoped Robocop was embarrassed.

"Try to take your emotions out of it and look at the facts as they present themselves," Ellis instructed the junior officer.

"You're one to talk," he shot back. "Believing in ghosts because some girl told you to."

"Oh, good. Drinks," Melody said as our wine arrived. "Verity, you made a friend. Alec, you said your piece. And I'm having a birthday dinner with my favorite people." She took a first taste. "Mmm...I ordered a Muscadine," she said, sparing a wink at Duranja. "Like the one we took on our picnic last weekend."

Duranja blushed. "I'll toast to that," he said, as if the past few minutes hadn't happened.

"I'm going to hit the restroom," I said, tossing my napkin on the table. I needed to calm down if I was going to make it through the rest of dinner.

I tried a deep breath, then a couple more as I headed down the hall to the door at the left of the stairs.

"Hey," Melody said, catching up. "Girls can't go alone to the bathroom, you know."

"It is kind of a rule," I admitted, a grin tugging at my lips. "I love you to pieces, but for all that is holy, please tell me what's wrong with Duranja," I said, pushing open the door. "It's like he's extra feisty tonight."

Or maybe I'd never spent this much time with him.

"He really wants to win." Melody stopped in front of the long mirror. She dug in the pocket of her sundress and plopped her keys onto the countertop. "He's also not used to sharing outside his investigative team." She fished some more and drew out a lipstick. "I mean, think of how police departments work. They're not the type to bounce their ideas around with the neighborhood."

"This is different." I leaned against the counter. "I'm trying to build alliances, and he's launching torpedoes."

"I know. That was painful back there," she said, applying her lipstick. "I'll talk to him."

Good. "He can at least try to be nice. This is your birthday." This was a fun trip. "Why is winning so important, anyway?"

Her cheeks went pink as she smoothed her hair behind her ears. "If I tell you his secret, will you promise not to tell a soul?"

Chapter Six

Melody clasped her hands under her chin. "I shouldn't tell you this. You're sworn to secrecy."

"I promise I won't tell," I said, crossing my heart and hoping to die.

"All right." She shook out her hands. "If we win, Alec is going to use his portion of the prize money to buy me a ring!"

My heart did a flip-flop, and my brain froze. "A ring?" I stammered. I had to have heard her wrong because my ears were buzzing and the world felt like it had tilted sideways. "Not like *a* ring."

"Yes, like an engagement ring, Verity," she explained, as if she were one step away from getting out the hand puppets.

I pushed off the counter. "That's impossible," I assured her. "You've only just met."

Well, maybe they'd known each other for years. But they'd only connected and started dating over homecoming, which was only a few months ago, and I really didn't understand what she could be talking about. Marriage? Melody and Duranja?

"I love him," my otherwise sane, sensible sister declared. "He's sweet and loyal and *passionate*."

"Okay." *Think*. Admittedly, it was hard with my brain

screaming *no, no, no.* "I love Ellis, but we're not rushing to get married." Not that he'd asked.

Of course, his mother hated me because I'd almost married his brother. But Beau and I were on good terms now. And besides, we had time. And this wasn't about me.

She poo-pooed my concern. "I adore how you're always so cautious."

"Please tell that to your boyfriend."

She snorted while she fluffed her bangs in the mirror. "What I mean is you think too much. You worry about what's best. I bet it's half the reason you went for Beau in the first place."

"I also ran out on our wedding," I pointed out.

She stopped to look at me. "But you didn't leave him until it was the obvious choice. There's nothing wrong with analyzing your relationships," she was quick to add. "I love you for it. You spend more time in your head when it comes to romance. Whereas I just...know."

"You're scaring me." Absolutely terrifying, if I was being honest.

Our father had passed long ago. Our mother was off gallivanting with her second husband. I was Melody's last line of defense between reason and...whatever this was.

"It was like that with school, too," she observed, holding out the lipstick to me. "Take this. You chewed all yours off."

"Thanks," I said, barely registering it in my hand. "I'm not following your train of thought. What does any of this have to do with school?"

Besides the fact she'd attended four universities and dropped out of three of them before getting her degree.

And it was a lot easier to change one's mind about a school than it was about a marriage.

"It's like that when I go on road trips," she added.

Uh-oh. I was beginning to get it.

She liked to open the United States atlas to a random page and then pick.

Sweet heaven, one did not choose a life partner by flipping a coin!

I tipped the lipstick at her. "That's how you ended up at Barney Smith's Toilet Seat Art Museum in Texas," I warned.

"And at the Ben and Jerry's flavor graveyard in Waterbury, Vermont," she countered. "Both places were awesome. For different reasons."

"How am I not talking you out of this?" Logic was on my side.

"Because I know when something feels right to me," she said as if it were obvious. "It's instant. Boom. And that's how it felt when I got trapped in the library with Alec." Before I could find a paper bag and start breathing into it, she added, "I know you've had your issues with him, but he's a good person. And he's perfect for me."

"Melody," I said, treading carefully through the minefield of bad ideas, "forget what you think I think about Duranja." Because none of it was great, and none of it had stopped her. Or at this rate, slowed her down. "Consider that this is not about him." Even if it was a lot about him. "There's nothing wrong with easing up and taking your time. You don't need to rush a big decision like this. Give it some thought." She was exceptionally skilled at deep thinking, research. I didn't see why this couldn't extend to her personal life.

Especially now.

"Maybe I shouldn't have told you, but I wanted you to know," she assured me. "And it's not happening tomorrow."

I opened my mouth. Closed it. Opened it again.

"You still need lipstick," Melody reminded me.

As if that was my biggest problem.

I dutifully swiped some on and handed it back. "Promise me you'll..." I wasn't sure what. *Think? Run? Come back to your senses?* "Date. Have fun. Make sure this is what you want."

Yeesh. Now I wanted my sister to date Duranja?

I drew a hand down the side of my face.

What kind of world was I living in if that was the best alternative?

"Do you see why I want you two to get along?" she prodded fondly. "Now let's get back. We've been gone too long already. And don't tell him I said anything," she warned.

"I won't." If anything, speaking aloud would make it too real.

And so we returned to the table. Melody beamed as we sat down. My martini had arrived, but I didn't feel like toasting anymore.

If Melody married Duranja, she wouldn't just be my sister. She'd be *Alec's wife*. She might not see the distinction, but I did.

All her priorities would change, and her loyalties, and if the start of this treasure hunt had shown me anything, it was that Melody could and would turn toward him and away from me. Not dramatically. Not with malice or fireworks—at least not on her part. But she might not have my back the way I'd counted on since we were kids.

I shot a smile at Ellis that felt more like a grimace and tried to calm the tilt-a-whirl that had taken place in the bathroom.

"You okay?" Ellis asked.

"Sure," I insisted, not fooling anybody.

Duranja, the jerk who sat across from me and lifted my sister's hand to kiss it, could be my brother-in-law.

Melody positively glowed. "Now while we have a break," she said, "I'd love it if you could open the gifts I gave you earlier."

Um. Duranja shot me a terrified glance. Good to know he was scared of *something*. "I think Alec should open his first," I suggested. He deserved to be tortured a bit.

"Oh, no. After you," he insisted.

"I would love to. It's just...I'm not sure where I left it." A ribbon of guilt wound its way through my stomach. Melody always put a lot of thought into her gifts, and I hadn't treated it as graciously as I knew I should have. Duranja snorted. "Well, where's yours?" I asked. He hadn't exactly been eager to grab it.

Duranja swallowed hard.

Then I remembered. My chair screeched across the hardwood as I popped up. "Wait! I know. I left mine at the front desk before we started the hunt." Luckily I hadn't been trying to hang onto it on my mad dash to the bell.

"Me too," Duranja volunteered, standing.

"It's not a race," I warned as he edged ahead of me in the lobby.

He kept his lead. "It's important to Melody, so I'm not going to waste time. I'll do right by her no matter what it takes." He blocked me when I tried to get around him. "I do what's right. Always."

"Are you implying I don't?" I asked, spotting the bright yellow gift precisely where I'd left it on the reception desk.

"You really want to die on that hill?" Duranja reached for the present on the counter seconds before I snatched it out from under him. "Look, I'm not trying to start a fight here," he insisted.

"And yet, here we are," I said, present in hand.

He continued his reach and pulled out a gift from the shelf behind the counter. He held it like a waiter would a tray. "You always think I'm up to something, Verity. When really, it's you."

I gritted my teeth. "Can't you just *try* to get along with me?"

"I *am*," he said, as if he'd surprised himself.

"Seriously?" He couldn't have shocked me more if he'd started singing opera. Although I knew he had an ulterior motive—provided he could get his hands on the money for a ring.

"What?" he asked. "Your sister is an amazing woman, and she deserves that happiness."

"For once, we agree."

"I always give my best effort," he added to himself.

"I do, too." Just usually in the opposite direction.

"Look, Verity." He ran a hand along the back of his neck and sighed. "If you want to make your sister happy, maybe you should stop getting in the way and let me handle things."

"Hold the phone. Did you just hear yourself?" No one could be that dense.

"Think about it." He strode away.

"This. Right here. This is exactly the problem," I called after him. "You think you know everything, but you don't!"

But naturally, he wasn't listening.

Bless my sister—I got the last laugh when we returned to the table and he unwrapped his present. The stiff-backed officer crumpled the festive wrapping in his hand and stared down at his gift like it might bite him.

It was one of those custom books you buy online—with a smiling picture of me holding an ice-cream cone smack-dab on the front.

"*Getting to know Verity*," he said, reading the title as if he'd rather French-kiss Medusa.

"It's a book of questions you need to ask Verity so you two can bond," Melody said. "Scientists have used these types of questions to help people talk, connect, even fall in love."

"It's not a magic book," I said, stopping the crazy train at the station.

"You may learn you're not so different after all," Melody insisted, smoothing a lock of hair behind her ear. "And you have to answer each of those questions honestly. As a gift to me."

"As long as he doesn't try to twist my words and make me look bad," I warned.

"I don't need to twist anything," Duranja said under his breath.

"They need this more than we thought," Ellis remarked to my sister.

He didn't know the half of it.

"Now open yours," Melody said to me.

"This is fun," I said, trying to mean it. But I was no dummy. I knew what was in store.

I cringed a little when I unwrapped a book like Duranja's with a picture on the cover of him cuddled up to a French bulldog puppy.

Getting to know Alec.

"That's Arlo," he said when I let out an involuntary *aww*.

I didn't realize he had a dog. Not that it made a difference. Much.

Alec's expression softened when thinking of his dog. "I had Arlo's dog sitter booked three weeks ago and made sure to have all his food and toys ready yesterday. With special treats every night I'm gone."

That was both adorable and irritating because of course it was aimed at me.

I forced a smile. For Arlo.

"See? This is what I want," Melody said. "In celebration of my birthday, please take time this weekend to get to know each other. These books will help. I want you to be at least to question number five by the time we leave on Monday. After that, you can do a few questions a week at home."

"How many are there?" Duranja asked, horrified as he flipped to the end of his book.

"Thirty-six questions that lead to love," Melody said, as if that weren't about thirty-five too many. "I'm confident you both understand how much this means to me," she said, taking Duranja's hand. "You'll always be my friend as well as my hero," she said to him.

Oh, barf.

"And you'll always be my favorite sister," she added to me as Ellis took my hand.

"She's your only sister," Duranja couldn't resist pointing out.

"That's right," she said, smiling at him as if he'd said something nice. Then to me, she said, "How many times have you told me you'd do anything for the people you love?"

"A lot." Because it was true.

"How many times have you preached to Frankie about

finding common ground with people he doesn't like?" Ellis prodded.

Even more times than Ellis had overheard.

"You're right," I said, caving, seeing Melody's relief and happiness as its own reward. "At least I'll try."

I'd approach our weekend activities—and this book of questions—in good faith. I'd do my best to get to know Alec because he was more important to my sister than I'd realized.

Even if I didn't want to look under that particular rock.

"What's the first question?" Ellis prompted as the waitress arrived with a hearty stew paired with homemade bread.

"Wait." Duranja hesitated. "We have to start now?"

"Go ahead," Melody said, delighted.

Duranja cracked open his book as if something nasty might jump out at him. He smoothed the first page and cleared his throat. "Given the choice of anyone in the world, who would you want as a dinner guest?"

That was easy. I finished a bite of the rich, warm stew before saying it plain. "Our dad," I said, glancing to Melody. "I mean, he died when I was in fifth grade and you were in third. It would be nice to get to know him as an adult and to tell him what a great dad he was. He really cared."

"He was so much fun. We used to laugh all the time," Melody mused, dipping her bread.

"Remember how he taught us to grow one extra sweet potato plant outside the garden netting so the bunnies could have some?" I asked, belatedly realizing I'd neglected my salad.

"He was always taking in strays," she said.

"Like you," Ellis said, squeezing my hand.

"I suppose you mean Lucy," I admitted, spooning another bite.

"And Frankie," Ellis added.

That was twice he'd mentioned my ghost in front of Duranja. I really loved how Ellis went out of his way to encourage his friend to accept me the way he did.

Duranja tossed his spoon down hard. "Okay, I'll ask the questions, but I'm not pretending her imaginary friend is real."

"Alec, we've been over this," Melody said sweetly with a tinge of steel in her tone.

"Right," he said, glaring at me like it was my fault he was so closed-minded.

But he did as my sister wished. Alec wrote down my answer in his journal. His pen dug into the paper, and his jaw ground tight.

I swirled my bread in the stew. This could be fun.

"Why are you smiling?" Ellis asked, as if he wanted in on the joke.

"Just happy to be with you," I said, earning a warm smile from my sweetie.

"Okay, that's enough of the books," Melody said. "Maybe put them away for later." Duranja and I happily obliged. "It's clear that teamwork is the way to get you two talking this weekend."

She did not give up easily.

We ate in silence for a bit. Then I caught the author's frantic wave a few tables away. He cocked a thumb toward the twins' table up front. It appeared they'd pried their lid open with a butter knife.

"Hey, look," I said to my table.

Duranja leapt to his feet. "That's cheating!"

"Hold it," Ellis cautioned as our host approached the table where the culprits sat.

"They're getting a head start," Melody said, forgetting about her dinner.

"Not on my watch," Duranja pledged.

I finished my dinner quickly while the twins talked in rapid-fire hushed tones to our host. Ellis observed them closely. Meanwhile, Duranja tested the flashlight he'd pulled from his pocket while Melody took a couple of steps toward the window overlooking the beach. "It's getting dark out there."

"We're ready," Duranja said, flicking his light on and off.

"Always," I agreed, rising to join my sister.

The first task had been a lot of fun, even if we'd barely finished in time. We'd do better this next round.

I followed Melody's gaze out the window to the rapidly darkening beachfront that had seemed so interesting to Frankie as we'd left the boat. I wondered what my ghost friend had found while casing the island.

With any luck, the gangster hadn't offended any of the undead inhabitants in his short time out there.

It never took him long.

In any case, we might be able to use him on this next task, especially if he'd gained any knowledge of the island. Duranja would just have to suck it up. As *Alec* would be sure to point out, we hadn't had much time to explore on our own.

"Attention!" our host bellowed, clapping his hands. "It seems most of you have finished your dinner."

No kidding. Most of us were standing, ready to go.

Our host rested a hand on his sword. "That's good, because one of our team's treasure boxes has unexpectedly...broken open."

"Please." Duranja rolled his eyes.

"I thought I was the one writing fiction," Rick drawled.

"Their knife is bent," the professor called, slinking over for a closer look.

Zara grabbed their box and turned it away from him.

The pirate held his hands out. "In any case, they haven't had more than a minute to look at things, and I can easily even the score." He didn't appear one hundred percent convinced of that, which worried me. Still, I supposed there wasn't much we could do.

"Eyes on me," our host insisted. "You found your first treasure. Now the real game begins." He rested a hand on his sword hilt. "On the island are four keystones. The treasure and the map inside your box might help you find one. But beware! This is a game of piracy. Each event, we unlock a different part of Captain Bill's story. So I hope you paid attention earlier."

"Always," Ellis murmured.

"We've got this," I assured him.

Pirate Bill hooked a thumb under his belt. "The keystones fit into capstans located in different parts of the island. You must turn the capstan completely to reveal a hidden doubloon. At the end of the weekend, the team with the most doubloons wins. But there will be four keystones and four coins. It will take teamwork, alliances, and possible piracy to steal a prize from the others in order to win."

Rick shot us a thumbs-up, and Duranja scowled.

The twins began talking animatedly, and our host raised his voice to speak above them. "I'm going to walk around right now and open everyone's boxes. Then I'll set you on your final task of the night. You'll be exploring the island by lantern light, using the tools inside your treasure box to search for your team's keystone. A team without a keystone is a team that can be left behind," he warned.

"Please be careful with them," the professor called to the group.

"In this case, Dr. Fielding is correct," Pirate Bill continued. "The keystones are quite old and valuable themselves. You'll know yours when you see it," he added mysteriously. "The location of your team's keystone is on your portion of the map that is contained in your treasure box. Secure it quickly," he urged. "You are allowed to take another team's keystone, and they can take yours."

"That's not fair," the professor choked out.

"That's life." Zara shrugged.

"That's piracy." Our host chuckled. "The game is designed so you either have to work with another team, or steal from them."

"Thievery or cooperation," Ellis mused.

"You know which one I'd pick," I told him, ignoring Duranja's huff.

"The trick is, you will know the location of only one stone, and that is the one on your individual map." He held up an old-fashioned alarm clock with a double bell at the top. "I'm going to set this alarm for five minutes. In that time, I will open your boxes and let you see your maps. After that time, when the bell rings, you can join me in the lobby, where I will provide you with a lantern to begin your search for your keystone, or for anyone else's." He made a show of setting the alarm and twisting the knob. The alarm began ticking. "You're done when all the keystones have been located."

"Who's first?" Duranja asked, moving to deliver our box into the pirate's hands, or more accurately, toward his key.

"I'll go in order of your team's finish in the last task," he said, ignoring Duranja's groan. "However, you won't need more than a minute to know where to go."

"The twins found their box first, and theirs is already open. He's trying to make it fair," Melody said, leaning close.

And he was holding everyone back until we all had our boxes unlocked so no team had an advantage. I had to admit, I appreciated that.

"Now, are you ready to explore Phantom Island?" he asked, motioning to the author as he held aloft a key.

Chapter Seven

Our host made a show of holding aloft his key ring while he strode to the front of the dining room, the photographer snapping pictures in his wake. The twins' treasure chest lay open, the lock gouged and broken from the butter knife.

And they'd thought we wouldn't notice.

Ten bucks said they didn't care.

"See what you find inside," the pirate invited, as if they hadn't already peeked. With a satisfied twist of her lips, Zadie withdrew a thick parchment map, rolled tight and secured with a red ribbon. She slipped it off and unfurled her prize. It was torn along two of the edges.

Duranja cleared his throat. "Okay, they have the northwest quadrant," he said under his breath. "The edges are raw at the bottom and on the right, where the map got torn."

Zadie's eyes glittered as she spread the portion of the map onto the table in front of her while Zara weighted down the edges with drinking glasses and soup bowls.

"There," Zadie said with great satisfaction, planting a finger down toward one edge.

"That is the location of your keystone," our host boomed,

hooking the keychain under his belt. "You'll see it as a green diamond on the map."

"What does it actually look like?" Zara asked.

Our host touched the tips of his fingers together. "I won't say. Follow the map. I promise you'll recognize the keystone when you see it."

The pirate turned his attention to the author, while Zadie hastily rolled their map and Zara reached into the box and withdrew the object that would help them on their questing this weekend. It appeared to be an antique watch on a chain, the gold finish mottled with patina from time and use.

She flicked it open and nudged her sister. "It's a compass," she said, holding it out in front of her, turning toward the kitchen as she did. "This way is north."

"And our keystone is three hundred and twenty-two degrees northwest," Zadie said, with no small amount of satisfaction.

"Why would she say that?" I muttered.

"She could be lying," Melody said under her breath.

Zara turned a little more to her left, the compass pointing the way. "This'll be easy," she said, her excitement paired with relief.

She could just be confident.

Zara caught my eye and winked. "We'll go after your keystone once we find ours."

I felt like she'd pinned me down where I stood. "I hope she's joking," I said to a horrified Melody.

"Don't count on it," Ellis warned.

"But why us?" People usually liked me. I'd made an honest effort to get to know Zara and Zadie.

Zara shot me a satisfied smirk as she slipped the compass chain over her head and wore it like a necklace.

"We're the weakest link," Duranja said. "We finished last on the previous task. She sees us as an easy kill. Low-hanging fruit."

"That was one task," Melody was quick to point out. "And we were kind of thrown into it."

"Let's hope we have something really helpful in our box," Ellis said.

I didn't like the resignation in his voice.

The twins had a huge advantage with that compass. Each treasure chest was supposed to contain something of value. But what could be more useful than a compass and a map on a treasure hunt?

"And"—he strode toward Rick's table near us—"let's see what Rebel Bill Brown has for you."

"Yes, please," Rick said like it was his birthday.

Our host twisted his key into the lock on the author's box, and Rick kept his eye on the prize as he lifted the lid.

"First, the map," he said with great relish, lifting it out and theatrically releasing the red ribbon. "I've always wanted my own treasure map," he blurted, unfurling it for all to see.

"He has the dock and the haunted beach," Ellis murmured.

"You're fast," I said.

"The edges are raw at the top and on the right," Duranja pointed out.

"Wait. How do we know the beach is haunted?" Melody asked.

Because I'd met a pirate on the dock. "Frankie went that way after the boat landed," I said, ignoring Duranja's disbelieving sneer. Every place Frankie went became haunted by default. "I didn't make up the rules."

And now Rick was showing the front of his map like a teacher presenting a picture book to a bunch of kindergarteners.

It appeared to be an old map of the island, hand-drawn and crude. I looked for the green diamond, but didn't see one. It must be small.

"There's a guy who doesn't want to win," Ellis murmured.

"He's in it for the research," I told him under my breath. "He said so earlier."

"You see? He also has a portion of the hotel," Melody whispered.

"The hotel is at the dead center of the island," our host said with a hint of mystery. "You'll see it superimposed on the edge of each of your maps. Use it to orient yourselves if you don't have a compass," he added with a nod to the twins.

"And now for my tool..." The author reached into the treasure chest and pulled out an old wooden tankard. Tarnished silver bound it at the top and bottom, and a rough wooden lid rested over the top. "Now this is cool," he said, holding it up. "Tell me this belonged to a real pirate."

"Check out the name inscribed on the handle," the gamemaster prompted.

"Bill," the author crooned. "As in pirate Bill?" he asked our well-pleased host. "You gotta see this, Verity," he said, motioning me over.

"No fraternizing during the reveals," our host said, waving me back with a flick of the wrist.

"Can I drink out of this?" Rick asked as if it were a revelation.

"I have," the pirate said. "You can. We'll grab you a bottle of ale at the bar later. But first, lift the lid on the tankard."

"Ha!" Rick said, looking down into the cup. "Check it out." He held it up so that we could see him through the thick glass bottom. "It's a kaleidoscope."

"Magnifying glass," the pirate corrected.

"No kidding?" Rick asked. "This is wicked cool."

The glass-bottomed tankard made a neat party trick, but I wasn't certain how it would help us solve anything.

"What do you make of it?" Duranja asked Ellis.

"Not sure," Ellis said, glancing at me, "but we don't have one of our own, and Pirate Bill said it would come in handy."

That went for all the tools we'd seen tonight. "We'll have to make alliances," I said, catching sight of the twins at the door and the professor, who stood over his box.

Pirate Bill joined him. I exchanged a glance with Ellis as the gamemaster turned his key in the lock and waited for the professor to lift the lid on his box.

Dr. Fielding didn't bother with the reproduction treasure map. He tossed it onto the table with barely a thought, his mouth falling open at the artifact inside. He planted his hands on the table on either side of the chest. "It's exquisite," he gasped. "Please tell me it's not original." He looked to the pirate. "It can't be."

"It's bona fide." Our host beamed with pleasure. "In more ways than one. Every object in these chests will help you solve the mystery," he announced. "And they are real living history."

"I love this place," Rick burst out.

"That's horrifying," the professor erupted, the color draining from his face. "These artifacts could get broken or damaged. Breathed on wrong." He dragged his chest closer, as if he could safeguard his object and every single historical artifact inside the hotel. "They belong in a museum."

"They belong to the Phantom Hotel," our host corrected. "To my family who lived here before, and to me now." He surveyed the room as he added, "I say we should enjoy these things and remember the people who lived here, rather than locking their stories and their memories away to gather dust." He turned back to the professor. "Go ahead. Pick it up." When the doctor hesitated, he shrugged. "Or you can be out of the game, forfeit your entry fee, and spend your time in the library while the others enjoy these bits of history."

Dr. Fielding's cheeks mottled with pink. "I don't have a pair of cotton gloves with me," he sputtered. "It's not too late for you to donate—"

"I won't and you know it. Now pick it up and show the group," our host said. "It won't bite you," he added, reaching into the box himself.

The professor cut him off. "No. I'll handle this gently, if at all," he admonished, turning his back and hiding his box from the rest of us.

"No wonder he's on a team by himself," Duranja said, sliding his hands into his pockets as he watched.

"He has a point about the history," I said. We didn't want

anything to be damaged during the hunt, and I had a feeling some teams might not take care like ours would.

"You use your great-grandmother's blue flowered teapot, don't you?" Duranja prodded.

Yes, but... "How do you know?" I asked, feeling put on the spot. Of all the things for Duranja to know about my personal life.

"It's one of the things I enjoy when I go to your place," Melody said, with a tinge of guilt. "I might have mentioned it."

"Fair enough." I'd inherited the house from our grandmother, and she'd used the teapot, so I used the teapot. Mostly for company. And for special occasions.

"Some objects are sturdy enough to be used and appreciated without getting damaged," Melody asserted.

"A metal compass is a lot less fragile than a teapot," Ellis reasoned.

He had a point, I decided, reserving judgment. "Let's see what Dr. Fielding has."

So far, the professor had refused to turn around to face us.

"Show us," Zara called to the professor, but he kept his shoulders rounded, studying his prize.

Our host tucked his thumbs under his thick leather belt. "Dr. Fielding is in possession of the retractable maritime telescope once owned by Rebel Bill Brown, captain of *Fortune's Revenge*," he announced. "Zara and Zadie are holding Rebel Bill's compass. And"—he strode toward Rick's table near us—"let's see what Rebel Bill Brown has for you."

I couldn't wait to see which of the late captain's treasures we'd discover in our box.

"Last but not least," our host said, selecting the key.

"The sun is almost down," Zadie admonished from the doorway as if we were the ones holding them up.

"You said five minutes, and it's already been more than five minutes," Zara added.

"Huh," our host said, glancing at the old-fashioned alarm

clock he'd left on the twins' table. "Is it still ticking?" He waved off their frowns. "I'll fix it later. Just be patient. We only have this last box," he said, inserting his key.

We hovered close and heard the click of the latch.

"You do the honors, Melody," Duranja said. And with great joy, she lifted the lid.

"We have our map," she said, withdrawing the rolled parchment and sliding the ribbon free. "Of course, it's going to be the southeast quadrant," she added, low for our table.

It was the only quadrant left.

"But what's on that part of the island?" I asked.

Duranja helped her hold the edges of the parchment down. The map had been photocopied from an old map of the island, drawn by a deft hand in black ink.

"Where'd you find this?" Ellis murmured.

"My grandfather found it in a cave near the beach," our host said, leaning shoulder-to-shoulder with us. "I like to think the pirates drew it."

"You can't just 'like to think' history," the professor huffed, drawing a bit too close to our table. "You have to prove it."

"No fraternizing during the reveals," the pirate said, leaving our group to wave the professor back.

Though crude, the map seemed fairly detailed. The outline of the hotel had been photoshopped in the upper left corner. We saw a winding path from the hotel that skirted the edge of the cliffs overlooking the sea and what appeared to be a rock bridge. The path dead-ended at the old lighthouse.

"Be careful," our host cautioned. "Your way is definitely haunted."

"We'll manage," I assured him.

If anything, it gave us an advantage.

"Just don't be surprised if your lantern dies when you cross the rock bridge," he warned. "Flashlights tend to fail as well. But it'll be better once you make it to the other side."

"Great," Duranja said, clearly not believing a word of it.

"What happened there?" I asked.

"That is where Captain Bill's kidnapped bride leapt to her death," our host said solemnly.

"No fair," Zara said from the doorway. "They're getting to check out part of the game board."

"The entire island is part of the game," our host said. "And giving the ghost hunter a haunted portion makes it more exciting for everyone," he teased. "Sure, the clues leading you to your boxes were earned by the order of your arrival, but the boxes themselves are no accident. The twins are experts at navigation. Professor Fielding knows the island topography like the back of his hand, but he can see it differently with that telescope. Our author friend is a detail man. Every team has expertise to offer."

"I can't believe you're our expert." Duranja winced, looking right at me.

"Charmed," I said. "But how'd Bill know?" I wondered aloud. I hadn't had a chance to mention it.

"They asked for background on the signup form." Melody hitched a shoulder.

"So you told them everything," Duranja concluded, fighting a wince.

"Of course," Melody said. And I noticed he didn't lecture her.

"Let's focus." Ellis turned his back to our competitors and drew our attention to the map. "Our keystone is in the lighthouse," he said, planting a finger near a crude green diamond drawn in crayon. "Let's try to get there as quick as we can and then use the lighthouse as a vantage point to check out what the other teams are doing."

"It'll be dark," Duranja said.

"They'll all be carrying lanterns or flashlights," Melody said.

"What's our item?" I asked, nudging my way toward the box, stopping short when I saw the tool we would use to help find the gold. "Oh no."

"What?" Duranja pressed.

"This had better not be what I think it is," I said, gingerly reaching inside.

Of course, we wouldn't get anything useful like a compass or a telescope. We wouldn't get the pirate's cup with a magnifying glass and who knew what else hidden inside.

No. I blinked hard and prayed I was wrong as I withdrew a very real, very dead parrot. It had been taxidermied, the feathers preserved over a carved wooden form set with shiny glass eyes. Stiff wooden legs had been reinforced with metal bands and claws.

For once, even Duranja was speechless. "Is that—" he sputtered.

"She has a little hat," Melody stammered, as if that were the important thing.

"Like a little leather headscarf," I cooed.

Our host beamed. "I present you with Rebel Bill's pet parrot. Say hello to Pearl."

"It can't be," Ellis managed.

"It is," our host assured us.

"It has wooden feet," Duranja pointed out.

"So did Pearl," the gamemaster said. "That's how we know it's real."

Melody crossed her arms over her chest. "I'm pretty sure that would be impossible given the limits of avian veterinary medicine two centuries ago."

Pirate Bill tsked and dove back into actor mode. "June 14, 1731." He raised his hands to the sides as if he could conjure it. "Captain Bill's fierce and loyal parrot, Pearl, died in battle while saving him. As a tribute, Captain Bill had her preserved and vowed to carry her into battle with him until the end of time." At the looks on our faces, he dropped his hands. "I'm serious. He'd clip her on his shoulder and away he'd go."

"Truly?" I wasn't sure if I was ready to hop on that particular crazy train despite our host's insistent nod.

"According to legend, anyway," the professor said as if he

couldn't quite believe he was backing Bill up. "Where'd you find her?"

"In my dad's old trophy case. Isn't she a beauty?" our host crooned, as if that made it fact.

"Well..." I turned the bird over and found a steel clip attached to the bottom of her feet. If she was real, then she'd been a sweet and loyal pet. And she was cute, in a dead-parrot sort of way. Pearl had gorgeous red feathers, with a bright blue chest and back and a wide black beak. She held her head cocked to the side, her beak slightly open as if she were about to speak. Her feathers were softer than I'd expected for an old bird. All in all, she was a pretty girl, if a bit dusty.

Ellis wasn't as impressed. "How is a two-hundred-year-old bird going to help us solve a weekend pirate adventure?"

"She's an artifact," Pirate Bill assured us. "A treasured member of the crew. You'll learn how valuable she is tonight...if you succeed on your quest."

Chapter Eight

Duranja couldn't keep himself from pacing at the back of the line. He truly was the most impatient man I knew.

Meanwhile, our host held court at the roaring fireplace in the library to provide final instructions to each team before we headed out. Each team would also receive an old-fashioned iron lantern to light the way. We'd lined up in the order of our finish in tonight's treasure chest hunt, which meant our team stood dead last.

"Ooh, look." Melody sidestepped out of line. "Pirate Bill is using an eighteenth-century method of lighting the lanterns. I've never actually seen anyone use a spill before," she said, earning a wry grin from our host.

"I'm beginning to like all of these authentic touches," I said, taking a look, glad when her potential maybe future fiancé didn't join us.

She ran a finger along her chin. "His spill is made from twisted wood. Probably driftwood."

"My sister is so smart," I said, noticing the gamemaster's extra flourish with the spill as he lit a lantern for the twins.

"Just well read," she corrected.

The twins high-fived and skirted past us out the door of the inn.

"First again," Duranja said under his breath.

"For now," Ellis added.

I gave him a squeeze on the arm. There was nothing to do except rock this next task, and we had faith in our team.

"The twins got a compass," Duranja huffed as the professor stepped forward to receive his lantern. "Rick got a magnifying tool. The professor has a working telescope. And we got a bird. A dead one."

"You can keep saying it, but it won't stop being true," I said, pointing Pearl at him.

Let our feathery friend see what I was dealing with.

"A bird." Duranja halted in front of me, hands on his hips.

"Loosen your buttons," Melody said, sweeter than he deserved.

"It's not Pearl's fault," I said, giving her a stroke on the head. "I'm sure she'd rather not be our treasure-hunt clue, either."

We'd do our best with the lot we were given and hope our little piece of pirate history would be a blessing. I mean, Frankie did love animals. Maybe he could keep an eye out for ghost Pearl.

Melody weaved her arms around one of Duranja's outthrust elbows. "We're just going to have to play it by ear on this one. Trust me," she added fondly. "We've got this." He melted, but she wasn't finished. She kissed him on the cheek and murmured, "I've done plenty of research on this island, and I know where we're going tonight. And after we take first place this round, I also know where all the good kissing spots are."

"You just make everything better, don't you?" he asked, nuzzling her ear.

My word. I covered Pearl's eyes. "She's found a way to tame the savage beast."

Truthfully, it was a bit frightening.

"Let's look at this objectively," Ellis urged, drawing close so as not to be overheard. "We don't need the twins' compass—at least not right away. Not to find a keystone in the lighthouse. We could do without the professor's looking glass"—he spared a glance for the professor at the fireplace—"although so could he at night. I'm not sure how Rick's magnifying tankard will help him down on the beach unless his keystone is small or partially buried." He looked to Pearl. "Maybe she has...hidden talents."

"You hear that, Pearl?" I clipped her up on my shoulder and winked at my man.

Ellis winked back.

Duranja was not amused. "Let's focus on the prize. And keep things moving," he added in a louder tone as the professor and our host bickered over the proper way to light a lantern. "The twins are getting a huge head start."

Rick turned around to watch. "He's feisty."

"You don't know the half of it," I said, glad to see Duranja's outburst had at least gotten the professor to drop his argument.

"Hey, why did you let the professor go ahead of you?" Ellis asked the author.

That's right. Rick had come in second in the treasure chest hunt.

A pained expression flashed across Rick's features. "My wife said she'd try to join me after dinner. I ran up to check on her, but—"

"She was gone," the professor finished. "I saw."

"She likes to walk," Rick insisted, optimistic and a little defensive. "With any luck, she'll walk in the door any second."

"I don't see any lights out front," Melody said, peering out the window.

"You didn't need to mention that," Duranja told her gently as the professor scurried for the door.

"Next team," the gamemaster prompted, waving the author forward. "We have to keep this moving," he added, as if he weren't enjoying every second of it.

Without the prospect of his wife's imminent return, Rick reluctantly moved to the front to have his lantern lit.

"That could have been us right now," Duranja muttered.

Maybe so, but Rick deserved a break. I felt bad to think of him out there alone. Especially when he'd signed on as part of a team. "I'd offer to let you come with us but..." I glanced to Robocop. Duranja would never go for it. I focused back on the author. "I can help you look for your keystone after we find ours."

"Thanks. But I'm used to working by myself. Besides"—he shrugged—"I'd like to take first place this time."

So would we.

Duranja filled the space in front of me, the veins in his neck bulging. "How many times do I have to tell you, he is not our friend."

"Did you hear what Pirate Bill said about alliances?" Or had he tuned that part out?

"I heard what Bill said about playing like a pirate." Duranja stood stiffly, watching our host light Rick's lantern.

The author hadn't had to help us back on the first quest. "If not for Rick, Pearl would be sitting on Zara's shoulder."

Duranja's gaze settled on the bird. "I'm not sure that's a loss."

"This is a friendly competition," I reminded him.

"To win thousands of dollars each," Duranja said.

And to sink his claws further into Melody.

I realized she wanted a ring, but I didn't think Melody would like his single-minded focus on the prize rather than teamwork during her celebration. She tried to put on a brave face, but I could tell she was disappointed.

"Let's all do our best," she said, pushing through it. "If we finish first tonight, we'll have the advantage in tomorrow morning's quest. That should even the score a little."

"Exactly," I chimed in before Duranja could object.

The author left with a salute to our team. He hurried out the door and into the night while Ellis stepped forward to accept our lantern.

This would have to be an exercise in teamwork if we hoped to place high. Too bad our team wasn't as solid as one would like. We had all of the essential skills covered, but we needed to learn how to cooperate to make use of them. Or, in some cases, to acknowledge those skills existed in the first place.

Ellis held up our lantern to be lit.

"Carry it down at your side with your arm low," our host instructed. "Stay behind everyone else to keep the light steady. If you put the lantern down, tilt the wire down below the flame, or it will burn your hand. Keep the lantern lit at all times so I can track you. First place team on this task gets to go first on tomorrow's quest—and it's a biggie. Your quest is over when you return with the keystone, the lantern, and the bird."

"Right," Ellis said. "Anything else you can tell us about the bird?"

The gamemaster nodded with pleasure, flattered Ellis wanted to learn more. He tented his fingertips. "Pearl is an eclectus parrot that hatched from an egg Captain Bill planned to eat for breakfast."

"That can't be true," Duranja balked.

"That's the legend," our host insisted. He glanced to the door, as if the others had somehow decided to hang around. "Pay attention to what she says, and you'll make it inside the lighthouse," he assured us.

Duranja stared in disbelief. "She can't talk. She's stuffed."

"Details," our host said, waving away the officer's concern. "I shouldn't say this, but yours is my favorite quest." He closed the lantern door with a flourish. "Good luck."

～

"Favorite, my rear." Duranja took an early lead as we hurried down the path leading from the inn. He moved fast despite the graying edge of the light. "I'll bet we have the farthest to go."

"What did he mean about the parrot talking?" I asked, trying to peek inside her beak.

"Maybe it's another play on words," Ellis suggested in that

pragmatic way of his. "We'll figure it out." He kept a strong, steady presence at our backs. "This way," he said, map in hand as he cast the lantern's glow over a break in the shell-strewn path that wound toward the sound of the ocean.

"I can't believe we're doing this." Melody nudged me, giddy and slightly out of breath.

"Happy birthday." I made a twirl, keeping up the pace.

That was when I spotted Rick's light to our right down by the beach.

"Hey, look." I turned and saw the faint flicker of a pair of lanterns to the north of us. To my surprise, they seemed to be moving closer together. "I hope the twins didn't find their keystone already. The way they're going, they might have decided to go for the professor's as well."

"The gamemaster would love it if they did," Ellis said, his lantern bobbing behind us.

"So would I," I admitted. It might hold them up long enough for us to finish first.

Rocks crunched under Ellis's shoes. "When I talked to Pirate Bill in the lobby earlier tonight, he told me he's hoping to make a big splash with this treasure hunt, even though our kickoff weekend hasn't attracted the number of teams he wanted. It's no mistake we have so many high-profile guests."

No kidding. "Why didn't I think of that?" It made sense with the reality show sensations and the author. Maybe the professor. "But then why are we here?" I wondered. "No offense," I added to my sister, who laughed.

"You've been in the media more than a few times on all your ghost-hunting adventures," she pointed out.

"Sometimes, more than I'd like," I admitted.

Make that most of the time.

"If you're trying to sell people on visiting a haunted island, it helps to have someone who can confirm whether there are ghosts on the premises. It wasn't hard to get in when I told them I was signing up a ghost hunter and a pair of police officers," Melody said.

"All four of us are credible witnesses," Ellis suggested.

"You make it sound like someone is going to run into trouble," I said, pressing forward as the lonely path emerged bit by bit out of the darkness ahead. This was a treasure hunt, pure and simple. "Besides, we're planning to win this thing," I reminded them, "not stand around and watch."

"Oh, we'll beat the snot out of them," Ellis agreed. "Still, the twins bring drama and lots of Instagram followers. Bill couldn't ask for better publicity."

"They're nothing without a Wi-Fi hookup," Duranja said over his shoulder.

"I don't know about that." I imagined they were pretty photogenic. I doubted Steve had captured any photos of Zadie or Zara slurping soup.

Duranja pulled farther ahead while I was talking. "I think I see the cliffs. According to the map, the lighthouse stands over the sharpest drop. Let's pick up the pace."

"Our host is hoping reality TV producers take an interest in the hotel and the story of Captain Bill," Ellis explained, maintaining his quick, steady stride.

"No doubt the twins will be posting about this like crazy," I said, "especially if they win."

"Or maybe Rick will decide to set his next book here on Phantom Island," Melody suggested.

"It worked for the Stanley Hotel with *The Shining*," I admitted. Our host may be a little eccentric, but he seemed determined to be a showman like his great-grandfather all those years ago.

Melody tucked her hair behind her ears. "I'll bet Bill is hoping you see some ghosts so he can publicize his hotel as 'officially haunted.'" She glanced out over the rocky island. "The place isn't very big, and the logistics of getting people and supplies out here is a hurdle. The only way he can make any money is to have people so interested in staying here, he can put a premium on rooms."

"Makes sense," Ellis said. "When I talked to him, I got the impression he's bleeding money."

Well, then. "A certified haunted hotel definitely attracts a certain clientele."

"Or a different angle for a reality show," Melody said, shooting me the side-eye. "Maybe you'll meet some pirate ghosts," she teased.

Little did she know, I'd already met one.

The air chilled as we drew closer to the cliffs. I shuddered as a piercing wind off the ocean cut through my thin windbreaker. I'd packed more for s'mores on the patio than a moonlight adventure to the old lighthouse.

Then I saw it.

A rock bridge lay dead ahead, longer and narrower than I'd like. The shadowy outline of a lighthouse stood farther up the hill on the other side.

"Can't we just swing north and go by land?" I asked, halting a few feet short of the ominous strip of rock buffeted by blackness on both sides as it gave way to the ocean.

"That way is rocky and full of holes," my sister said. "I researched it."

Of course she did.

"It's what the map says, too," Duranja said, looking past it up the hill. "It'd take longer, especially at night. And we'd risk injury."

Ellis's lantern cast a milky glow over the uneven rock. "Let's take it single file," he suggested.

"I'll go first," Duranja volunteered, stepping onto the precarious expanse, sending pebbles cascading over the edge.

I'd give him one thing—the man had guts.

He wrapped a hand around a flimsy iron handrail, dented from years of use and leaning drunkenly outward. He thought twice and decided against the rail.

Melody followed on his heels, and it took everything in me to resist asking her if Duranja jumped off a cliff...

The sharp call of seagulls pierced the air.

"Come on," she urged, pressing forward behind the all-or-nothing Duranja.

"We're running out of light," he grumbled, fading to shadow as he stepped beyond the glow of the lantern.

I hesitated.

A blanket of stars glittered overhead. And below, the deep, dark undulation of the ocean splashed ominously.

"You don't have to go," Ellis said, too softly for our team-mates to hear. "I'll take the bird," he offered, holding a hand out for Pearl.

"I'm good," I assured him. I couldn't let Melody do this without me. If something happened to her, I'd never forgive myself.

I took a deep breath and tamped down my natural fear of the decrepit bridge and a dark, most likely wet rock structure I knew nothing about.

Had Duranja taken Pirate Bill seriously when the gamemaster told us lanterns and flashlights tended to fail on this bridge?

I said a quick prayer of thanks that I wasn't tuned in to the other side.

Then I took one step onto the bridge. Two steps. I grabbed the handrail and felt it give a little. Oh boy. I snatched my hand back. *Focus.* I forced myself to keep walking. I'd faced down murderers and phantoms. I could handle whatever was on Captain Bill's island.

"It'll be fine," Melody assured me from up ahead. "Did you know there were five rock bridges in Captain Bill's day? This is the only one left. It's a treat to get to see it up close, let alone walk on it."

"What happened to the other ones?" I asked, keeping my gaze forward, as much as I wanted to look down at my feet.

"Oh, um...they all collapsed."

"Goody." Tiny pebbles rolled under my sneakers, making the whole thing feel...slippery.

"There's no logical reason the bridge would pick this time to go," Duranja said over his shoulder, echoing my fear.

Why not? Now was as good a time as any.

Especially with four people weighing it down.

I'd caught up with them, which comforted me until I realized our weight was now concentrated in one small area.

"It's only about twenty feet long," Melody said, though it felt like twenty miles. "And it's supposed to be the most haunted spot on the island."

Peachy.

I attempted to put on a brave face despite the roar of the ocean pounding against the rocks below. "At least I won't be distracted by any spirits. I'm ghost-free this weekend."

"And every weekend," Duranja muttered.

I ignored him, choosing to focus instead on the strange, icy chill that overtook us as we neared the halfway point. Melody slowed, listening to the hollow whistling of the wind.

Ellis cursed under his breath as the lantern died.

The darkness crashed over us.

"What happened?" Duranja demanded.

"The lantern failed," Ellis gritted out, sounding a lot calmer than I felt. "Try your flashlight."

"It's the haunting." I didn't need to be tuned in to detect the heaviness in the air, the prickling at the back of my neck—telltale signs the dead lingered.

"I can feel...something," Melody whispered, reaching back for my hand.

"My flashlight's not working," Duranja snapped.

"It won't." I rasped. My throat felt tight. "Not if the ghost doesn't want it to."

"I'm sure there's a *reasonable* explanation. We'll figure it out when we get to the other end of this bridge. Let's keep moving," Duranja urged.

"It's the only way out of this," I said, agreeing with him for once.

The air grew colder with every step forward.

"Verity...if that's a ghost...why can I feel it?" Melody whispered.

"It's strong." Most of us could sense spirits if we were open and they were as powerful as this one. I felt the iciness in my teeth and in my bones.

"No offense, but I don't know why Bill needs a ghost hunter." My sister whooshed out a breath. "He's not going to have trouble convincing anybody this island is haunted."

Duranja let out a grunt. "The lantern got blown out by the wind. And the salt air is probably interfering with the batteries in the flashlight. This is nothing more than a technical failure that we will solve when we get off the bridge."

Bless his heart.

"Steady," I warned Melody, who had stopped dead.

"I'm fine," she assured me. "There's just a...break in the rock." More like a gap that dropped straight down. She took a giant step over it.

I held my breath and did the same, clutching Pearl as we hurried forward toward the outline of Duranja with a blanket of stars at his back, eternally grateful to get out of that space and away from the cold, icky wetness that set the hair on my neck standing on end.

We spilled out onto the stretch of land beyond, tripping over each other as I clutched my sister and the stuffed bird. Ellis emerged from the bridge behind us a moment later, his eyes wide and his expression hard.

"You good?" he asked.

"Good as I'll ever be," I assured him, gazing up at the black-and-white-striped lighthouse before us.

"I've never felt a ghost like that," Melody whooshed.

"It wasn't a ghost," Duranja assured her, hands on his knees, staring at solid ground as if he would be eternally grateful for it.

"Just...the wind."

"Then it was a hell of a wind," Ellis gritted out.

"Oh no." Melody's voice edged up. "Bill said we have to keep the lantern lit."

She was right. "Anybody have a lighter?"

Duranja dug around in his pockets. "I think I have some matches."

But there was no need. Because right then—in front of our eyes—the cold, dead lantern light sprang to life once more.

Melody gasped.

Ellis stood speechless, staring at the flame as it flickered and danced.

Duranja huffed out a breath. "Oh, come on. The wind kept the flame low, and then the wind went away."

"Whatever lets you sleep at night," I told him.

"Let's go." Duranja charged off toward the lighthouse.

Rough steps had been cut into the rock hill ahead, probably not long after Captain Bill's time. I glanced behind us to the bridge half-enveloped in the fog, hoping to spot the lanterns of the other teams in the distance. But no light pierced the gray. It felt like we were standing in the clouds, cut off from the world.

"When we get the keystone, I'm going to run back," Duranja said, already halfway up the stairs in the dark. "You all can follow me. Be careful going back over the bridge."

"Take the lantern when you go," Ellis said, hot on his heels.

"And the bird." I hurried to catch up. He'd need all three for our finish to count.

"Will do." Duranja flashed a beam on and off. "My spare flashlight is working." He looked to Melody. "You can have it when I go back."

"Mine's been fine since we got off the bridge," she said, giving hers a flick.

I tested mine as well, and it worked perfectly.

Not that I'd tried it on the bridge.

"Let's keep moving," I said, overtaking Duranja in the rush to the stone lighthouse.

It stood at least three stories high, a stark shadow outlined by the light of the moon.

My flashlight beam caught a small sign in the grass that read:

Brown Bar Lighthouse
1803

Ellis arrived first. "This is it." He planted the lantern next to an ancient brown wood door.

Duranja grasped the handle, rattling it on its hinges as he attempted to fling it open. "It's locked."

Chapter Nine

Melody shone her light on a high-tech electronic keypad fitted with a keyhole at the bottom. Hopefully, it only took one or the other. "Pirates didn't have Master Locks," she protested.

"They also didn't have safety pins holding their sleeves together," I said as we determined how to make it inside.

The modern lock looked strange on the solid old door.

"Type in the numbers 1803," Ellis urged.

"Got it," Duranja barked, stabbing in the code.

Duranja turned the handle and yanked, but the door didn't budge.

Meanwhile, I inspected the parrot we'd been given, shining a light between her wooden toes. She was supposed to help us retrieve the keystone.

"Are there any numbers written on her?" Ellis asked.

"Not on her legs or feet," I said, which would be the only place to write or engrave a door code. "I hope it's not on the feathers." I ruffled the feathers on her red back and bright blue chest. Ellis joined me with his flashlight to help me see.

Melody and Duranja focused on the door. "Try 1722," she suggested.

"The year on the anchor from the lobby." Duranja nodded, dialing it in.

I sincerely hoped that was it, because there was nothing between the parrot's little wooden toes, nothing on Pearl's soft leather hat... Ellis held the light as I attempted to peek under a wing.

"The Phantom Hotel opened in 1902, right?" Duranja asked.

"Right," Melody agreed as he tried it.

He yanked on the lock. "Not it."

"Try June 14, 1731," I insisted, checking under Pearl's stiff red tail feathers.

Duranja shot me a squirrely look.

"That's the year Captain Bill's fierce and loyal parrot, Pearl, died in battle while saving him," Ellis said, in an excellent recall of pirate Bill's presentation.

Duranja rolled his eyes and tried it a few ways.

"No good," he said.

Well, dang. Pearl was cute, but a bust. I ran a hand through my wind-rumpled hair. "Maybe we missed a combination or key in our treasure box."

"We didn't," Melody insisted. "I double-checked. There was only the clip-on bird and the map."

"She's right," Ellis said.

Duranja planted his hands on his hips. "Pirate Bill also seemed to think we were set when we'd left the hotel."

"Let's think," I urged.

"Because we haven't been?" Duranja shot back.

"Don't get saucy," I warned him.

We could do this.

Duranja dropped to his knees and shone his flashlight on the keyhole under the punch pad. "I'm going to try to pick the lock."

"You brought tools?" Melody balked as he reached into his back pocket and drew a thin sleeve out of his wallet.

"I always have tools," he said, inserting a slim piece of metal into the underside of the lock.

Well, that was one thing he and Frankie had in common.

"While he's working on that, let's try to find another way in," Ellis suggested.

"Or around," I offered, clipping Pearl onto my shoulder. The way the map was drawn, the symbol for the keystone had been etched on top of the lighthouse. "The keystone could very well be tucked outside."

"Then what's the point of Pearl?" Melody asked as she and I went left and Ellis went right.

"I'm not sure how Pearl figures in," I admitted.

We'd figure it out.

Our lights illuminated the worn rock and scrubby grass surrounding the old stone lighthouse. "If we find this quick, I really think we can come in first," Melody said, her light darting as she searched. "Alec ran track in high school. He's fast."

I'd remember that the next time I was trying to get away from him.

We encountered Ellis at the back. "Nothing," he said, training his light up the back wall to a tiny high window. "And no other way to get inside."

Melody dug her hands through her hair. "Okay, well, if Alec can't pick the lock, then we have to break down the door."

She really wanted Duranja to buy that ring.

As if on cue, Robocop came charging around the curve of the lighthouse. "Verity, I will not allow you to damage property or even attempt to break and enter," he announced.

"Oh, that was your girlfriend suggesting it," I said, watching his face fall. "If she tries it, maybe you should arrest her."

His mouth dropped open.

Melody was right. This weekend was fun.

My sister crossed her arms over her chest. "Well, do you see another way in?" she asked her boyfriend, who still hadn't quite recovered his composure. "You said it yourself. We absolutely have to come in first on this challenge."

"Less talking, more doing," Ellis said. He directed a sharp nod to Duranja, paired with a glance up at the high window. "Let's see if the keystone is in there."

Without another word, Ellis bent and held his hands down to hitch the slightly shorter, leaner Duranja up on his shoulders. Duranja complied, and in a few seconds, we had eyes inside the lighthouse.

I glanced to my sister. "I think they've done this before."

She smoothed her hair behind her ears. "We are dating the best of the Sugarland PD."

Robocop stared intently through the glass. "I see the keystone! Smack-dab in the center of the floor." Ellis began to ease him down. "Hold up." Duranja stiffened, causing Ellis to sway a bit. "I see a paper on the back of the door. Like a Post-it. What if it's the punch code key?"

"Can you read it?" Ellis asked, his voice strained from holding the other officer's weight.

Duranja huffed. "Not without Rick's magnifier or the professor's telescope. But oh wait—we have a bird."

"At least nobody else can get it," I said, searching for a bright side.

He looked at me like he wanted to use me as a battering ram.

"That's it. I have to put you down," Ellis barked. As he eased Duranja off his shoulders, he drew in a sharp breath and added, "See if Frankie can go in and read it."

He didn't know what he was asking.

Melody clapped her hands together. "That could have been Bill's plan all along."

"No, it wasn't," Duranja said dryly.

"I'll try," I promised. Although it had been a miracle the gangster had showed up the last time. Frankie didn't respond well to being summoned.

"We're at our wits end, here, sweetie," Ellis said by way of apology.

"I know," I said, drawing away from the lighthouse, looking for a little space. "Frankie?" I called, feeling the cool sea air coming in off the ocean. "Sorry to do this again, but we could really use your help."

"A ghost?" Duranja's voice floated after me. "That's our solution? A ghost?"

When he put it that way, it made me more eager to try.

"I'm going to pick the lock." Duranja stalked toward the door.

I hoped he could. In the meantime, I called again. "Frankie." I spotted a fleck of gray down near the cliffs by the rock bridge and glanced back at the others. "I hope that's him." I wasn't tuned in, so it wasn't as if I'd be seeing anything else ghostly.

"Tell him it's urgent," Melody pressed.

Yeah, that didn't tend to motivate Frankie.

"Be safe," Ellis said, giving me space as I hurried down the hill. "And don't tune in if you can help it."

"Believe me, I won't," I called over my shoulder. Because I really didn't want to meet whatever was on that bridge.

My light danced over the uneven ground as I rushed toward the outlook on our side of the haunted bridge. "Frankie!" The gangster crouched with his back to the cliff, his hat in hand, completely ignoring me.

"Frankie!" I clattered down the stone steps. "I'm going to keep calling your name until you answer."

He slammed his eyes closed.

As if that would make me go away.

He stared at something on the ground in front of him.

"The lighthouse is locked," I told him.

He ground his jaw. "Oh no. Whatever shall we do?"

I was so glad he asked. "There's a Post-it note—" I began.

"Cut it." He threw up his hands and stood. "I'm not doing any favors for you. This is my time. You said so."

"All you have to do is go through the wall." Easy as pie. "There's a Post-it on the back of the door. Check and see if the door combination is written on that, and you can help me break and enter," I added, sweetening the pot. "I also need you now because we're in a hurry."

He shook his head slowly. "Using a door code is *not* breaking and entering."

He would get caught up in semantics. "Then you can sneak through the window. Let's go!"

But the gangster didn't move. He held his jaw stiff and his body tight as he looked at something over my shoulder. "Her? I don't know her. Never seen her before in my life."

"Are you talking about me?" I asked, turning even though I knew I'd never be able to see anyone besides Frankie.

Frankie's gray skin went almost white.

The bird on my shoulder grew cold. The metal clasp went frigid.

"What's going on?" I asked, not sure I wanted to hear the answer.

But Frankie wasn't paying attention to me anymore. "Hey, calm down. Join me in a little game of liar's dice."

Pearl's feathers ruffled in the wind.

A trickle of dread wound through me. "Are you talking to pirates? I have Captain Bill's parrot."

"Pearl?" Frankie asked as if hearing the word out of thin air. "No," he stated with a straight face. "Different bird. Now, go. Leave. Now!" he insisted. *Run.* His disembodied voice sounded in my ear.

If I knew one thing about Frankie, it was that he didn't fool around when it came to scary ghosts. I turned and fled. I clutched Pearl to my shoulder as I hightailed it up the hill and back toward the lighthouse.

Ellis met me halfway. "Did you get Frankie?" he pressed.

"No," I said, disappointed, double-checking to make sure nothing had followed me.

As if I could see.

"But I don't think his new friends liked the fact I have Captain Bill's bird. The sooner we get out of here, the better."

"Agreed," Ellis said as I unclipped Pearl from my shoulder.

"There has to be something we're missing," I said, inspecting her once again. Ellis lent his beam.

I suspected the Post-it note was left behind for the other teams to steal our prize if we couldn't solve the puzzle of Pearl. So that meant our clue was still on her. "Pirate Bill said to listen to what Pearl has to say." But I'd checked her feet, her feathers, her beak. I ran my fingers over the leather hat she wore, feeling the supple leather. If the hat were as old as she was, I'd expect it to be stiff or cracked.

I took a closer look. As I lifted the edge, I spotted a glob of hot glue.

"That's not exactly vintage," Ellis said as I attempted to pry the glue off her and perhaps see under her cap.

"I don't want to tear the feathers." I winced. We had to be super careful with the real bird.

My fingers danced over the soft cap and felt a small, hard disk. "Hold on a sec." I pressed it and felt it give.

"Squawk! Birthday bird in an egg... March 5, 1724. Squawk! I'm a pretty bird!"

"Yes." I fist-pumped.

"Come on," Ellis urged.

We dashed to the front of the lighthouse, where Duranja knelt, cursing.

"It's Pearl's birthday," Ellis hollered.

"March 5, 1724!" I roared as Ellis punched in 03051724. Duranja stood back, and Ellis swung open the door in triumph.

"I love you!" I gushed. And I meant every word.

There on the floor lay a beautiful blue stone as large as my palm. It appeared to be made of sea glass.

"That's got to be it," Melody said, rushing in to grab it.

"We did it," I whooshed, ten kinds of relieved. "That stone is gorgeous!"

"We need to get back now," Duranja warned, checking his

watch. "Hopefully the other teams ran into similar trouble, but we can't count on it."

Right. "Time to go," I said, fetching him the lantern. He'd also need the bird. I searched for a panicked second until I realized I'd clipped her back onto my shoulder.

He clutched the lantern, stuffed the keystone into his pocket, held out his hand for the bird, ready to run.

I unclipped her, when Frankie stumbled into the space between us, wild-eyed, clutching his neck.

"What the—" A thin line of blood bubbled from his neck.

I gasped in horror. "Frankie, are you all right?"

"Sorry," he gurgled. An unseen force lifted him a half foot off the ground. "They aren't giving me a choice."

"No." My voice thudded low in my throat as I felt the icy-cold stab of Frankie's power flowing over me, in me. Through me.

The air around us shimmered.

Odd shapes emerged in the night.

Ghosts took form in front of me, behind me. A gang of dirty, sneering pirates.

Ellis rushed to my side. "Verity!" He held me up. I hadn't realized I'd slumped.

Melody broke away from Duranja. "Is she okay?"

I stiffened and stood my ground as more and more pirates appeared out of thin air. A half dozen. A dozen.

Before I knew it, I was surrounded by the dead.

Chapter Ten

Duranja held out a hand. "Give me the bird so I can go!"

"Don't." A pirate with a pocked face and rotten teeth glared at me.

"Can you all give me a second?" I asked to the clink of metal, the unsheathing of blades as the pirates drew their weapons. "Pirates," I whispered to Ellis. "I'm surrounded."

He squeezed my shoulder. "What can I do?"

"Nothing."

"We'll see about that." He edged over to Duranja and turned the lantern key, dousing the flame. "Look," he said, redirecting Robocop. "We can't finish without a lit lantern."

Robocop cursed and slammed the lantern down. "Where are my matches?"

"I think you put them in this pocket," Ellis said, fumbling with Duranja's jacket, in Robocop's way as he helped. "Check his pants," he said as Melody joined in. "Be quick," my boyfriend added to me.

"I will," I promised, feeling the cold prick of a ghostly sword at my back.

I'd like nothing better than to skedaddle out of there.

"It's Pearl all right," murmured a ghost behind me.

"That bird never leaves the captain's sight," gruffed a pirate to my left.

"Except the captain's dead," I told them. This bird was in the realm of the living. They had no reason to bother me.

Pock Face scoffed. "Captain Bill is as alive as I am."

Uh-oh. I turned to Frankie. "Do I really have to explain to these guys that they're dead?"

"I wouldn't," the gangster said.

My heart sped up, and my mouth went dry.

"What are you doing with the captain's bird?" the pock-faced pirate demanded. "And why is she wearing a hat?"

"Go get the captain," I suggested. Maybe I could run while they left to fetch him.

"He's busy," snapped Pock Face.

"With the wedding," Eye Patch added, as if I should know.

I did. Sort of.

I tucked Pearl closer to me. "The captain asked me to look after her." I notched my chin up. It wasn't a complete lie. "He'd tell you that if he were here," I said, growing more confident. "As for the hat... The captain wants Pearl to look her best for the wedding."

Pock Face chuckled. Four more pirates behind him joined in.

He leaned close, his breath smelling like alcohol and smoke. "That bird is the most fearsome pirate on our ship."

"She's the captain's most prized treasure," said the pirate next to him. This one had a real eye patch. The air went frigid as he ruffled his fingers through the feathers on her neck.

"Mighty brave of you," Pock Face cackled. "After she took your eye."

"I looked at her funny and lost half my nose," said the scallywag on his other side.

"I never touched her," Eye Patch insisted. "I never said an ill word against her, and she still attacked me when Mack knocked her cage with the mop handle."

"That was your mistake," a voice thundered behind me.

I turned and saw a man who could have made it as a pro wrestler. His scraggly hair hung down over his shoulders, woven with beads and bits of bone.

"Don't ever touch the cage." Bony Beads spat onto the ground. "Even after she died in battle, touching her cage has been a curse to anyone near it."

Pock Face nodded his agreement. "We toasted her the day she died."

"We toasted *because* she died," added the man behind me.

"So why'd the captain trust her to you?" Eye Patch demanded.

"I'm...Catherine's sister," I fibbed, glad I'd remembered the name of Captain Bill's bride. "In for the wedding." I smoothed a lock of hair behind my ear. "I have a knack with bloodthirsty birds. After her last battle, Pearl here lost a couple of feathers, so Bill asked me to fix her up. She must look her best for the nuptials."

Pock Face eyed me like he didn't believe me, which, to be fair, was a smart move. But he didn't argue. Maybe Captain Bill could be as vicious as Pearl.

He exchanged a glance with Eye Patch. "Well, you'd better hope Pearl likes what you done. Misfortune follows those fool enough to upset her. You don't want what happened to Old Squigs to happen to you."

Oh my. "What happened to Old Squigs?"

Bony Beads licked his lips. "He bumped into her cage five years after her demise. He fell overboard that night."

Pock Face cocked his head. "Cursed he was, as is anyone who crosses Pearl."

"Well, it's a good thing I'm making her look fabulous," I said, radiating a confidence I didn't feel.

Eye Patch stared me down. "Since we know a little whelp like you couldn't kill a man so mighty as the captain, he must have his reasons for trustin' you with his precious Pearl. But mark my words, you'd best guard her well. Or deal with the consequences."

"Seriously?" I managed.

Pock Face laughed. "We'll make you sorry if you don't."

Bony Beads made a show of cracking his scarred knuckles. "Oh, yes, my darling." His front lip hitched up. "Never let Pearl out of your sight. Keep her secret. And make sure there isn't a feather out of place when we see her next."

"How am I supposed to keep her a secret and also keep her with me all the time?" I asked, struggling to understand. It would be impossible to hide a large parrot on my person. Her feathers would get mussed if I kept her in my bag too long, and we would be running around a lot this weekend. "Or does she *have* a secret? And if so, I'd like to know."

"Do your job," Pock Face snarled. He tilted his head and stared at me as if he could see into my soul. "Fail at your own peril. We have our ways of making people pay."

"All right." I nodded frantically. "I'll take good care of her."

"You do that," Bony Beads ground out as the pirates began to fade.

"We'll be watching..." rasped a hollow voice.

Chapter Eleven

The ghosts disappeared. Frankie, too.

"Let's go!" Duranja stood with a lit lantern, Melody's soft grip on his shoulder the only thing holding him back.

"Right." This might be one of the few times Duranja had a point. "Race you," I said, taking off toward the hotel, keeping a tight hold on Pearl.

Duranja cursed and ran after me.

Ellis caught up first. "Talk to me. What just happened?" he pressed as we dodged rocks and brush, the beams of our flash-lights dancing over the ground ahead.

"Pearl here is precious to Captain Bill, and the crew wants to make sure I take good care of her. Also, she may have a secret. Or I have to keep her secret. The pirates seem to think I know which one it is." To be fair, I'd told them I'd talked to Captain Bill.

He clearly hadn't been expecting that. "Is that going to cause a problem for us?" His attention darted to the darkness behind me as if he could suss out Pock Face or old Bony Beads.

"No more than usual," I admitted.

"That bad, huh?" he quipped, earning a grin from me.

He steadied me as I stumbled over a rock. "What I'd give to lend a hand. Or some muscle."

"Just help me keep a close eye on this bird."

We hustled down the slope of the hill to the narrow rock bridge. The chill off the coast tore through my jacket and sent goose bumps up my arms.

"Do we really have to do this all together?" Duranja demanded, barreling ahead with Melody on his heels.

"Yes," Ellis and I said together.

Duranja paused at the edge and whipped out a flashlight, ready to take the lead. "Watch the rail. It's wobbly. Be smart. Be careful. Keep pushing even if our lights fail again," he said, reaching behind him to take Melody's hand.

I grabbed his arm instead. "Wait!" Now that I had Frankie's power, I could see exactly what was wrong with the bridge.

"It's a lady," I said, pointing, though nobody else could see the apparition glowing gray in the moonlight.

She stood alone in the middle of the expanse, blocking our escape. The wind off the ocean whipped her white gown around her legs and chest. A white veil shrouded her face and streamed out behind her.

"We can't wait," Duranja said, shaking off my grip. "We've had enough delays." He reached for Melody's hand once more. "We have to get going, or we'll lose."

I got it. I did. But he didn't. "There's a spirit out there. I think we found the pirate bride!"

"For real?" Ellis stopped short behind me.

"It's got to be." This was Phantom Island, after all.

"Not for real!" Duranja shot back. "None of this is real."

"I can't walk across this bridge without walking through her." It was too narrow. When I didn't have Frankie's power, contact with a ghost would feel chilly and eerie. But fully tuned in? Both the ghost and I would be in for a terrible shock. It felt frigid and piercing and invasive on a soul-deep level. "She could really hurt me if she felt threatened."

"What should we do?" Melody asked, holding back.

"Let me think." Maybe I could help her move on. Or at least convince her to let me pass.

"No," Duranja said before I could formulate a plan. "Nope. No. Nopety nope. You can stay back, but we have to go." He began to lead Melody across.

The ghost held up a hand to stop them. "Don't do it," I said. "She's not keen on having people on her bridge."

"Verity," Duranja warned, "I'm cold. It's late. We're not stopping for you or for any ghost brides, ghost pirates, or ghost parrots."

"For the love of Pete. You just don't get it."

Now that I was tuned in, I didn't see a ghost parrot anywhere, but according to the crew, maybe that was a good thing. She sounded vicious.

Melody halted in her tracks. "If Verity says there's a problem, there's a problem," she insisted.

Duranja looked set to chew nails.

Ellis stiffened. "If we tick the ghost off, she could go after Verity, and we'd be helpless to stop it."

It had happened before, and it had been awful.

I looked to Duranja. "I know you don't believe in any of this, but a powerful enough ghost can do real damage in the real world, and this one is strong." The apparition was fully formed. She clearly haunted the bridge. And I'd bet dollars to donuts she was the entity who had killed our lights. If that had been her warning, who knew what she would do if we pressed on? "We shouldn't upset her."

"So we're supposed to stand here all night?" Duranja asked. "In case a ghost might get mad?"

He didn't even believe in it.

"I don't know," Melody said. "You both have a point."

"Give me the bird, and I'll run ahead," he said. "The ghost isn't going to bother me."

"I can't." Or we'd have more than one angry ghost on this

bridge. "Just give me the time to talk to her, and we can get past her without our lights going out."

Or any more trouble.

"We don't have time," Duranja insisted.

Melody looked from me to Duranja, chewing her lip as she did.

"Maybe I can take the bird," Melody offered. "The pirates won't notice the difference between Verity and me."

"That's not a good idea," I warned. In no way, shape, or form did I want those pirates going after Melody while she was on such a precarious expanse.

"It could work," she maintained, looking to her boyfriend, who nodded. "We have to try it."

"I don't like it," I said as she eased the bird from me.

"Trust me," she insisted.

"I do trust you," I promised. But he was leading her down the wrong path, and I had no way of knowing what the ghosts on this island were capable of.

"I'll stay here with you," Ellis vowed.

I'd still worry. The pirates had gone. The lady in white didn't appear angry. But that could change in an instant.

"We'll be fine," Duranja said. "I've got you." He smoothed a lock of hair from Melody's cheek and tucked it behind her ear. "Trust me. It's important that we remain focused."

Melody clipped the bird to her shoulder.

The ghost floated inches above the rocky expanse, watching us.

"We can turn back if it gets bad," she said, squeezing his hand as he led her onto the bridge, straight for the apparition.

"With any luck, they'll pass straight through," Ellis said, running a hand along the back of his neck.

"We did before," I reasoned.

Oh, who was I kidding? I had a terrible feeling about this.

I took a deep breath.

The lady in white couldn't hurl them from the slippery

expanse. At least I hoped and prayed not. But a deathly cold shock or nudge could force them to make a tragic mistake.

If she were strong enough, she could bring the whole bridge down.

The woman in white shrieked as Duranja and Melody made a steady advance toward her. This wasn't good.

The ghost retreated with every step they took, stumbling dangerously close to the gap in the rock. She whipped off her veil and let it billow into the wind.

Delicate curls clipped with glittering pins and combs quivered in a high mass above her head. Her heart-shaped chin jutted out as she held out a hand to block him. "Don't come any closer! I'll make you sorry."

Duranja's flashlight flickered and went dead.

Now did he believe me?

"She just killed your light." Ellis's voice went a little thready.

"I'm scared," Melody said, gripping Duranja's arm with both hands, as if she could haul him into a full retreat.

"We're fine," Duranja insisted, doubt creeping into his voice even as he doubled down on his denial.

The ghost began shaking all over.

Then the bridge itself started to tremble. Pebbles tumbled over the edge in the real world.

Terror threaded through me. "Get off the bridge!" I ordered.

"What's going on?" Ellis demanded.

"The ghost is the one making the bridge shake." It hadn't done that when we'd crossed earlier. She was desperate.

"We're almost halfway," Robocop said. Naturally, he couldn't be prudent when it counted. "I'll keep you safe," he assured my sister, blindly pressing forward though he had no way of knowing what he faced.

The spirit began to weep, taking a wavering step backward toward the break in the rock.

"You have Pearl," she wailed. "He's gone. He's gone."

I should never have given Melody that bird.

"Verity?" Melody glanced back at me, as if seeking my permission to follow her fool man.

"It's a lady in white, and I think she's mistaking Duranja for someone who wants to hurt her, maybe one of the pirates." He was certainly obnoxious enough. "She's backing down, but I don't know for how long."

I skirted along the edge of the cliff, trying to get the spirit's attention. Perhaps she'd listen to me even if half our team didn't. "You're safe right now. I promise," I called to her. "The man on the bridge isn't a threat. He's just a jerk."

"Verity," Melody admonished.

A piece the size of my hand broke off the bridge and tumbled down onto the rocks below.

"Move!" I told my sister.

The woman in white stared at me. Through me. Pain shone in her eyes.

The lady's entire body shook. "You won't win," she cried, ripping a pearl necklace from her throat, the beads exploding across the bridge and into the night. She pointed the broken remains at Duranja. "You'll never win!" She threw her jewelry down into the ocean.

The pebbles near the center of the bridge began to roll and shift. "What's happening?" Melody cried, gripping the railing.

Exactly what I'd warned her about.

"We have to help them," Ellis said, making a move toward the bridge.

"Not you," I insisted. "Let me."

I focused on the ghost. "We don't want your necklace or anything else from you," I stated, trying to think what I could do to calm the spirit. "We're from Sugarland, Tennessee," I added, as if that would make our case. "We only need to cross the bridge so we can get back to our hotel."

Duranja braved another step forward in the dark. "This is all Pirate Bill's fault."

The ghost recoiled.

"Don't talk about him," I warned.

"Who? Pirate Bill?" Duranja asked, causing the ghost to shriek.

Dang it. We might be able to calm her if he'd only halt his advance. I might even be able to help her see there was more to the afterlife than haunting a rock bridge on a remote coastal island, but I couldn't do anything while he made her feel like a trapped animal.

The shaking intensified. The railing broke loose in Melody's hands. She dropped it and fell into Duranja, forcing him off-balance. He stumbled forward, sending a cascade of rocks careening over the edge.

The woman in white gripped her throat with both hands. She had nowhere else to go except...

I watched, petrified, as the poor girl clutched her fists to her chest. She screamed and wavered backward toward the gap.

"Don't move," I ordered as Duranja regained his balance and drew within touching distance. I focused all my attention on the ghost, afraid I might start screaming with her. "Don't mind him. Just talk to me," I pleaded. But she didn't speak again. She refused to look at me.

The ghost stared at Duranja for a long moment. Then she turned and took a swan dive straight off the bridge.

I rushed forward, too late to stop her from falling. I was halfway across the bridge before I saw the faint gray glow of her spirit crumpled on the rocks below.

"She's gone," I said dully. She lay dead and broken, the ocean waves tousling her hair. I had a feeling it wasn't the first time she'd died that way.

She'd keep haunting this bridge.

She'd keep dying.

It was a horrible way to go, and she'd almost taken my sister with her.

Ellis had already made it to Melody, and I hurried to join him, gathering up my shaking, terrified sister, and helping her across.

Now that the ghost had departed, our flashlights flickered on.

"All right," Duranja said, gripping his light, completely missing the implication. "Steady," he said, taking the lead once more.

At least the winds had died down. I could watch where I was going and avoid a lot of the slippery rocks.

But I couldn't stop thinking about how I could have lost my sister.

Or picturing that poor woman crumpled on the rocks.

It was a relief to step onto solid land. Another gift was that Duranja appeared as shaken as I felt.

"*Now* do you believe Verity?" Ellis demanded.

My entire body quaked. "You never should have taken your chances with an unhinged ghost. You could have gotten yourselves killed tonight!"

"I don't know what we were thinking," Melody said, clutching her forehead.

"Here," I said, taking the bird off her hands. The ghost on the bridge had reacted quite strongly to Pearl, as had the pirates. I wasn't about to risk my sister again.

Duranja planted his feet firmly on solid ground and shook his head. "I admit that was scary. The rail was loose, and a wave hit the rocks. They should never have sent us this way. But nothing about that was supernatural." He didn't sound as convinced as before. Still, he ground his jaw at my disbelieving huff. He flicked his flashlight on and off a few times. "This is ridiculous. The bridge is a menace," he said, hitching up his pants, "and enough of the ghost drama."

He directed his light toward the hotel and began walking.

I glared a hole in his back. "I'm going to kill him," I said to Ellis. "He's always accusing me of murder. Well, this time he's going to be right."

∾

We kept a strong, steady pace on the way back, pressing as fast as we could in the dark. Duranja took the lead with Melody close behind. Ellis and I brought up the rear. We'd been gone at least an hour, which was a problem when every second counted.

Duranja had been correct in that respect.

I brightened when I realized we might be doing better than we'd imagined.

"Look," Melody said, pointing down toward a light bobbing along the beach near the dock. "Rick's still down there."

"I figured he'd come in first," Ellis murmured.

"Why?" I asked.

"His keystone was placed along the main drag from the docks to the hotel," Ellis said. "It's well-lit, familiar territory and close to the finish line."

Duranja's light found the main path, and we veered north.

"You got that good a look at his map?" Melody asked, out of breath as we began climbing up toward the hotel at a good clip.

"We both did," Duranja said, keeping up a blistering pace.

Then it clicked.

The vivid blue keystone we'd found on the floor of the lighthouse bore a striking resemblance to the green stone Duranja had grabbed on the way up from the boat. Both stones appeared to be made of sea glass, both with a hook on the end.

"Duranja," I said, stomach sinking, breath burning in my lungs, "I think you took Rick's keystone."

"I know I did," he said, focused on the warm yellow light shining through the windows of the historic inn.

And he thought Rick had double-crossed *us*?

We couldn't just leave the author down on the beach. "We need to give his keystone back."

Melody slowed. "You think we should go down there and tell him we have it?" she gasped between breaths.

"Absolutely not," Duranja ordered, barely winded. "For once, we have an advantage. Thanks to me."

"To be fair, we didn't even realize we had it," Ellis said, "until—"

"We recovered our keystone from the lighthouse," I finished.

I'd been so focused on the pirates it hadn't registered fully.

Well, it did now.

"We're not the sneaky types," I insisted, renewing my uphill battle.

"Since when?" Duranja wondered out loud.

Okay, that was aimed at me.

"It's part of the game." Melody hustled alongside me.

"Melody, our parents taught us to play fair," I reminded her. She was hanging out with Robocop too much. "What about you?" I asked, glancing over my shoulder to Ellis, who always had my back.

The lantern cast its light forward onto the group, making it impossible to read my boyfriend's expression. "The gamemaster said it's fine to snag an extra keystone," he pointed out. "He practically encouraged it."

"That doesn't mean we have to do it," I said, tossing my hands up, almost forgetting I carried a stuffed bird. And I thought Pearl would be my biggest problem tonight.

Ellis shook his head, resigned. "This is a game, and the goal is for the four of us to work together and win."

"I don't know." It still felt wrong to me.

My boyfriend's mouth formed a grim line. "I get being friendly with the others." He ignored a huff from Duranja. "I get helping out when we can. But we can't forget we're in a competition."

"We don't know Rick or his motives," Melody said. "You only met him tonight. I mean, his wife was supposed to be upstairs sick, and then we learned she's out for a walk?"

That bothered me as well. "I don't have all the answers," I admitted.

Duranja slipped his hand into Melody's. "We're playing by the rules," he stated, taking the hotel stairs two at a time.

"I suppose I'm used to working alone," I said. "Or with Ellis." But we thought alike most of the time.

"We're your team," Melody pointed out as we clambered up behind Duranja. "Trust us."

I was trying. The author's lantern was now a speck on the beach. He was in the dark, out in the cold. All because of us. "I'm still not sold."

"You're outvoted." Duranja flung the door open for my sister. "I'm keeping it."

Melody shot me an apologetic look and slipped inside.

They really were just going to walk in with Rick's keystone stashed in Duranja's pocket.

I hoped we wouldn't regret it.

"I think it's the right call for now," Ellis assured me, taking my hand and leading me into the warmth of the hotel. Leaving my new friend in the dark.

Chapter Twelve

Any further debate ended when we blasted into a lobby rich with the ghosts of tourists past. The men wore sports jackets; the women were draped in pearls. A pair of children dueled with wooden swords before their mother shushed them, and a look from their father had them sheathing their weapons.

Amazingly, the hotel itself appeared just as it had in the ghosts' time.

It seemed Bill wasn't big on change.

I found it nice that the ghosts had chosen to spend their after-lives in a place they'd enjoyed.

Or maybe they were just here for vacation, like we were.

I tried to appear as natural as possible as I dodged a little girl who'd run to see a boy holding a small box. A live frog peeked out the top. He closed the lid a second before his mother arrived to take his hand and lead him to dinner.

As the spirits chatted and filed toward the dining room, I saw Professor Fielding conversing with a woman near the curve of the stairs.

She was petite, wearing all black. Her brunette hair, cut into a bob, shielded most of her face. He noticed me and waved while she headed up the stairs. That must be Rick's mysterious wife.

. . .

Robocop charged straight ahead, toward Pirate Bill, who hurried out from behind the front desk to greet us. "Congratulations! You've snagged second place."

"Second place?" I figured we'd be rolling in dead last.

"Do you have your keystone?" Bill asked.

Melody held up the bright blue artifact, and the professor's eyes went wide as he joined us. "You've got the Jewel of the Ocean." A pained expression crossed his features. "These belong in a museum."

"Gathering dust." Our host waved him off.

"Oh, we'll take care of our keystone," Duranja said, giving it a big, sloppy kiss. "This is our ticket to winning the weekend."

"How romantic," I remarked.

"Bathroom," Melody intoned, easing the keystone back into her pocket. The pirate pointed her toward the hallway near the stairs, but she was already on her way. I watched her pass straight through a pair of ghostly young men with shovels bent over a trinket.

"Please. Do be careful with that artifact," the professor called after her. "It is real, living history. In fact, it dates to the time Captain Bill Brown and his crew used this island as a hidden base."

"Broken record, thy name is Kevin Fielding," the pirate shushed. He directed his next question to us. "I see you have your lit lantern. Do you have your tool and your map as well?"

"Right here," I said, producing the bird while Duranja held up the map.

"Then you are officially our second-place finishers!" Our host grinned from ear to ear. "You can keep the map, blow out the lantern, and return it and the bird to the library."

"About that..." I shifted uncomfortably, lifting a hand for the high-fives Duranja had begun showering on the group. "I'd like to hang onto Pearl." Like, for the entire weekend. "Having Pearl around would be great for my—" Life, weekend, ability not to be haunted by pirate ghosts...

Our host clapped his hands together. "Tell me you've seen the ghost of Pearl the pirate."

"Not exactly," I hedged. Plenty of other pirates, though.

"Well, did you see any ghosts out there? I sent you over the haunted bridge."

What a stellar call that had been.

"I saw a pirate by the lighthouse," I admitted, not sure I wanted to be drawn into this particular aspect of the weekend. The last thing the upset bride needed was more people tromping over her bridge. It wasn't safe for the living, either.

"I knew it!" Bill quickly waved his cameraman over. "Our ghost hunter has made an official sighting! This is big. Huge!"

The photographer hustled through a trio of ghosts wearing headlamps and arguing over a map, and he motioned for me to pose with Bill. Then pose alone. Then pose again with Bill. Spots danced in front of my eyes from all the camera flashes.

"No doubt the pirate you saw was Captain Bill," our host enthused.

"It definitely wasn't Bill," I told him.

"Who's to say that?" he countered.

I believed that had been me.

At some point, Bill had unclipped Pearl from my shoulder in order to pose with her. I gently retrieved the bird. "If you don't mind, this is my good-luck charm," I said to our host. When he hesitated, I added, "If you leave me in charge of Pearl this weekend, there's a chance the real Captain Bill could seek me out."

I'd never seen a pirate swoon, but this one almost did. "Take her. Keep her!" Bill enthused.

"I'll be sure to return her," I insisted before the professor could protest. "And I'll take super good care of her."

"Of course you will," our host boomed. He took me aside. "It would be great if you could dredge up a ghost for Pearl, too. Show our spiritually inclined guests we have plenty of spirits fit for a real ghost pirate adventure."

"I'll see what I can do," I said, clipping Pearl onto my shoulder.

I left our host chuckling and rubbing his hands together.

"Are you seriously going to keep walking around with that dead bird on your shoulder?" Duranja looked at me cock-eyed while Ellis returned the lantern to the fireplace in the library.

"I don't know where else to put her." I had to keep her with me, pirates' rule.

Duranja stared at me. "We've got the keystone. We don't need it anymore."

"The pirates told me to." It was the truth. And bonus points —it made his cheeks all splotchy.

He stood speechless for a long moment before his expression clouded over. "You just have to be different." He leaned close, hands planted on his hips, clueless as the ghost of a fat striped cat peeked out from between his legs. "This is what gets me about you, Verity. This is your sister's weekend, not yours, and we might have taken first tonight if you hadn't been so focused on using your 'special gift.'" He added air quotes to the end as if my ghost-hunting skills were anything but special. "I've got news for you; there are no extra points for crazy."

"Crazy?" If Pearl's cage were around here, I'd tell him to hug it. "Look, you rushing out onto a narrow, slippery bridge in the dark, that was crazy. I was trying to help you."

He scoffed. "How about you filling Melody's head with nonsense, making her so afraid she nearly fell. That's what put her in danger."

"Melody believes me because she has good reason to. So does Ellis."

"That's almost worse," he said, as if their belief was my failing as well. "Two sane logical people let you 'talk to ghosts' tonight and hold back the team." He closed his eyes briefly. "All I'm asking is that you cut it out. *Try* to be normal."

Okay, that hurt. "Believe me, there was a time I'd have given anything to be normal." But that ship had sailed. "Now I do my best with the world I'm living in, and I at least try to understand people and care about them."

He dug a hand through his hair. "Your entire job was to work with us to get into the lighthouse and then back to the hotel. Instead you got all woo-woo and jeopardized our standing on the leaderboard. We could have made it back first if you'd just helped us the way you were supposed to."

"Help? I got us in." Thanks to Pearl.

Melody breezed back into the foyer. "We secured the stone thanks to Verity." She squeezed me on the shoulder, "and we made it across the bridge with Alec leading us." She kissed him on the cheek. "We are an awesome team who came in ahead of two other great teams, right?"

"I could have made it into the lighthouse without her," Robocop muttered.

"And I would have found a better way across the bridge." Without terrorizing my sister or a wayward spirit.

The professor looked from me to Duranja like we were a few feathers short of a duck. "I'm not exactly sure what went on with your team, but you probably couldn't have beaten me with a head start and luck on your side. My task was almost too easy."

"How so?" I asked, spying our host in animated conversation with Ellis at the entrance to the library.

The professor adjusted his glasses. "My map showed a diamond-shaped smudge on the north end of the island. It would have been hard to know where with no landmarks. Even with my knowledge of the topography."

"You would have had to trace the coast in that general area." And hope to get lucky.

"Ah, but I had my telescope." He winked.

"At night." It would do no good after dark.

"Yes." He glanced toward our host engrossed in his conversation. "Bill was in no hurry to get us out before dark. Bombastic as he is, he's no fool. Therefore, I decided the telescope had to be a clue rather than an instrument."

"Can I be on your team?" I asked, letting Melody playfully smack my arm.

Duranja took a more analytical approach. "If you couldn't see through the telescope, how was it helpful? Was there something written on it?"

The corner of the professor's mouth tilted up. "Not quite." He tented his fingers, in full lecture mode now. "Sailors used telescopes to navigate by the north star. So I used the compass on my Swiss Army knife, found the northernmost point and—boom—there was my keystone."

"A perfect display of logic," Melody enthused.

"Doesn't sound like you wasted any time, either," Duranja said.

I didn't know why he eyed me when he said it.

The professor shook his head ruefully. "I'm lucky I had my own compass, or I would have had to negotiate to use theirs."

"Your spyglass could have helped us," Melody said. "This would be easier working together."

"Yet here we are regardless." He shrugged. "I'm still shocked I came in first. I figured the twins would have beaten me, seeing as they had a head start and exact coordinates for their stone."

"They seemed pretty sure of themselves." Duranja moved to the window a few yards away and gazed out.

Dr. Fielding took off his glasses and began fiddling with them. "When I left here, I followed the twins. Not on purpose, mind you. Their path was the same as mine at first."

"Did you hope to snag their keystone if they overlooked it?" Duranja asked from his post.

Dr. Fielding cast an annoyed glance in Robocop's direction. "I admit I kept an eye out. I'd preserve it and keep it safe." He huffed. "I didn't think the coordinates they announced were real. Three hundred and twenty-two degrees northwest? The twins are too smart to give away the location of their keystone." He straightened his shoulders and placed his glasses back on. "I knew I was correct when they veered hard left about fifty yards up the path."

"Three hundred and twenty-two degrees would have taken them almost directly north," Duranja agreed.

"Which would have also put them on my map fragment," the professor said. "Anyway, I kept going north and...first place."

"Your keystone is gorgeous," Melody said, drawing my attention to the cloudy pink stone cradled in the professor's palm, cushioned on a white silk handkerchief.

"It's made from Brazilian rose quartz." He held it out for Melody to enjoy a better look. "Well, that's according to Captain Bill's diary, at least. But it appears that way, doesn't it?" He tilted it this way and that so that we could fully appreciate the beauty of the marbled pink stone. "Legend has it, the four key stones are inserted into four guard posts, and when all four have been turned, it unlocks Captain Bill's treasure."

"Do you think that's true?" Melody asked, running a finger over the pink stone.

"If it were, our host's grandfather would have unlocked the treasure decades ago. I caught Bill fiddling with the green stone down by the dock when I arrived."

"So there's a guard post down there?" I asked.

"It's down the beach from the main dock, holding up a much older ship's landing," the professor said. "Bill won't tell me where the others are, and I haven't found them yet."

"Thanks for sharing," I said. He didn't have to.

He looked to my sister. "You seem like the type to care about these objects. I'd rather you handle them than someone who is just out for money. Or to use them as trinkets."

"Want an up-close look at our keystone?" Melody asked, reaching into her pocket. "It doesn't really look like a stone at all."

His eyes lit up when she pulled it out of her pocket. "May I?" he asked, excited when my sweet sister obliged. He carefully wrapped his artifact, then withdrew another silk handkerchief to receive our stone from Melody. His lips moved softly as he examined it. He didn't utter a word as he turned it over in his silk-shrouded hands. "This one appears to be made from ancient sea glass," he said at last, "just like the diary described."

Melody gathered closer. "I helped coordinate an ancient Roman glass display when I worked at the library at Auburn. We showed cups and pitchers and an almost complete window. Which was amazing."

"Imagine looking through the same glass as an ancient Roman," the professor said reverently.

"I know, right?" Melody gushed. "But this glass is thicker than most I've seen."

"Probably from a small statue base or a cremation urn," Dr. Fielding extrapolated.

"Yikes," I muttered. I didn't need to deal with any more urns. The last one had left me saddled with a ghost and access to powers I was still trying to figure out.

At least most of the spirits from the lobby had made it to the dining room, leaving the space clear.

Belatedly, I realized I'd drawn Dr. Fielding's attention. "So, tell me more about Captain Bill's diary," I said, recovering my focus. "Have you read it?"

"We have a copy at my museum, and it's fascinating. I should try to have it published. The diary is more of a captain's log, but that's what they called them in those days. It details bounties, divisions of treasure among the crew, ship supplies, and some personal observations here and there. Do you realize how much the weather patterns have changed since Captain Bill's time?"

"If it's anything like the Matthew Flinders diary—" my sister began.

"It is!" the professor enthused.

"Can I see it?" Melody asked. From that point on, I might as well not have existed.

"I have it up in my room," he said, leading the way. They

reminded me of my grandmother and her friends discussing soap operas, or their "stories," as they liked to call them.

I was tempted to join them, and would have had no qualms about it, except those two had bonded fast and hard, and a niggling part of me wondered if Melody would get more information on her own. It would also be interesting to see if Duranja was going to be as grumpy about Melody making an ally in the game, or if that attitude was reserved only for me.

I was saved from speculation when the twins burst in the door like they were on fire.

"Argh!" Zara spun a circle when she saw me by the bell. "We got beat by *them*?"

"And the professor," I added. Although he'd been quite content not to gloat about his win.

"Hey, we took a chance," Zadie said to her sister, catching the eye of Dr. Fielding, who had halted at the stairs when the twins made their grand entrance.

"So that means Rick is last," Duranja said, "and it's definitely his light down on the beach."

"Or his wife's," I theorized.

"No, I saw her when I got back," the professor said. "Bill said she returned shortly after all of us went out on our quests. She was, of course, disqualified from competing. She would have had a head start."

She wouldn't have known what she was looking for anyway without participating in the opening of the treasure chests.

"Let's see your keystone," the professor prodded, closing in on the twins.

After a moment's hesitation, Zara shrugged and pulled it out of the knapsack on her shoulder. She held it up like a trophy, a rich brown and amber tortoiseshell stone.

"Tiger's eye," Melody said. "Some pirates used it to protect them on raids."

"But not one that big," the professor added, gazing at Melody as if she were his new favorite colleague.

"Can I see it?" I asked. The twins' keystone had the same proportions as ours, just a different base stone.

"I don't think so," Zara said, depositing it back in her sack.

"Was it where your real coordinates stated?" I asked.

If I couldn't get cooperation, I'd at least try to get a better handle of the nature of the game.

"On point exactly." Zadie grinned. "It was simple."

How nice for them. I wondered if the twins and the professor had gotten more straightforward tasks because they'd placed higher in the contest to get here first, which I'd been completely unaware of. Or if the hotel owner merely saw them as more influential in terms of publicity for the hunt.

Then again, Rick's task would have been super easy if his stone hadn't been in Duranja's pocket.

And, naturally, we'd gotten the haunted portion of the island. We'd barely made it in the door before we'd been photographed and asked for our story.

But if the twins were as good as their reputation, and if they had an easy task, it made me curious. "Why were you the third team in?"

Zara winked at me. "We were playing the game."

The twins' fist bump was interrupted when the door flew open and Rick practically fell inside. He held a smashed lantern in one hand and clutched his bloody leg with the other.

"Oh, my word. Are you all right?" I rushed to help while Duranja closed the door behind him.

"It looks worse than it is," he said, avoiding my probing fingers, hopping sideways on his good leg.

"Are you sure?" I asked, trying to see.

"I hope so," he said. I did, too. There was a lot of blood. "I was coming up the steps, and one of them gave way under me."

"That's awful." The gray slate had seemed sturdy and well maintained. Then again, this was an old hotel.

"It's fine," he said, though it probably wasn't. "I can't find my keystone anyway." He stiffened when he laid eyes on Zadie. "Did you take it?" He wiped his runny nose. "I saw you take a picture of my map."

"You held it up," Zara pointed out.

I couldn't believe I hadn't noticed her snapping a shot. Then again, the twins had been standing in the doorway behind all of us.

Rick stared Zara down. "Did you go for my keystone before I had my lantern lit?"

The professor rubbed his eyes under his glasses. "Rick, you can't talk about the twins taking your stone when you tried to take theirs."

"What?" I wouldn't have thought he had it in him.

Even Duranja appeared surprised.

Rick drew back to compose himself. "I happened to bring a compass. And I was curious. I didn't find anything."

"Too bad, so sad," Zara mused.

"It worked." Zadie did a little dance. "I had a feeling someone would go for those coordinates, and it worked!"

"Wait. How did you know?" I asked the professor.

"I didn't." He shrugged. "I killed my light when I saw another lantern coming behind me. It had to be either your team or Rick, and he just admitted it."

"This is not my night," the author muttered, shaking sand out of his hair.

"Trust me," our host boomed, making a show of rejoining us, "it'll all look better in the morning!" He caught a look at Rick's leg. "Except maybe that. Come, I have a first-aid kit in my office."

"Thanks." He limped to join our host. "Once I get fixed up, I'll head back out."

"Nonsense." Bill shook his head. "It's getting late. I'm locking the hotel for the night. You can rest up, heal a little, and look for your keystone in the morning."

"Is there anything left for me to go out and find?" Rick asked the group. I tried not to look as guilty as I felt. His eyes lit on me, and he waved off his own question. "No. Forget it. You won't tell me either way."

I was a terrible almost-friend.

Bill ushered Rick to his office while the rest of us headed for the stairs and up to bed.

"I can show you that diary if you'd like," the professor said to Melody.

"I would like that," she said, and I caught Duranja's grin.

So there was a double standard. Not that I was going to point it out. I liked the idea of Melody learning what she could from the professor.

Ellis and I would have to stop by their room afterward to see if she'd discovered anything we could use.

"While you were talking downstairs, I did some digging," Ellis said to me when he'd led me to the door to our room. I was glad at least one of us had the foresight to grab a key.

"Yes?" I asked as he unlocked the door.

"Your friend Rick has a secret."

Chapter Thirteen

"A secret?" I asked as Ellis led me inside a nautical-themed room overlooking the south end of the island. "I mean besides the sick, maybe not-so-sick wife?"

"Yeah." Ellis closed the door. "I got Bill alone to tell him the bridge wasn't safe. Structurally. I didn't mention the ghost."

"Thanks," I said, glad he'd had the foresight not to direct our host's attention to the poor bride on the bridge.

Then again, this was Ellis.

"Of course," he said, as if it were nothing. "Fair warning; Bill wants to add your ghost sighting to his treasure-hunt presentation, so be careful what you say when he asks you about it."

"Yeah, I dodged that bullet in the lobby," I said, reaching up to stroke Pearl. At least I'd secured the bird in the process.

Ellis slipped off his shoes. "In any case, we came up with a way for him to rejig the weekend to keep people off the bridge."

"That's a relief," I said, easing out of my shoes as well. It was too dangerous to risk another bridge crossing. Although I would try to find time to see if I could help lead that ghost to the light. Or at the bare minimum, assist her in finding a more pleasant place to haunt. Bill knew she was stuck on that bridge. I didn't want him turning her into a tourist attraction. And if by some miracle he decided to leave her alone, she deserved better than to be trapped and reliving her death for eternity.

Ellis took a seat on the bed, and I joined him. "Afterward, I got Bill talking about the island itself, specifically how his great-grandfather and grandfather unearthed most of the pirate artifacts we're using this weekend."

"Did he tell you where he found the bird?" I asked, depositing Pearl onto a decorative bed pillow embroidered with anchors. I reconsidered and added another pillow at her back to prop her up.

The pirates said to take care of her, and I had a lot of practice pampering pets.

Heck, if I had her long enough, my mom might make her a few costumes.

Ellis paused as if he couldn't quite believe it himself. "Pearl was interred by herself in a small iron coffin. Bill's grandfather dug it up on the beach near the caves."

"I wouldn't have expected that." Pearl's final resting place was fancier than Frankie's. "It's strange because according to both Bill and the ghosts, Captain Bill had Pearl stuffed and would even take her into battle with him after she died."

Ellis furrowed his brow. "Maybe they buried her after Bill died? In any case, the coffin's been lost," Ellis said, his attention lingering on Pearl's pillow throne. "After the hotel's heyday as a tourist mecca in the 1940s and '50s, Bill's father let the place fall into disrepair. He sold off several of the artifacts, including the pearl bracelet and earrings Captain Bill's bride was wearing when she fell."

"Jumped," I corrected.

Ellis winced. "I'm sorry you had to see that." Then gentler, he asked, "Would you like to talk about it?"

"Later," I promised. "I can tell you now that I didn't notice any earrings or a bracelet, but I saw for a fact she had a pearl neck-lace." Before she ripped it away and tossed it into the ocean.

Ellis ran a thumb along his chin, rubbing like he did when he was working things through. "The pearls were a wedding gift from the pirate and evidently worth a lot." He dropped his hand. "Captain Bill had his crest etched into them, which makes them both valuable and one of a kind. They were sold in 2005 to a wealthy collector of American nautical history—a guy who goes nuts for pirate artifacts and anything with a good story behind it."

"Don't tell me you're talking about Rick," I said, letting it sink in.

"It's Rick."

The author had pretended to have no real interest in the island or its history other than for a fun, fanciful "research" weekend getaway. "He lied to us."

"He bid against Kevin Fielding."

Unbelievable. "The professor lied to us, too."

"More like both failed to tell the whole truth," Ellis said.

"Or even acknowledge they knew each other before this weekend."

"We might have simply missed that," Ellis said, shaking his head. "They don't owe us their life stories."

"True." I was used to Sugarland, where personal secrets were an endangered species.

"This is a game, and your friend Rick is playing. He can present himself as the doe-eyed jokester all he wants, but you need to know it's at least partly an act." He leaned back onto his elbows. "And bonus—now I feel less bad about taking his keystone."

"I think I might as well," I admitted, flopping down next to him. "So, you felt bad?" It bothered me thinking he hadn't.

"It's not in my nature to take things from people, Verity. But it's expected this weekend. What I'm wondering is why Rick feels it necessary to hide his interest in the artifacts and the island. Bill obviously knows, along with Professor Fielding. Heck, I'm surprised Bill didn't tell us himself. Seems he loves to stir the pot, especially if he's got an interested party who can help him promote the island and its story."

I slid off the bed and cracked open the window so that we

could hear the sea. "Maybe Rick is here to fanboy over the artifacts." He had been excited about the tankard.

Ellis shrugged. "Rick's trying to win, or at least do well, as evidenced by his frustration tonight."

Good point. "Okay, but Rick doesn't need the money he'd get from a replica gold medallion, so it's got to be about the passion for the historical pirate goodies we get to use." I thought for another second. "Or he could have lost all his money, and he's living off his reputation."

"According to Bill, Rick tried to buy some of the artifacts we're using tonight," Ellis said soberly. "He wanted all four keystones."

"Obviously, Bill didn't sell," I said, unsure how valuable they'd be. The stones were pretty. And one had been carved in ancient glass, so that was neat. But that didn't always translate to a high price tag on the open market.

"Bill wanted them for the game. He's convinced he'll bring in more money as the next hot adventure tourism destination, and he might not be wrong. I admit, I've never been to a place like this."

Or risked his life on a bridge like the one we'd crossed. "The island needs some work, but I admit it's one of a kind. Quirky." Despite our run-ins tonight, I kind of liked it.

"So if Rick has a passion for the place and the artifacts, why is he hiding it from us?" Ellis asked, trying to work it out. "Dr. Fielding certainly isn't shy about it."

"Maybe Rick is the type to play it cool," I said, joining him again on the bed. "I mean, I love ghost hunting, but it's not like I go around talking about it."

"Maybe you're not the best example. I love you, but you can hardly keep a secret when you're excited about something."

So maybe Rick had a bit more self-control in that department.

Ellis glanced to Pearl on her pillow throne. "It's also noteworthy to me that Bill's family possesses so many artifacts. I'd expect him to have a few. His family is directly related to Captain Bill himself. But the pearls, the keystones, the compass, the tankard, *and* the telescope? Let's not forget the bird. I think they all add up to something else."

"Hoarding?" We were all guilty of that to a degree.

"Think about it," he said, shifting on the bed. "If the hotel has been in financial distress, wouldn't Bill have sold off some of these artifacts, just like his father did?"

"Maybe he has, and that's how a collector like Rick got them."

"But why keep these particular ones?" Ellis pressed. "More importantly, why not let go of any of the four keystones? I mean, according to the legend, each of the four keystones must be inserted into one of four guard posts, and when all four have been turned, it unlocks Captain Bill's treasure. You'd need to keep them if you were on the hunt for the mother lode."

That made me pause. "Okay, so we know Dr. Fielding witnessed Bill fiddling with a keystone at the old guard post attached to the main dock." I drew in a sharp breath. "You don't think..."

I was usually the fanciful one.

"I'm just looking at the facts," he said simply.

"Yes, but could the treasure really be real?" I hardly dared think it.

Ellis hitched a shoulder. "We've seen stranger things."

I could see his point. "Did you ask Bill about it?" I asked, scooching onto the bed behind him so that I could play with his hair.

"Naturally." Ellis didn't tend to beat around the bush. "Bill avoided the question. Said I should focus my energy on the treasure hunt." He closed his eyes. "I'm going to have a tough time thinking when you do that."

"Then you might have a tougher time in about two minutes," I said, kissing him lightly on the ear.

After all, this was a weekend with my man, a chance to reconnect and have a little fun that didn't involve ghosts, pirates, or double-dating with Duranja.

Ellis ran a hand down my arm and drew me into a long, sweet kiss.

A flurry of knocks hit our hotel door hard and fast. "You in there?" Duranja called.

Gah! He thought *I* had bad timing?

Ellis groaned as I sat up and went to answer the door.

Duranja stood on the other side, frowning. "Oh, good, it's you," I said, brightening when I spied Melody behind him.

"The professor might want to team up tomorrow," he said, stalking into the room.

Interesting. "I thought you were against teaming up with anybody."

"I am," he said crisply, keeping a tight hold on his frustration. "It seems Melody has taken a page out of your book."

Then I was proud of her.

Melody planted her rear on the edge of the dresser across from our bed, unimpressed by Duranja's snit.

"I should have been consulted." Duranja tried for a shrug, but it came off as a twitch.

"You would have said no," Melody reasoned.

Maybe I liked how this double-date weekend with Duranja was working out.

Melody braced her hands against the dresser. "I've been talking to Dr. Fielding about the history of the island. The keystones we're working with are delicate and need to be used correctly, or the curved tips could break off. Dr. Fielding is going to help us use and preserve ours. In exchange, we'll help him keep an eye on the twins."

"Okay..." Ellis grunted as he eased off the bed, making sure Pearl remained secure as he stood.

"I'm not even going to ask," Duranja said, raising an eyebrow at the reclining parrot.

Ellis planted his hands into his back pockets, thinking. "What else is Dr. Fielding bringing to the table?"

"Exactly." Robocop ran a hand across the back of his neck. "We'll naturally be taking great care of our keystones and our... artifact," he said, side-eyeing the bird on the pillow. "We have absolutely no reason to work with him."

"You didn't tell him we have more than one keystone." Ellis made it a statement more than a question.

"No. Of course not." Melody closed her eyes briefly. "Look. I just have this feeling that the professor is holding back on us."

"Exactly," Duranja said. "Everyone in this game has an angle."

"I don't mean it that way," Melody insisted. "I think the professor wants to confide in me," Melody added earnestly. "I can feel it."

Duranja eased next to her. "I get that you feel deeply. You connect with people, and I love that about you, but how can you trust the word of someone you barely know? People need to earn that trust, and I don't think the professor has."

"Sometimes you just know," I said, defending my sister. "The alternative is you close yourself off and become..." Robocop.

He shot me a put-upon look.

To the group, Melody added, "I know you all think I'm the research whiz, and I am, but I'm smart enough to realize Dr. Fielding knows a whole lot more. And knowledge is power, right?"

I did believe in giving people the benefit of the doubt. And I trusted her instincts when it came to getting the information we needed to solve a mystery. Still... "Are you sure we can trust the professor to tell us the truth?" To Duranja's earlier point, it was becoming quite clear that everyone had an agenda. "Dr. Fielding already has one keystone, and he could win if he somehow tricks us out of one of ours." Duranja huffed, and I shot him the side-eye, only to recognize that I'd won his approval for once.

Ellis jumped in. "I also think it's important to keep in mind what I learned about Rick tonight." He filled the group in on the author's double motive. "Going forward," Ellis said, addressing the group, "let's check ourselves when we start to think we should trust a competitor just because we like him. Or her."

"Okay, but the professor is different," Melody insisted. "He's only concerned about the artifacts."

"Maybe so, maybe not," Duranja concluded. "Sure, that's what he says, but this isn't Sugarland. You can't take everything he says at face value."

No place was Sugarland. "I understand the not trusting," I admitted. After Rick's omissions, I saw all too clearly. "But it doesn't mean we can't work with another player for our mutual benefit. Rick included. It's built into the game. As long as we're not putting our team at risk, it benefits us to share tasks and knowledge with others. Look at how much faster we'd have gotten into the lighthouse tonight if we'd had the professor's tele-scope when we looked through that window for the door code."

"Exactly," Melody said. "And we should probably be keeping a closer eye on the twins anyway. If they win a challenge again, the best we can hope for is a tie for the medallion."

Duranja frowned and glanced down at Melody's hand. Seemed he really wanted that ring.

But the temptation was short-lived. Instead of agreeing, he began to pace. "The fewer strangers we work with, the less we have to worry about."

"Truth be told, I'm not crazy about teaming up with anyone at this point," Ellis admitted. "We have two keystones, which gives us the advantage. Dr. Fielding's ability to contribute to our team is questionable. I don't think the twins will want to work with another team, and Rick is—I hate to say it, Verity—but Rick is pretty much out of the race without a keystone."

"I would also feel bad about using his knowledge, seeing as we double-crossed him," I felt obliged to add.

Duranja halted his pacing. "It's a pirate game, Verity. It's supposed to be cutthroat."

"Professor Fielding said in exchange for keeping an eye on the twins, he'll show me something from that diary that will give us an advantage," Melody said. "Provided we're still in the game by the time we can actually use the information."

"Oh, good," Duranja mused. "A promise for a later date."

"No," Melody corrected him. "I'll make him show me right away." She looked to the group. "Dr. Fielding doesn't know we have two stones. He doesn't know how close we can really get. And nobody else has read the diary save Dr. Fielding. This is a unique opportunity."

"You are a master at getting things done," I said to her.

"Trust me. He's the real deal. I can't learn what he knows in one night, no matter how many great books are down there in the library. But this? This is original source material. It could be huge."

I looked to Ellis. "It might say something about the bird."

"Or something to help us on our hunt," Duranja said, as if my reasoning were completely absurd.

"Let's do this," I told her. "You know I believe in you."

Duranja nodded. "Me too. I mean, if you're this convinced, Melody, then yes, let's go for it."

We looked to Ellis, who held up his hands. "Okay. But we're using both of our keystones before we consider helping the professor with anything else," he cautioned.

Melody clasped her hands together and gave a little squeal. "This is so exciting, you all."

"Happy birthday," Duranja said, giving her a hug and a wink.

He'd beaten me to it, but just this once, I didn't mind.

Later, as I finished brushing my teeth for bed, I couldn't escape a niggling thought.

I walked out of the bathroom and found Ellis propped up in bed, reading with Pearl on the pillows next to him.

"An enthusiast wants to talk about his passion," I said,

picking up a bottle of lavender hand lotion from my overnight bag on the dresser. I mean, it couldn't just be me who tended to do that. And when you're excited, you have to let it out. "So why isn't Rick all over Bill and his hotel full of history?" I asked, rubbing lotion in to my hands. "Why is he playing it cool?"

"You see my point." Ellis propped his book on his chest and considered the question. "I think he's after something else."

"The keystones he tried to buy?" If that were the case, he'd have been doubly frustrated tonight.

"Maybe it's one of the artifacts Bill hasn't added to the game," Ellis suggested. "It would be a lot easier to nick something that's off the radar. Or something that's already been used and returned."

I gathered Pearl from her throne and made her a new home on the dresser across from the bed.

"Did the pirates say why she's so important to them?" Ellis asked, amused when I planted her on top of my travel jewelry box.

I mean, pirate bird. Jewels. It fit.

"They just told me to keep her with me and safe under threat of perpetual haunting."

I returned to Ellis and climbed into bed next to him. "I find her name very interesting considering Captain Bill's wedding gift to his kidnapped bride." Poor girl. Taken from her home and forced into marriage against her will. I'd be happy if I could help the ghost move on. She deserved some peace. And Melody would be thrilled if our treasure hunt resulted in not only a win for the team, but also a ghost girl gaining her freedom at last.

Ellis wrapped an arm around me. "Let's get up early and sneak out to the rock bridge," he suggested with me snuggling warm at his side. "You can help the ghost. I'll be there to back you up. And maybe you can have a chat with her about the pirates while you're at it."

"I'd like that." I gave him a little kiss on the chest.

"The more we know, the safer you'll be," he said, holding me close. "And you may discover something that will help us win the scavenger hunt."

"You always know what to say to make me feel good," I said, drawing him down for a kiss. He was my friend, my partner. And a great kisser to boot.

Afterward, I fell asleep listening to the waves through the open window.

That night, I dreamed of lights on the beach.

I woke suddenly in the predawn, bleary-eyed and chilled to the bone.

"Finally!" Frankie declared on an exhale, his cigarette smoke tickling my nose.

"What are you—?" I sat up with a jerk and sneezed.

"I thought I was going to have to use more than my jacket to wake you up," he said, taking a hard drag. "The pirates wouldn't have been so gentle."

"I've got Pearl," I said automatically, motioning to the dresser as another chill seized me.

Dang Frankie and his ghostly touches. He knew better than to do that.

Unless it was important.

Or maybe he wasn't alone.

I clambered out of bed, my mind instantly clear. I scanned the room for Bony Beads or Pock Face and heaved a relieved sigh when I realized I had only one annoying gangster to deal with.

"What is it?" Ellis asked, awake and staggering to his feet.

"See for yourself." Frankie pointed to the window. I drew Ellis to the window with me. He inhaled sharply. I saw it, too—lights coming up from the beach.

"Somebody's sneaking around on the beach," Ellis said low under his breath.

"They messed with something that isn't theirs," Frankie growled. "The Bloody Bandits aren't happy."

I stopped short. "They have a gang name?"

"Everybody's got a gang name," Frankie said.

I hurried to the window. "Did you see who it is?"

Frankie glanced out the window. "Two live girls who look exactly alike."

"The twins." Naturally. It wasn't the first time the twins had gotten a head start.

They'd wanted to go out earlier, most likely to grab Rick's keystone. That's why they'd lied and said they already had it—to keep us from looking.

It had been sheer dumb luck that Duranja had found it first.

Now, evidently, they'd found something else—something valuable enough to stir up the pirates.

"Here." Ellis tossed me a pair of shorts and a T-shirt. "Get dressed." He was already pulling his jeans on.

"What's the plan?" I whispered.

"We'll make it up as we go," Ellis said, more confident than I felt.

I had to admit the glow of the ghost helped me find my shoes. And Frankie did have the decency to turn around.

We dressed quickly in the dark and snuck down the hallway toward the stairs.

But that didn't mean my ghost was ready to give me a break.

"Red Jack blames you," Frankie said, floating next to me. "You showed the entire living hotel the bird tonight, and look what happened."

"Who?"

"The guy with the bones in his hair!"

Bony Beads? He couldn't possibly be blaming me for any of this. "I pulled it out of a box in the dining room. Of course anyone could see it."

The gangster took an aggravated drag on his smoke. "After that. In the lobby. You announced to everybody that you were keeping it. Did it ever occur to you to hide it?"

"Not when our host was expecting me to give it back. Besides, how am I supposed to hide a stuffed bird?" I hissed as we came up on the landing.

"Shh..." Ellis urged. "Let's not wake the entire floor."

"Yeah," Frankie agreed as if he hadn't been pestering me.

Ellis paused at the top of the landing. "It looked like they were coming toward the hotel. We can ambush them in the lobby, or if they're headed somewhere else, we'll track them from the front porch."

"Got it," I whispered, commando-style.

The old oil paintings on the landing loomed in front of us.

"Got what? You can't even protect a stuffed bird," Frankie said, crushing out his cigarette on the portrait of our host's great-great-grandfather.

"Sure I can. I've had her for the last twelve hours, and she's been just fine."

"Okay, bodyguard. Where is she now?"

I froze. I'd left her back in the hotel room.

"You said you'd keep her on you at all times," Frankie lamented. "If Red Jack catches you breaking your promise, I'll owe him a ruby the size of my eye, and those things don't grow on trees, you know!"

"I'll be right back," I whispered to Ellis.

"What? Why? Where are you going?" he protested.

"Ghost issue," I said, giving him a peck on the cheek. "Keep going. I'll meet you in the lobby."

Meanwhile, I booked back to the room for the bird with Frankie on my tail. "I never told you to bet a ruby," I whispered, unlocking the door and struggling to shove it open. Ellis made it look easy, but the dang door was sticky.

"I figured it was a sure thing, seeing as you don't want pirate ghosts haunting you for eternity," he said as I grabbed the bird from her perch on top of my jewelry box. "Jeez-o-Pete, Verity. I expected you to be more responsible."

"I *am* responsible! And why do they care so much?" I asked, stuffing the bird under my arm and dodging past Frankie out the door.

"The captain likes his bird," Frankie said noncommittally.

"Then why doesn't he come and get her himself?" I struggled to relock the door in the dark.

Frankie planted his back against the wall. "Pirates are as petty as gangsters," he said, with no small amount of pride.

And Frankie was as deep as a puddle.

The gangster shrugged. "All I know is that the bird is important. And worth killing for."

"Does she have a secret?" I asked.

"We all have secrets." The gangster chuckled.

My breath caught as a door down the hall cracked open.

"Hello?" a woman's voice called.

"Sorry to wake you," I called, cringing hard, wishing Frankie would lean closer so I could see the lock better in the light of his ethereal glow. "I was just grabbing a drink from the kitchen."

"Verity?" Rick's voice sounded behind her. "The kitchen's closed."

"Yep, and I'm going back to bed," I singsonged, finally able to twist the door locked.

Did I really have to unlock it again?

The doorway across from ours clicked open. Duranja's silent shadow loomed. "What are you up to?"

Of all the rattlesnakes in Texas...

"Sneaking," I admitted, turning to face them. There was no use hiding it now. "Ellis and I saw flashlights coming up from the beach."

"Let's go," Rick said under his breath.

"We're here." Melody slipped into the hallway. Duranja closed the door behind her.

"We don't need your help." This was morphing into less of an ambush and more of an angry mob. "Ellis is already down in the lobby," I assured them.

"So you figured you'd bring the bird?" Duranja asked with a pointed look at Pearl.

"Are we going or not?" I hedged, avoiding the debate. I kept the bird tucked under my arm as I led them down to the landing and into the darkness below.

"Still showing everyone the parrot," Frankie grumped.

Truly? "What do they expect? It was made to clip on a shoulder."

"For Captain Bill," the gangster lectured.

"Fine. Is this better?" I said under my breath, hiding Pearl in the fabric of my shirt.

"That doesn't change anything," Frankie lamented. "I hope you got lots of rubies for Red Jack, because I don't."

I pinned Pearl to my side with an elbow and hunched over to protect her from who knew what, no doubt looking like Igor lumbering down the staircase.

We neared the bottom of the steps and saw shadows at the door.

Fire crackled low in the library hearth.

Ellis stood partially hidden behind the anchor.

I wasn't sure how to join the ambush. Time was up, and I had four people in tow.

But I didn't have time to worry about it much before the door flew open and a light caught me square in the chest.

Chapter Fourteen

"Told you she was nosey!" one of the twins declared as they barreled into the hotel.

Her light shifted and hit me straight in the face, blinding me for a second before I hopped down off the last stair. "Don't blame me," I said, seeing spots. "I'm not the one sneaking out at night." Well, I was. But only because they did it first.

"What were you two doing out?" Ellis asked, flicking on the lights by the door and catching them by surprise.

They looked a mess. Yet worryingly triumphant.

Seaweed and gunk tangled in Zara's hair. Zadie had a chunk of moss dripping from her dragon cuff earring. Both stood soaking wet with bloody hands and an awestruck, almost manic energy.

"We used our keystone," Zara announced.

"We were supposed to do that this morning, all together," Melody protested, coming down behind me.

"It was wicked cool," Zadie added. "Take a look at our prize." She held up a thick silver coin. "Isn't it beautiful?"

My heart sank. "You've got the first doubloon." Already. Before we'd even had a chance to look.

"It won't be the last," Zara taunted.

"I feel like this entire game is passing me by," Rick said, joining us with his wife in tow.

"I haven't started," his wife said, her face falling.

I recognized her. Or at least her brunette bob. If I wasn't mistaken, she was the dark-haired woman I'd seen with the professor last night.

Mindy, was it?

"You snooze, you lose," Zadie mused.

Duranja stood with his arms crossed, off to the side, observing.

Ellis slammed the door closed behind the twins. "How did you find it?"

"We haven't been given our instructions yet," I pointed out.

"You've been sleeping on the job," Zara said, tossing a bit of seaweed from her hair onto the floor. "Which is why we win. We take things into our own hands."

"And break the rules," Melody spat.

Zadie tossed the silver coin to Zara to admire. "There was no rule against going out."

"It was an implied rule! Bill locked the door," the professor admonished, fiddling with his glasses as he hurried down the stairs, late to the party.

"Bill didn't specifically order us to stay inside." Zadie strolled toward the center of the lobby, as if she enjoyed any kind of attention she could get—including the negative kind. "The game is on 24/7. In case you hadn't noticed."

"It's not fair," Mindy said, looking to Rick.

"Life's not fair," Zara retorted. Nobody attempted to contradict her.

Duranja remained the coolest of the group. "Well played," he said, closing the distance between them, arms crossed over his chest. "How'd you do it?"

"Why should we tell you?" Zara balked, still defensive.

"We need to in order to bargain." Zadie shrugged, looking

down at her bloody hands as if she'd just realized the state she was in.

Zara immediately glanced to the professor of all people. It was subtle, but I caught it.

"Oh, right," Zara said, with a predatory grin.

"Told you there might be more to him," Melody whispered in my ear.

Yes. And it also seemed the twins already had another plan in the works.

"So lay it out," Duranja said, matter-of-fact. "Tell us what we're dealing with."

For the first time, I saw Zara hesitate. "We'd like to see Dr. Fielding in the library."

The professor stepped forward. "I'd rather talk here." To the twins' frustration, he added, "I meant it when I said I'm not playing a game."

"Fine," Zara hissed. "We'll win anyway," she muttered to her sister.

Zadie took the lead. "Bill talked about the first guard stone being down where an old dock once stood." She notched her chin up. "We took a chance and headed down to the modern docks, figuring it might be nearby."

"It was," Rick said stiffly. "I saw it earlier tonight."

"Yep." Zara tucked her thumbs into her belt. "It was in your quadrant. My theory is the guard post you need will be in a different quadrant than where you found your keystone."

"If you found your keystone," Zadie said, unable to resist the taunt.

"We'll get it," Rick's wife assured him quietly.

Not when it was in Robocop's pocket.

"So you found the old dock," Duranja repeated, leading them like the "good cop" in an interrogation.

"About fifty yards down from where we arrived," Zadie added. "Three of the posts were basically rotting wood. The fourth one was made of thick stone and old. Super old."

"It's the only remaining support from the original pirate dock," Bill said from near the door of the library. He wore a robe instead of his pirate getup, and his hair stuck out in tufts. "Good morning," he added. "I think."

I hadn't seen him walk in.

Zara hadn't either, based on her startled expression. "Hey, Bill," she said, by way of recovering. "So, yes, we found the old support. On closer look, we realized it was an old capstan."

"A vertical-axled rotating machine," Bill explained, with no small amount of pride, "used by sailors to multiply their pulling force when they needed to haul ropes, cables, you name it. It has holes, and it turns."

"Our keystone fit into the base like it was made for it," Zadie boasted.

That's because it probably was. Bill's objects were the real deal.

"We twisted the keystone, and it slid a portion of the stone aside, revealing a lever hole in the capstan."

"I would have loved to see that," Rick gushed.

"I can't believe it worked after all those years," the professor said, right on his tail.

"We needed a board if we were going to make use of that lever hole." Zara shot a dare-to-question-me look at Bill. "We found a bunch near the house."

"We picked a good, strong one and whittled it down with our pocketknives," Zadie continued, "and voilà—we fit it into the lever hole and pushed."

"Hard," Zara added.

"I don't know how you had the strength," Bill said, shaking his head. "It took me and the ship captain who brought you out here to insert the coin."

"It was tough," Zadie admitted.

"We made it work," Zara said proudly. "It was pretty neat when turning the capstan made the other hole open up, and a coin drop out. Ping! Right onto the dock."

"Glorious," Zadie agreed. "Then I tripped and fell through the dock before I could grab it." She winced. "The whole section by the capstan gave way."

"Took us both down into the water," Zara said, rubbing her hip.

"The coin was fine. Still on the dock," Zadie said, "but it looked to me like somebody sawed through the wood on the bottom."

"Which is a nasty trick, but it didn't work," Zara said, eyeing all of us.

"None of my guests would do that," Bill said, brushing her off. "Even if they had the means, which they don't. You must have stepped wrong."

The photographer walked up behind Bill, bleary-eyed but with his camera in hand.

"You can go back to bed," Bill said, waving him off. "We're not documenting this."

"A dock is made for stepping on," Melody pointed out.

"I can show you," Zara said. "I was going to bring a piece of wood up, but then we got distracted by the coin."

"I'm sure it was a rotted board, an unlikely accident. I wouldn't knowingly put you in any danger," Bill vowed, ignoring our incident on the bridge.

"You fell on the stairs out front," Rick's wife said to him. "You're usually a lot more coordinated."

"I'll show you where," he told her.

"Yes. I'd like to check it out," she agreed.

"Things happen when we get excited," Bill soothed. "I'd like to take this opportunity to remind you all to be careful out there. The waivers you signed indemnify the hotel of any responsibility for your safety, so you must use your best judgment and watch yourselves. Also, please try to refrain from damaging hotel property."

Zadie looked him up and down as if she couldn't quite believe he'd tacked on that last bit. "Anyhow, now we're ahead 1-0," she said.

"And we both need showers," Zara said with a grin.

"And a penalty," Bill added.

Zara's jaw dropped open. "Excuse me?"

"You left before you were supposed to," Bill said. "I can't have guests running around the island at all hours."

"The rules don't specifically state—" Zadie began.

"Which is why I'm letting you keep your coin," Bill said. "As your penalty, I'm giving the board you made to the team with the next keystone," Bill announced. "And I'm giving you a task here at the hotel to complete before you can go out and join the quest to unlock the second capstan."

"That's not fair," Zadie protested.

Zara eyed him. "What task?"

"Kitchen duty," Bill said with no small amount of satisfaction.

"That'll teach them," Mindy smirked.

"We hope," the author said.

Zadie crossed her arms over her chest. "We'll make it quick," she vowed.

Melody smoothed her hair back, and I could tell her mind was already working on what to do next. She looked to the twins. "According to the brochure, the treasure hunt will take us to the lip of the cave where the brothers faced off. Is that where you were?"

"Yes," Zara said. "The old dock stood in front of the cave."

"So according to Bill's presentation in the library, our next stop is the cliff where the bride took her fatal leap," my sister concluded.

"Correct," Bill beamed, seemingly relieved that the hunt was back on course.

"At least we know where to go," Melody said to me.

"The question is—who has the keystone we need?" I murmured to Melody.

Not quietly enough, since Rick looked our way. "I still have to find mine."

My sister pulled me toward the deserted check-in desk. "The answer is in the diary Dr. Fielding showed me." She glanced past me to make certain no one was listening. "It's the green one—the one we took from Rick."

Great.

We were about to be outed.

"You'd better keep looking for your stone, Rick," Zadie said. "I know *we* haven't found it yet."

"Last night, you implied you had," Rick accused.

"You shouldn't believe everything you hear," Zara said, all innocent-like.

The twins must have already checked the path while they were out and knew it wasn't there.

"Are you sure kitchen duty is enough?" the author asked Bill, only half joking.

"I vote for toilet scrubbing," Melody pitched in.

To Duranja, Zara said, "We may be held up prepping your breakfast, but I promise not for long. When we get out, maybe you'd better work with us. You too," she added to the professor.

If she was offering assistance to both teams, she must not have known which of us had Rick's stone.

"I was going to have each team fashion a board from the precut wood out back," Bill offered. "But the twins beat you to it," he said, eyeing the pair. "So I'm awarding you the one they cut. You can use it for this next quest."

"Two penalties?" Zadie balked.

"Two people snuck out in the middle of the night," Bill reasoned. "And if these other teams had to fashion their own boards, you'd be off to the capstan with yours before they finished."

"It took hours," Zadie lamented.

"We'll catch up soon enough," Zara vowed.

Of that I had no doubt.

They were good at this game. Too good.

Little did they realize Duranja was as sneaky as they were, even if mister perfect would never cop to it.

Bill held up a finger. "Remember, it's not who has the keystone. It's who snags the silver doubloon."

"Right." I nodded, eyeing my worried sister.

We didn't know how the guard posts worked, but the ever-confident and clever twins did. We'd have to keep on our toes so that we didn't end up doing the work while they caught up and snatched the doubloon.

"Fine. Take it. We left it outside," Zadie said, pressing a bloody hand to the hem of her black athletic shirt.

"Let's get you cleaned up and to the kitchen while the rest of the teams head out," Bill said, leading them away.

"I'd like to get some shoes on," Ellis said, his feet bare on the polished oak planks of the lobby. "Let's meet back in five minutes."

"Come on," Zara said, heading toward the kitchen with her twin. "Let's hurry up so we can get back in the game."

"You think they'll be able to catch up?" the professor asked, watching them go.

"Knowing them? Yes," Melody said. "But at least we have a head start."

And a keystone.

"Let's find our keystone," Rick's wife suggested, ever hopeful.

She slipped her hand into his and headed for the door.

"What is it?" Melody asked, noticing how the couple had captured my attention.

"Nothing." Maybe. "For someone who officially skipped all of yesterday's game, she seems super motivated now."

"She was sick," Melody said. "A walk and a good night's sleep did her good."

"You're probably right," I conceded.

Five minutes later, we were fully dressed and back in the lobby. The twins were nowhere in sight.

"You'd better get a move on," Bill said, still in his pajamas. "Zara and Zadie have already made coffee, cracked two dozen eggs, and are chopping fruit salad like a pair of ninjas."

"Don't they ever let up?" Melody lamented.

"No," the professor said.

"We're not going to be eating breakfast," I said. We had too much to do.

"Believe me, the staff and I will enjoy it," Bill said, rubbing his belly.

"Let's go," Duranja said, leading the way.

"I'm with you," the professor said to Melody as they followed on his heels.

"We've got this," I said to Ellis, tightening the laces on my white tennis shoes.

He bent close to me to do the same. "Remember, don't trust anybody."

I nodded.

"Good luck," Bill said—as a wish or a warning?—as we headed out to even the score.

Chapter Fifteen

We found the twins' board tucked to the side of the front stairs. Ellis and Duranja hefted it up and took the lead out toward the cliffs, maintaining a brisk pace, like a military team ruck marching.

We now had everything we needed—the board to turn the capstan and release the coin, and the keystone to unlock the entire mechanism.

"Hurry. Let's figure this out before Bill releases the hounds," Melody said, urging our group toward the rock bridge over the water. It might have been less scary in the light of morning—if I'd thought to ask Frankie to take back his power.

Ellis carried the tip of the board over his right shoulder, while Duranja had the tail end perfectly aligned behind him. They made the awkward look easy, and I worked to conceal the fact that I was breathing hard as I kept up with them.

I glanced over my shoulder, noticing the professor trailing farther and farther behind. "I think he might have an alliance with Rick and Mindy. I saw him talking to her last night when we came back, and she didn't stick around to chat with us or even see our keystone."

Duranja huffed. "Like I said, don't trust anybody."

We neared the narrow expanse of rock over the waters below, and I fought back a shudder. I couldn't see the ghost yet, but the bridge alone made my blood run cold.

Melody halted. "I can't believe we crossed that."

Now that we had more light than the beam of a flashlight or the glow of the lantern, it was clear the rock bridge could collapse at any time.

Fissures ran from the surface down deep into the structure. Scraggly bushes and vines forced them even farther apart, dripping muddy water that ran like bloody tears. The left railing had fallen into the sea, leaving rusty fastenings in its wake. The railing on the right—the one I'd grabbed on our first crossing—clung to the supports with little more than rust and luck.

The pebbles we'd felt under our feet were due to the surface disintegrating under us. Entire sections of rock had loosened in sheets. The bridge seemed to be crumbling in on itself as if it were made of wet sand.

"Bill is insane," Ellis growled.

"A menace," Duranja agreed.

At least the ghost bride hadn't appeared.

Dr. Fielding caught up to us, out of breath, the diary tucked securely under his belt buckle. "Stay away from that bridge," he admonished. "It's not safe."

"Somebody should tell that to Bill," Duranja said.

"I have." The professor nodded hastily. "Over and over..."

"Bill said the capstan is located where the bride took her final leap," Melody insisted.

"There's no documentation on where that is." Dr. Fielding took off his glasses to wipe the sweat out of his eyes.

I exchanged a glance with Melody.

He didn't know where the bride had died, because nobody else could see her!

We needed to locate the capstan before the twins ever got out of the kitchen. That way, we'd unlock the puzzle, scoop up the doubloon, and win the quest before they could do anything to stop us. That would knock them down a peg.

And even the score.

Dr. Fielding slid his glasses back on and straightened. "My sources say the capstan we're looking for is on this side of the bridge, over by the cliffs." He pointed slightly behind us, toward the water. "Possibly closer to the beach."

"I don't get it," Ellis said. "The first capstan is part of a dock. What do these capstans do?"

Dr. Fielding appeared to enjoy the question as he dragged a hand across his sweaty brow. "The first capstan was used to unload ships. This capstan hauled goods up from the shore to a pirate hideaway that once stood near the lighthouse. Can you believe it?"

"Yes," I said, surprising him.

As for the location...

"Let's check it out," Melody said.

The professor nodded. "I hope our capstan didn't fall into the sea." He absently touched the book where it lay semi-hidden under his shirt. "The diary is old. The cliffs are crumbling."

"Surely Bill would have planned better," I said. He'd hid the doubloons before we arrived. That had to mean everything was in working condition.

Dr. Fielding shot me a long look. "Bill also sent you across that bridge."

"And now I stand corrected," I decided, earning a smile from the professor.

"The capstan's got to be around here somewhere," Melody insisted. "Alec and I will go look with Dr. Fielding."

"I'll stay at the bridge," I offered. Maybe the ghost bride could help me find it.

No doubt the ghost knew the area, having haunted it for centuries.

Melody caught my eye and gave a quick nod. She knew what I

was up to and was most likely keeping the professor busy while I tried to make a connection with the bride.

Duranja guessed as much and frowned.

"I'll keep a lookout for Verity," Ellis said, taking up a position to guard my back.

"I don't mind losing her, but you?" Duranja protested.

Ellis remained firm while Duranja grew red in the cheeks.

"It's not here, and there is no bride," Robocop gritted out.

"Then you're wasting time here," Ellis said to his friend.

Duranja swore under his breath and took off.

Melody winked at me. "He'll come around," she assured us, taking off to join him.

I wouldn't count on it. But I was glad I could depend on her and on Ellis.

He watched after them to make sure we were alone. "Do you see the ghost?"

"Not yet," I said, eyeing the rickety bridge.

Last night, the ghost bride hadn't appeared until we'd begun crossing. In fact, we'd made it near to the center both times before she'd been roused. I really wasn't looking forward to stepping on that bridge again, but if that's what I had to do to get her attention...

"Hello?" I called. "Catherine?" I added, remembering her name.

A lone seagull cried, circling the cliff before diving down to the water.

"Remember me?" I asked earnestly. "Verity. From Sugarland. I was here last night."

Nothing.

"Guess I'm going to have to come to you," I said to myself more than anyone else.

"You can do this without setting foot on that bridge," Ellis said, his voice rich with warning.

The trouble was, I didn't think I could.

She wasn't answering my calls. She hadn't been much of a

conversationalist when we'd met earlier. It wasn't as if I could summon ghosts on the spot. They had to be present and willing to have a conversation. But I was pretty sure why she'd shown up last night—both times.

"Keep an eye out for the others," I said. It might make it easier on him to have his back turned.

"Verity—" he warned.

"It's not like I have a choice," I said, stepping onto the scattering of pebbles at the start of the bridge.

"It's not safe," Ellis said, rushing for me.

"It'll be worse with you distracting me," I said, clipping the bird to my belt behind me for safekeeping. "Also, a lot more treacherous with both of us on here."

He halted, and I purposely didn't look to see his expression.

At least I didn't have to worry about losing the light this time. I'd be able to see exactly when the rock crumbled out from under my feet.

"I hate this," Ellis growled. "I really hate this."

"I'm okay," I assured him, holding my hands out to the sides for balance, avoiding the railing.

"Damn it, Verity. This is just a treasure hunt," he insisted. "It isn't worth your life."

"It's more than that. Some poor girl is doomed to spend her afterlife killing herself every night. I have to try to help." This might be my only chance to connect with her and coax her off this miserable stretch of rock. I maintained a slow, steady pace.

He swore under his breath, but I was right, and he knew it. "I'm watching out for you," he promised.

It was the only thing he could do.

I kept my focus trained squarely on the section at the middle where the rock bridge had already given way, exposing a gap the length of my foot. The ghost had retreated to that very spot last night before she'd jumped.

"They must have found something over there," Ellis said. "They're all looking over the edge."

"Good, it'll keep their eyes off me." I didn't try to see what had caught their attention. I didn't want to see the ocean crashing against the rocks below. It was bad enough I could hear it.

I pressed forward, stepping steady and true, until I felt the air in front of me chill. I paused, keeping my feet planted, ignoring the wild beating of my heart as the spirit took shape.

Her eyes were maniacal, and her hands clutched her throat. Her white bridal gown fluttered in an unseen wind. "Stay away!" she shrieked.

"I don't want to hurt you," I assured her. "I know you've been hurt badly." I could see it in the way her fingers scrabbled against her pale skin, in the way her gaze darted to the waters below. "I'm here to help. Tell me what you need to find peace," I asked gently. "Please."

"No one can help me," she insisted. "I'm alone. No one knows I'm here. Except for *them*," she added, searching frantically behind me.

"I'm the only one here," I promised. I hoped. "Who can I locate for you? Who can I tell?"

She pressed her lips together hard.

Wind buffeted the narrow slice of rock. I felt the parrot bouncing against my backside. If she flew off...

"Excuse me," I said, unclipping her and tucking her safely under my arm.

The ghost shrieked. "You're with *them*."

"She's not mine," I insisted, clutching the bird to my side. "This pock-faced guy told me to take care of her. He was a bit of a jerk about it to be honest."

"Short John?" She stared at me, as if she could hardly believe it.

"Sure," I said, hoping it would help her relax. "Well, no." I couldn't lie. "The pirate I met was tall."

She let out a breath, as if I'd passed some test. "Short is his temper, I'm afraid," she said fondly.

"That's definitely true," I said, sharing a knowing look. "I also saw Red Jack," I added, remembering Frankie's name for Bony Beads. "Does he always do his hair that way?"

She brought her hand to her mouth and giggled. "He's very vain. He likes to attack French ships so he can hoard pomade and perfumes."

"That's hilarious." I laughed, much to her delight. "Seriously. I'd never peg him for it. He looks like he's out for blood."

"Oh, he'll kill anybody who offends him," she assured me. "He'll just smell nice doing it." She folded her hands in front of her. "Now I must ask. If you have Pearl, that means you've been in the caves. Did you see a pirate captain in the caverns?"

"Thank goodness, no," I answered, earning a frown.

Troubled, she stared at a spot near my side.

I didn't see anything there. "I know you've been kidnapped," I told her. "Hidden away." I shook my head. "I can't pretend to know what that's like."

She blinked hard. "That's not the worst part," she said in a voice so reedy I barely caught it. "Nobody remembers me. I'm just...here."

"Oh, sweetie." I drew a lock of hair away from my eye and tucked it behind my ear.

She looked toward the sea. "My William would come for me if he could find me. He's strong and brave." She straightened a bit. "He's an outlaw," she added with more than a little pride.

Wait. "What?" I glanced back to Ellis, who stood at the entrance to the bridge, ready for the word go. "Are you talking about Captain Bill? You *want* him to find you?"

"He is my love," she said simply.

Hold the phone. "Didn't you get kidnapped by pirates?"

She brought her hands to her heart. "Absolutely not! They rescued me," she said dreamily.

Well...good. "From whom?"

"That awful man and his hired crew who would force me to marry against my will." Her eyes grew misty. "I told them I'd rather die."

And she had.

"But you have Pearl!" She brightened. "And you know the crew. If they trust you, I do too. Find William. Tell him to meet me here," she said breathlessly. "Tell him to find me." Her expression darkened. "There are people coming to hurt me."

I turned and saw Melody and Duranja descending on us. "They won't hurt you," I assured her. They couldn't even see her. "I know them," I said, hoping to calm her fears. "We're looking for a capstan Captain Bill used to use. It's supposed to be on or near this bridge, but I don't see it."

She pointed to a place on the cliffs nearest the ocean, a place where a larger rock bridge had fallen. A narrow switchback led down to the beach below.

"They used it to haul their ale," she said fondly. "It's hidden behind that scraggly bush."

"Are you sure?" I still couldn't see it.

She nodded. "Find my William. Tell him I'm here. Tell him his princess needs rescuing. He'll know what I mean."

"I will," I told her. "I'm glad to do it."

A tear ran down her cheek. "I thank you," she said properly.

"I have to go," I said, retreating, not willing to risk the bridge any longer than necessary. "Thank you for your help!"

She nodded, disappearing this time.

I felt strangely heartened that she didn't jump. That maybe, just maybe I'd find Bill and deliver her message and she'd never have to hurt herself ever again.

Holding my hands out for balance, I hurried as fast as I could off the bridge, scattering rocks in my wake. I slipped, and a section of loose shale tumbled into the ravine below.

"Verity!" Ellis called, rushing for me.

But I made it into his arms, and together, we inched off the deadly bridge.

Melody and Duranja had made it back. "I know where we need to go," I said to the group.

"I knew you'd do it," Melody said, hugging me. "We left the

professor on a trail near the cliffs. He insisted on going down to check out the beach."

"There's not much down there. It won't keep him busy for long," Duranja warned. At Melody's side-eye, he added, "What? I still don't trust him."

"Come on," I said, taking Melody's hand. "We'll do this together, birthday girl."

Chapter Sixteen

We hurried to the collapsed rock expanse. It lay closer to the sea than the bridge I'd just been on—right at the edge overlooking the beach. A few large boulders clung to the cliffside. That was all that remained.

"I can't believe we're really doing this," I said, navigating the rocks erupting from the soil. If there ever had been a path here, nature had reclaimed it a long time ago.

Duranja grinned. "And that your pure and honest sister led the professor astray."

I almost tripped.

"Alec's exaggerating," Melody said, steadying me. "I only encouraged Dr. Fielding to follow his instincts."

"Which were wrong," Duranja added. "I'm proud of you, sweetie."

"You were busy stashing the board in case the twins caught up," she said, no-nonsense. "It was my turn to help the team."

I wasn't sure how I felt about my sister leading a potential ally astray, but I had to admit—if only to myself—I was glad it was just the four of us.

I led the group to where I'd seen the narrow switchback from the haunted bridge.

"Okay, let's make the most of our chance," I urged.

We'd prove to the professor we could be respectful while winning this round. Then if we were lucky, we'd find ourselves with an ally when it came time to gain the final advantage—a partner who didn't want to win anything for himself.

Talk about a rare commodity in this game.

"There!" I said, spotting the switchback trail leading down from the cliffside.

Ellis let out a low whistle. "We never would have found this path without you."

"Come on." Duranja bopped Ellis on the arm. "Let's grab the board."

"And avoid the professor!" Melody called after them.

After the men had taken off, I turned to my sister. "I should bring you with me on more ghost-hunting adventures. You're so good at this." She was smart, level-headed, and great in a pinch.

"It's fun." She blushed, smoothing her hair behind her ears.

I told her all about my recent encounter with the ghost bride on the bridge, and then I had to say it.

"I still can't believe Duranja is ready to buy you an engagement ring." Every time I thought about it, I was shocked all over again.

It was just so *soon*. Reckless. And it was Duranja.

"I can't believe you don't want one from Ellis," she countered. "You've been dating for a while, and you obviously love him. What's going on?"

I was saved from answering when I spotted the men in the distance.

"Here they come," I said, delighted to see they'd made such good time.

I half expected to see the twins at any minute.

Melody scanned the path from the hotel, same as I did. "Please tell me we might actually pull this off."

"Not without any wood to knock on."

"That's coming up," she said as the men arrived with the board.

"Now we just have to get this down the narrow switchback." Ellis wiped his brow.

And hope the capstan was where the ghost said it was.

And if we won, maybe talk Duranja into buying a motorcycle instead of a ring.

"I'm ready," Melody said, peering over the edge.

"Be careful," Duranja cautioned as he and Ellis set the board on the ground. "It's a drop to the trail. I'll lower you down. We don't want anyone jumping and slipping."

I shuddered at the thought of it. The narrow trail below hugged the cliffside, then dropped off hard. There was no room for error.

"Let's go," my sister said, letting Duranja carefully lower her down.

"Slow and steady," he murmured. I wasn't sure if he was talking to himself or to her. Although somebody needed to watch out for my sister, who tended to leap before she looked.

"Me next," I said to Ellis. I had to see this capstan. It was a piece of pirate history. The ghost on the bridge had known where to find it, so it was definitely from Captain Bill's era. With any luck, it could lead us closer to the ghost of the captain.

I still owed a promise to his bride.

My arms ached, and my front half dragged against the earthen cliff as Ellis lowered me down next to Melody.

Her eyes shone with excitement. "It feels pretty good to be the group leading the race."

"We're certainly catching up," I said as the guys handed down the board.

It was solid, but not as bone-crushingly heavy as I'd expected.

Duranja eased down and took Melody's end of the board before Ellis joined us and relieved me of mine.

"Let's go," Ellis said. He'd ended up in the position to lead, so he did, letting Duranja take the rear for once. Melody joined Ellis at the front, and I kept watch in the middle.

The switchback was steep and rocky, but manageable. At least so far.

Melody's ponytail bounced as she craned to see what lay beyond the next switchback. And the next as we inched our way down the cliffside.

I ran a hand along the rock face and tried not to look at the ocean churning below.

"That's it," I said, spotting a bush as we made a turn toward the ocean. It was half-yellow and scraggly, and slightly visible behind it—a thick mortared post.

Duranja inhaled sharply. "I can't believe you spotted it from the bridge."

"Oh, I didn't," I said over my shoulder. "Catherine's ghost told me."

Let him chew on that.

Duranja shot me a look as the men tucked the board against the cliffs. But we didn't have time to argue.

Ellis held the vegetation back to reveal a thick, weathered post constructed of rock blocks, the mortar infused with tiny seashells. Along the side, we found a slot with an opening almost identical to the carved edge of the board that had opened the first capstan for the twins. "This is it," I said on an exhale.

We'd done it!

I glanced up to the cliffs above, wondering how much time we had left before the twins tracked us down.

"Quickly," Ellis urged, probably thinking the same thing, while Melody crouched next to him, running her fingers along the post.

"Look," she said, brushing away the dirt to reveal a cut-out the exact size of a keystone, complete with space to fit the hook. "You did it, Verity!"

"How does it work?" Duranja demanded. "Does the keystone trigger something in there?"

"It looks like it sets off a mechanism," Melody said, examining it. "This is an incredible piece of maritime history," she added, tracing her fingers along the inside seam where the keystone would connect to the inner workings of the post. "I mean, think of how much work it took to build this and then to lift goods from the sea..."

"We'll look at it later." Duranja handed her the keystone and turned back to retrieve the board.

She held the glassy green keystone reverently before brushing away an errant leaf from the opening carved to fit it. Then, with both hands, she placed it directly inside the opening on the post.

It was a perfect fit!

"I'm so happy," she said, beaming at me. Then her face squinched as pebbles and sand rained down on us.

I squeezed my eyes shut and brushed it off my head as the rock above us crackled.

"Heads up!" Ellis cried. I stared at my sister, and our eyes widened with alarm.

"Melody!" Ellis grabbed her, tackling her away from the capstan as a boulder crashed down where she'd stood a fraction of a second before.

I screamed, or maybe that was Melody as she slipped and fell over the edge, taking Ellis with her. I reached for them, but it was too late.

They slid down the steep, rocky cliffside, tumbling out of control until they landed motionless on a narrow strip of beach below.

Chapter Seventeen

"No!" I barreled down the switchback, full speed. Duranja streaked past me, cursing because we were taking too long, and they weren't moving, and I needed to get down there faster.

Duranja stumbled down the last quarter of the hill, where the slope evened out and the rocks crumbled. I followed his lead.

I slid the last several yards and about cried in relief when I saw Ellis's head turn.

Duranja bent over my sister. "Don't move," he ordered.

"Don't want to," Ellis answered.

Then my hardheaded boyfriend sat up anyway.

"Cool it," I said, sliding down next to him. "You might have a back injury."

"I think it's more my knee." He groaned. His jeans had been sliced open on the rocks to reveal a bloody leg.

"Mine's the arm." Melody winced. She touched her hand to her elbow. Her cream jacket was bloody and torn, and she was missing a pink tennis shoe.

"Everybody stop moving," Duranja ordered as Melody sat up next to Ellis.

"Oh!" She flinched. "My ankle."

They both looked like they'd been beaten up.

I resisted the urge to tell them to cool it. "We need to get you out of here."

Before any more rocks decided to fall.

I looked up, way up, toward the top of the cliff. No way we could make it back the way we'd come. Melody and Ellis were in no shape for that kind of climb, even with Duranja and me supporting them.

We huddled on a narrow strip of gray, seaweed-streaked beach uncovered by low tide. It gave way to a series of slippery-looking rocks that led to the ocean.

Call me pessimistic, but I didn't think we could swim.

"Okay," I said, trying to think. "Either we wait, or we climb." Both sounded like terrible ideas.

"Waiting isn't an option." Duranja glared up at where the rock had fallen as he cradled Melody. "We can't afford for anything else to fall."

My sister nodded.

"I've got you," he said, gently lifting her up.

"Ow, ow, ow," she whimpered, clutching her arm to her side.

He might be able to carry her uphill and all the way back to the hotel, but I wasn't so sure how Ellis and I would manage.

"I'm fine," Ellis insisted, attempting to stand.

No, he wasn't. "Stop it," I ordered, for all he cared to listen. And when it became clear he intended to stand with or without me, I hurried to help.

"Ellis, you're hurt. I don't think I can carry you." Rocks and sand slid under my shoes as I supported him on his left side. He slipped, and I nearly dropped him. "Help!" I called up the hill.

The professor couldn't have gone far, and we could really use another hand.

"He's probably on the beach by now," Ellis managed, stumbling sideways with me while he favored his bad leg.

"Can you put any weight on it?" I asked, digging into the sand with both feet as best I could.

"No," he grunted.

For all I knew, he had two bad legs and he wasn't telling me.

"We're hurt!" I hollered, loud as I could. "Help!" I added before Ellis tried to scale the cliff with his teeth.

A head appeared at top of the cliff. It was one of the twins. Thank heaven. "Down here!" I waved my free arm.

"Amateur Hour?" she called back, clearly startled. "Is that you?"

What? No. Well, yes. "It's Verity!" I called, waving my free arm. "And Ellis and Melody and—"

"I know, hang on." She turned away then quickly back to us. "Zara is going for help. I'm coming down!"

Wonderful. Perfect.

"Watch out for falling rocks!" I called as Zadie lowered herself on her stomach, her feet dangling over the switchback path.

She dropped and landed neatly. "Hey, Doc. They're down here," she called to the professor, whose head appeared over the edge.

Zadie supported his waist to help him down, like she'd been born to the maneuver, then they hurried to join us. She moved like a gazelle, and the professor, well, he was human like the rest of us.

"What happened?" Zadie asked, making it down first.

Ellis staggered forward, and she propped up his other side.

"Rock fall," Melody said as the professor located a pink tennis shoe behind a rock and held it out for my sister.

Duranja took it and stuffed it into his back pocket. "Both our people need medical attention."

Zadie nodded. "Last I saw, Rick's doctor wife was out front of the hotel, looking for their keystone. She'll know what to do." She made a quick study of our situation. "Do you know how to do a two-man lift?" she asked me and Dr. Fielding. When we hesitated, she went into instruction mode. "Each of you grab one of Hot Cop's legs," she said, demonstrating where to grasp. "He'll brace his arms on your shoulders."

"Hot Cop?" I repeated. I didn't disagree, but still...

"Yeah, we have nicknames for all of you," she said, helping the professor get into position. "Okay, come on. I know a way out along the beach, but we'll have to hurry because the tide is coming in. I'll lead the way until we get out of here; then the three of us will switch off carrying Hot Cop so that one of us is always resting."

"I could get used to that nickname," Ellis groaned as we got into position.

"Where are you taking us?" I asked. "Those rocks lead right into the ocean."

The twin shook her head. "There's a narrow strip of sand between the rocks and the ocean. But the tide is due in. We have to be quick."

"Ready?" I asked Dr. Fielding. He didn't appear too sure.

Neither was I, but on the count of three, we lifted Ellis like a sack of potatoes.

"Sorry, babe," I grunted.

"I was about to say the same." Ellis winced as his knee jerked up and down with the motion.

But we had liftoff.

Meanwhile Duranja stood nearby, Melody gathered in his arms like she weighed nothing at all.

"Zara and I train for every possibility," Zadie said, scrambling over a few larger rocks leading down toward the water. "Don't worry. This isn't as bad as the time on *Stranded at Sea* when that pretty boy from LA thought he could fire dance his way through the lava challenge. The producers had to call in a helicopter to airlift that guy out."

My shoulders were going to pop out of their sockets. Or I was going to slip on a rock and take us all down. Or both. I gritted my teeth and took one step at a time as Zadie led us over the rocky shoal.

Just when it appeared we'd step into the ocean—and at that point, I wasn't sure I cared—she veered left on a wet, narrow sandbar that I could have sworn hadn't been there two minutes ago.

"You're lucky the tide is out," she said, glancing at us over her shoulder, "and that I don't hold grudges."

Duranja huffed. "We're not the ones who snuck out and grabbed the first keystone before this morning's game started."

"The game started when we landed on this island," Zadie said, leading us along the beachfront. "If you two hadn't faceplanted" —she glanced back at our injured friends—"I might never have seen the second capstan."

I was hoping she'd missed that.

"Thanks for seeing to us instead of the second coin," I managed, one foot slipping sideways in the sand.

I mean, the game was intense, but at least we all had our priorities straight.

If I weren't in so much pain, I'd be proud.

"I figure there's no rush. You're in no condition to go back and turn a capstan," she said, ever practical. And not quite as charitable as I'd given her credit for.

"Whoa!" Ellis slipped a little as the professor almost dropped his side.

"I've got it," Zadie said, relieving the professor of his side. "Trust me," she added when Dr. Fielding hesitated to let go.

The trouble was, I didn't trust her at all.

We'd made it halfway down the beach when Zara came running toward us with Rick's wife close behind.

Hallelujah.

Rick and Bill trailed behind them, each lugging a stretcher.

I regretted I hadn't at least talked to Mindy before we needed her help. Somehow being on the island had made me forget my manners.

"I'm Verity Long," I said by way of introduction as she examined Ellis prior to loading him onto a canvas stretcher.

"Dr. Stone," she said, immersed in her task.

It felt strange to see my boyfriend and my sister receive medical attention from someone we barely knew, but Rick's wife was smart, decisive, and quick about getting the people I cared about up off the beach and back to the hotel. That was all that mattered.

Ellis and my sister ended up side by side in the bed Ellis and I had shared last night. Melody lay with both her elbow and her ankle bandaged, iced, and up on pillows. Meanwhile, Dr. Stone tucked an errant lock of graying hair behind her ear while she examined Ellis's knee. It had begun to swell and turn purple.

"Oh, sweetie," I said, fluffing another pillow for Ellis's back. "You saved my sister's life. I just—" I still couldn't believe how close she'd come to that rock strike. She could have been killed in an instant.

"Yes, thank you again," Melody said from next to him in the bed. "I didn't even see it coming."

I'd heard it more than seen it. "I'm still shocked it happened." One minute we were fine, and the next—seconds away from a life-changing disaster.

"Your instincts have always been amazing," Duranja said to Ellis, who shrugged.

"There wasn't time to think."

All of Ellis's and Melody's major cuts and scrapes were clean and bandaged, but Duranja kept finding new ones on Melody to fuss over. "I should have stuck closer to you. From now on, I'm not letting you out of my sight."

I tried not to groan as he dabbed antibacterial ointment over a cut on her shoulder like he was restoring the glaze on the *Mona Lisa* before applying a tiny baby bandage.

He was going to run through the entire tin at the rate he was going.

"I'll tell you the same thing I told Melody," Dr. Stone said, applying an ice packet to Ellis's knee before she began wrapping it in an ace bandage. "You were lucky. It's just a sprain. Stay off it for the remainder of the weekend. You'll want to see your own doctor when you get home, but I don't think there's any permanent damage done."

"That's good news indeed," Bill said from the doorway. He carried a tray. "I brought you some soup and bread to warm you up, plus our famous roast beef sandwiches—a staple at our hotel since my grandfather's day." The sandwich toothpicks sported tiny pirate flags. He saw me noticing and winked. As if I were in the mood for another pirate adventure. "Do you have everything you need?" he asked the doctor, placing the tray on the dresser across from us.

"I need you to take safety as seriously as you take your sandwiches," I said.

"Hey, now—" he began to protest.

The doctor cut him off. "I need a step that doesn't slice up my husband's leg."

Duranja paused his ministrations. "I'd suggest a dock that stays in one piece and a cliffside trail that doesn't come with falling rocks."

Our host opened and closed his mouth like a caught trout. "I...I don't know how anyone is getting hurt. My treasure hunt is safe, I assure you."

"You really want to die on that hill?" Duranja asked.

Bill stood a little taller. "In case you're thinking of suggesting any different, I'll have you know it's libel to make accusations of that sort on social media."

"Not if it's true," Melody countered.

"That escalated fast," Ellis remarked.

"The rock bridge is a disaster," I pointed out. "The placement of the second capstan left us right under a falling rock."

"It's not as if it's up for debate," my sister said. "These are facts."

"I have your signed waivers," Bill said, "so it's not as if you weren't warned. Treasure hunting comes with inherent risks. Now let me know if you need any more soup," he added, snatching the last word as he left the room.

"That looked fun," Rick said innocently, leaning into the room from the hallway. "How are you all doing?"

"Come on in," Ellis offered. "We have sandwiches."

Rick wandered in and helped himself, handing a plate to Melody at her request.

"We chased Bill off before I could ask him about crutches," Ellis said, wincing as he tried to bend his knee.

"If he had stretchers, he might have some crutches, right?" Melody agreed. "We'll be staying off our feet that way," she said to the doctor.

Dr. Stone folded her hands in front of her. "Assuming I would suggest going back to the place where a gigantic rock nearly fell onto your head—" she began.

"I know that tone," Rick mused, munching on his sandwich.

"Your treasure hunt is over," she said to Melody.

Melody gasped. Duranja let out a low groan. "But we're only sore," Melody said. "No permanent damage done, right?"

Yet. She hadn't seen how close she'd come to getting hit.

The doctor's mouth formed a grim line. "With any luck, you'll be able to put weight on your ankle before you leave," she said to Melody. "And you, your knee," she added to Ellis. "But both of you have bad sprains. If you go running around on those rocks, you could end up inflaming your injuries to the point where it will take months of therapy to fix. I'm not kidding," she said when Melody appeared ready to argue. "Rick says you're a librarian, and if I'm not mistaken, you're a right-handed one?" she asked my sister.

"How did you know?" Melody asked, surprised.

"She's crazy observant," Rick said, biting into a sandwich. "Better than me."

She took the compliment in stride. "I assume you'd like to walk and type and go back to your job next week."

Melody chewed her lip and glanced to Duranja. "I can't afford to miss work."

"That goes for you as well," she said to Ellis. "I hear you're a police officer. If you irritate that knee, you could be looking at several months behind a desk, as well as occupational therapy."

He frowned. "I hear you," Ellis said, ever practical. "Do we quit the game, then?"

"I'll let you four talk," the doctor said, motioning to her husband as she gathered her medical supplies in order to slip out.

"I'm sorry, guys," Rick said, taking some of the Ace bandages she handed him. He hesitated, as if he wanted to say more, but couldn't quite come up with the words.

He wasn't the only one.

We sat in silence as they made their exit.

"We can't quit," Duranja said firmly the moment the door closed behind them. "We've come too far. Besides, this is important," he added, to Melody's chagrin.

"So is my health," she pointed out. "And Ellis's."

"I know." Duranja slipped his hand into Melody's. His thumb stroked the tender skin between her thumb and pointer finger as he thought. "Part of me wonders if Dr. Stone wants us out of the game. Or if her husband put her up to it."

There was suspicious, and then there was Duranja. "She's a doctor. She was there when we needed her, and now you're saying she's shady?"

"I'm not ruling it out," Robocop insisted. "All I'm saying is there are people who would take advantage."

"So what do you suggest?" Melody asked.

"Melody and Ellis can stay back here at the hotel. Take care of yourselves," he added to my sister. At her gloomy expression, he added, "We'll bring you books from the library. You can learn more about the island, help us with your brains instead of your bodies."

"And what will you be doing?" Ellis crossed his arms over his chest, looking at me. He knew quite well what kind of risks I tended to take.

Duranja released Melody and stood. "Verity and I will team up," he stated, choking out the words as if he'd promised to swallow a frog.

Sure. I'd abandon my injured sister and boyfriend to team up with my enemy in order to win some prize money so that he could possibly marry said sister and never leave. "I can't wait."

"It's not the worst idea," Ellis said.

"If we're going to do it, we should go back out right now." Before we lost too much time.

Ellis dug a hand through his hair, resigned. "The board is still on the path by the capstan."

Duranja's eyes widened. "I left the keystone in the capstan." He turned to Melody. "I was so worried about you, I wasn't thinking straight." He took her hand. "I wasn't thinking at all."

"Oh, Alec," she gushed, as if that were the most romantic thing ever.

"Focus," I said. We'd been so close before that rock fall. All we'd had to do was turn it. Of course, that was all anyone else would have to do as well. "Let's go," I said to Robocop. "We'll get the second coin," I promised the team.

We'd finish what we started.

"We'll be tied with the twins," Melody said, her excitement mounting.

"If Duranja and I don't kill each other first," I felt obliged to point out.

Then again, that might be fun, too.

Chapter Eighteen

"Follow my lead," I told Duranja as we hurried down the stairs of the hotel.

"I think that's my line," he said, trying to push ahead of me.

"This isn't a race," I insisted, wishing I could trip him. Luckily for him, I needed him to help me turn that capstan.

We were almost to the front door when the twins burst in.

"Winner, winner, chicken dinner!" Zadie declared, holding up a silver coin.

"Nooo." Duranja halted, and I nearly ran into the back of him.

"Please tell me that's the coin you discovered at the docks," I said, dodging Robocop.

We'd snagged the keystone. We'd uncovered the capstan. We'd done all the hard work.

"Hey, Amateur Hour," Zara said fondly, raising a hand for a celebratory high five.

I refused to give her the pleasure.

"This," she said, digging into the pocket of her cargo pants, "is the coin we found overnight," she said, holding it up. "It's not as shiny as the one we nabbed from the cliffs, but it's just as pretty."

"Now you and I each have one," Zadie said, kissing the coin she held.

"And you have none," Zara pointed out. "Sorry about that," she added, not sounding the least bit regretful.

No way. "That would have been ours if not for a falling rock."

"How's your sister?" Zadie asked with true concern.

That caught me off guard. Again.

"She's going to be fine, thank you," I answered crisply. No need to be rude. I mean, Zadie and Zara had helped. Before they'd both screwed us over. "You could have given us a minute to recover. We were dealing with injuries, and you took our win."

Zara scoffed. "My sister led you to safety, I brought in the cavalry, and newsflash—the game doesn't stop until somebody wins it all."

"One more coin and they *will* take it all," Duranja warned. "Best we can do now is a two-two split."

As if I didn't realize.

"Want to get the last coin before dinner?" Zadie asked her sister.

Now they were taunting us. "You don't have the keystone," I pointed out. The remaining two belonged to us and to the professor.

"Didn't stop us just now." Zara shrugged.

"None of us know where the next capstan is," Duranja said, both relieved and frustrated.

"We already have the board out there," Zara said.

"We always find a way," Zadie said, with no small amount of pride.

They were the team to beat. That much had been clear from day one.

The front door opened again for a sullen Dr. Fielding.

"Well, hello," Zadie said, very amused with herself. "Did you enjoy our performance?"

"He was spying on us while we bagged our prize," Zara said.

"Not like he could have turned the capstan by himself," Zadie added. "Honestly, I don't understand why you're playing in the first place."

"I retrieved both the keystones," he said, clutching a pair of cloth-wrapped bundles. "These aren't cheap game pieces to be left outside." He held them close. "Thankfully, they are undamaged."

"I'm glad to hear it," I said, with all sincerity.

"We'd have brought it back if you'd asked," Zadie said.

The professor's mouth tightened, but he didn't challenge her.

Zara laughed. "Okay, we need to put these three out of their misery."

Zadie slapped her on the shoulder. "Come on. Let's go find Bill. Show him our second coin and tell him he's almost got a winner."

Duranja scrubbed a hand across his forehead. "I should have taken the keystone out. I just love Melody so much, I lost my head."

"That's not exactly a bad thing," I admitted, even if I wished it weren't Robocop losing his mind over my sister.

I hadn't been thinking of anything else either, except getting Melody and Ellis safely off the beach.

And it wasn't as if we could have rushed back. We wouldn't leave Melody and Ellis alone until we knew they were well and safe —even if we'd imagined the twins would be racing back to take our prize.

We should have imagined.

The twins made a victory lap past the library, backslapping a few more times before heading for Bill's office. Meanwhile, we stood rooted in the lobby, feeling more than a little defeated.

"We need to get a jump on them for the next task," Duranja said under his breath.

"I know you have the third keystone," Dr. Fielding said quietly.

"I—" I wasn't quite sure how to answer that.

The professor adjusted his glasses. "The twins don't have it, or they'd be out there now. I didn't take it. Rick's still at a loss. So that means you took his stone."

"Nice work," Duranja conceded.

"Logic," the professor said simply. "Luckily for you, I have the diary."

"Does it tell us where to go?" I pressed.

"Following the twins and that board would tell him where to go," Duranja said.

"They were too careful," Dr. Fielding said. "And my first priority was preserving those keystones. But," he said, "I didn't need to follow the twins." His lips twisted. "I saw a map in the library earlier that details where to go. The entrance to the spot is hidden." He looked at me and then Duranja. "I'll take you with me under one condition. I get to turn my stone. I want to do it as gently as possible. After that, you can have my fake doubloon. I'm not going to win the main prize anyway."

"Are you sure?" The historian had been helpful so far, but giving us his doubloon was a bigger sacrifice than I'd hoped for.

"I only ask that I be included in the hunt," the professor insisted.

"Deal," Duranja said, offering a hand.

"With pleasure," I added.

We'd be tied with the twins!

Dr. Fielding nodded, excited. "Then let's go," he suggested, making his way toward the library. "They're so busy congratulating themselves, they won't see us coming," he said, glancing to where the victorious twins had disappeared.

Too bad we weren't as stealthy as we'd hoped.

We walked into the library to find Rick at the map table. His wife sat on the couch by the fireplace, thumbing through a weathered book titled *Pirates and Privateers: Medicine at Sea.*

"Oh." Dr. Fielding stopped short.

Duranja cursed under his breath.

The professor's gaze darted to the book Rick's wife held.

"Didn't I tell you to back off?" the author said, standing.

Well, this was awkward.

"I was just...leaving," Dr. Fielding said, beating a hasty retreat.

Rick rubbed a hand over his forehead. "Sorry," he said. "The professor and I go way back. He...asks too much sometimes."

"Sure," I said, giving him room to say more.

He didn't.

Maybe the professor would be more open. In the meantime, I couldn't pass up the opportunity to approach the good doctor. "Hey, thanks again," I said, making my way over to where she sat. "I know it wasn't fun to tell the action twins up there to take it easy, but I appreciate your willingness to help."

"It's what I do," she said easily, closing her book. "I'm glad they're going to be okay."

"They are two of the most important people on earth to me," I told her. "I'm Verity," I added, by way of introduction. Again. At least this time she seemed more receptive.

"Mindy," she said, taking the hand I'd offered.

"Now that we've got the Southern pleasantries out of the way," Rick said, strolling around to the front of the desk and planting his backside on it, "we all know the twins are playing dirty."

"Rick—" Mindy began.

"You said it first," he reminded her.

"I think they're extremely sharp and very good at this kind of game," I told the group. "Every move they make is testing the line, but they were really upset to be held back today."

"Good," Rick snapped.

I understood his frustration. "I don't think the twins will outright cheat again," I said, hoping to bring him some comfort. "Bill's not going to allow it. He needs this game to appear fair if he wants to sell an experience like this to more people."

"He should work on making it safe first." Mindy stood and

placed her book on the coffee table. "This has less to do with the capstans and more to do with the sheer number of accidents we're seeing this weekend. I think it's intentional."

That was a serious accusation. "I don't think anyone would be that vicious." The falling rock could have killed someone. "I mean, this is a game."

Mindy inclined her head. "I've trained in forensics. Granted, I'm retired now, and I left the actual crime scene investigation to others on my team, but I did look at the step where Rick stumbled. It appeared to me like the mortar had been deliberately chiseled out." She caught Duranja's eye. "I'll show you."

"Please," he said, suddenly interested.

Rick crossed his arms over his chest. "It's clear someone intended for one of the people here this weekend to fall and get hurt. Then they took advantage of my injury on the stairs to steal my keystone."

Not quite. Robocop had taken the keystone long before Rick's injury.

Duranja shot me a warning look, as if I were about to confess.

It had crossed my mind.

Rick stood up off the desk. "Neither of them got hurt, while we've got two teams who have taken hits."

True.

"The professor hasn't been hurt, either," I pointed out.

"His keystone is next, right?" the author said, as if it were only a matter of time.

Agitated, Rick walked around to the front of the desk. "If someone is willing to loosen a stone step in the hope of causing an accident, what's stopping them from sawing dock boards or pushing a rock? Or worse?"

"Because a trip is one thing, but skull crushing is way out of line," I said, feeling defensive all over again for my sister and boyfriend. And worried. Because if we'd escalated to potentially deadly force, then I didn't want to think about what we'd be dealing with on the hunt for the third keystone.

Duranja appeared similarly skeptical, which worried me all over again because when was I ever on his side?

"We need to take a look at the top of that cliff," Duranja said, strolling over to close the pocket doors. "Right now, there's no evidence that it was anything other than nature, gravity, and bad timing."

"I'll go with you," I said.

"I'll go alone," Duranja countered.

Bless his heart.

"I wouldn't mind tagging along," Rick offered. "If the twins went after you, it would be two against one."

Mindy rounded the couch, arms over her chest. "At the same time, I don't see any evidence pointing to the twins."

"Plus, they were victims themselves," I said. "The dock gave way while they were retrieving their own coin. If they'd sustained more serious injuries, they'd have been out of the game."

"We examined those boards this afternoon when your team was down on the cliffs," Mindy said.

"They were cut to the point of breaking," Rick added. He looked to me. "Sure. Like you said, the twins weren't seriously hurt. But they had plenty of time to saw through boards if they were out there all night. They could have staged it to draw suspicion away from themselves. Meanwhile, they got what they wanted."

"The twins are the only ones who benefited from the rock fall," Mindy said, slowly pacing in front of the bookshelves. "I mean, your teammates got injured, almost killed, and then the twins used that tragedy to take the coin out from under you."

"You heard?" Duranja groused.

"Couldn't miss it," Rick said.

"The professor was also near the cliffs," I said. "Melody encouraged him to go a different way." The wrong way. "But maybe there was a reason he didn't stick with us when we went down that trail."

Duranja rubbed the back of his neck. "Yes, but Dr. Fielding

couldn't have turned the capstan by himself. What good would it have done him?"

"He could have stolen the keystone by himself," I said. "Maybe the twins were simply faster."

Duranja took a moment to think. "We have to look at opportunity. The professor has been on this island multiple times for his museum. He could have chiseled the mortar or cut the boards before any of us ever got here. And he keeps disappearing."

"And showing up at inopportune times," Rick said, eyeing his wife.

"I think he's just awkward," Mindy said, a little flustered. "Not to mention intense."

Then again, she'd done some disappearing herself.

Duranja strolled over to where the pirate flag stood framed on the wall. He turned to face us. "The point is Dr. Fielding also has opportunity. And every single one of us has motive."

"That's true," I said, catching the author's strong, steady gaze.

Rick could have tripped on purpose. His injury hadn't been serious. And while he spent so much time down on the docks looking for his keystone, he could have easily damaged the dock beam. The only way back into the game for him was to get the coin from the cliffs—the one that should have been his.

Maybe he wanted revenge on us for taking it, and pushed the rock down while the twins were held back and the professor was down by the beach.

It could have been anyone.

Mindy clasped her hands in front of her. "Rick and I know we're out of the game. And frankly, with the rash of accidents, I'm glad." She turned to her husband. "I think it's our job to learn who the saboteur is."

The corner of his lip quirked. "I'm good at solving a mystery. It's a side benefit of making them up."

"And I'd like to avoid more people getting hurt," she said.

"To that end, do you think you can stick around this afternoon and keep an eye on the twins?" Duranja asked. "At least until Verity and I get done checking out the cliffs."

So I was invited now.

"After that, we'll go after the last coins," Duranja pledged. "Whoever is setting up these dangerous situations can't be allowed to win."

He slid open the doors to the library and found Dr. Fielding on the other side.

The professor stood in shock for a moment. "I still need to take a look at that...thing here in the library."

"Rick and his wife were just on their way out," Duranja prompted.

"Sure," Rick said, eyeing the professor as he and Mindy filed out of the library. "We have a few things to take care of, anyway."

Dr. Fielding watched them go. "What was that all about?"

"Sabotage," I said.

"Go on in," Duranja told him. "Find that map you need. Verity and I are going to check something out. We'll meet you here in twenty minutes."

Chapter Nineteen

The twins were nowhere to be found when we exited the library. Nor was Bill. There was no telling what the game penalty would be for sabotage, but I had to think disqualification was the only appropriate response.

Still, I couldn't help but wonder.

"Why all this over a weekend treasure hunt?" I asked as we hurried down the path toward the cliffs.

I mean, a step I could see. A rigged dock was borderline. But that rock? That could have killed my sister if not for the quick thinking of Ellis.

It wasn't worth that kind of danger to win a ten-thousand-dollar game token.

My sneakers crunched over the seashell-strewn path. "I think this is about something bigger than Bill's weekend treasure hunt."

Duranja kept his focus trained straight ahead. "You think Captain Bill's treasure is real."

I nodded. "And buried on this island."

Duranja flexed his jaw. "I think there's something big out there, too. It's the only reason anybody would go through this much trouble to incapacitate the competition."

"So our saboteur is playing one game, and we're playing another," I concluded.

"Not necessarily," Duranja said, thinking. "I think we're very much a part of the puzzle."

"To what end?" I asked aloud, the realization thudding low in my stomach. "Unless we're leading someone to a bigger treasure."

"Exactly," Duranja said under his breath.

"Heavens." I ran a hand through my hair. "I mean, if you can't find your pirate ancestor's treasure, why not call in a pair of professional treasure hunters?"

Duranja's mouth formed a thin line. "He did. Not to mention a mystery writer, a forensic medical examiner, a historian, two police officers, and a research librarian."

"And a ghost hunter," I added.

He frowned at that last part.

It didn't change the facts. "Bill could be setting us up to find the treasure, but not walk away with it."

In that case, every single one of us was in danger on this island.

"Or maybe the professor knows more about Bill's treasure than he does," Duranja said, tensing. "We can't rule anything out yet."

True. "It could also be Rick. I mean, he has a ton of money, or at least enough to waste it on pirate antiques. Why would he care so much about the medallion? His wife sure doesn't seem to."

We reached the cliff above the second capstan. Duranja peered down to where my poor sister had almost been crushed. "The rock was large. It would have had to be near the edge."

"Here," I said, locating a muddy spot with a few worms still digging their way back underground. "And look," I added, pointing to a deep indentation in the earth behind it. "You can see where the rock was levered."

"Looks like they used one of the boards," Duranja said, joining me. He tilted his chin down and looked at me. "That's good work, Verity."

"You don't have to sound so surprised."

Even if I was a little taken off guard by his acknowledgment.

"Truth be told, I was hoping we wouldn't find this," he admitted. "Anyone could have access to those boards Bill left at the side of the house."

And to the cliffs.

I knew how he felt. "I wanted the island to be safe, too." But it wasn't.

"That's okay," he said, nodding to himself. "It just means we have a job to do."

We returned to the hotel to find Dr. Fielding exiting the library.

"The rock that almost fell on Melody was no accident," I said.

The professor paled. "We need to find the last two capstans and fast. This game is getting dangerous, and it needs to end."

I couldn't agree more.

"You found what you needed in the library?" Duranja asked.

"Yes." He held up a rolled map. "This, along with Captain Bill's diary, will tell us where to go. Let's stop talking until we get up to my room. I'll show you everything, and we'll work out a strategy."

"Perfect," I said, hustling up the stairs after him.

The twins might have the two coins, but we had the map, and soon we would have the diary.

Duranja charged ahead of me and cut me off as we reached Founders Landing.

"Hold up a sec," he said, stopping me in my tracks, waiting for the professor to get well ahead of us. "About what we discussed on the way to the cliff—don't say anything to Dr. Fielding or to anyone." He stood, serious as sin under the watchful eyes of the generations of outlaws and innkeepers who had called this island home. "Remember, everyone besides us is a suspect. Except Melody and Ellis, but they're resting."

Like I was going to tell.

"You realize I've done this before," I told him, turning to hurry after the professor.

"That's what I'm afraid of," he called after me.

We caught up to the professor, who stood outside his open door, clutching the map. "It was open when I got up here," he said, worried. "The door. It was open by about an inch."

"Okay, let's check it out," Duranja said, walking in first.

Dr. Fielding's room faced the back of the island and was smaller than the one Ellis and I shared. Like the others, it was nautical themed. And despite the open door, it appeared neat and untouched.

"Maybe you left it open," I suggested. The door to my room was such a pain to open and close, I wouldn't have blamed him if he did.

"I did not," he said stiffly, depositing the wrapped keystones as well as the map on his bed before going straight for the bottom right dresser drawer and yanking it open.

He drew a hand to his mouth. "It's gone. The diary is gone."

Oh no. "Are you sure that's where you left it?"

"Of course I'm sure," he snapped, wrenching open the other drawers. "I kept it there, on a folded towel."

The white towel remained, covered with sand.

The men made a thorough search of the room while I pondered who might have taken the diary and left...sand. The twins had been on the beach. Then again, so had the professor. And the rest of us. "When was the last time you saw the book?" I asked while Duranja searched under the bed and the professor tore apart the bedding.

"I read it last night," he said, tossing a pillow. "I put it back in the drawer before I went to sleep." He peered under the covers. "Then I took it out on the cliffs today, and I'm sure I locked my room before I went out again."

"But you've been gone this afternoon," Duranja said. "Anyone could have snuck in here while you were away."

"Bill has the keys to everyone's room," I pointed out.

"He hangs them on the hook behind the front desk," Duranja added grimly. "Totally accessible to anyone."

He had to be kidding. "Anyone?"

"We had words," Duranja said crisply.

The professor threw his hands up. "So anyone could have taken it. Why didn't you warn me?"

"It's pretty obvious! And I thought you kept the diary on you," Duranja shot back.

"Okay, well, let's just follow the twins," I concluded. "We'll see where they go next."

"We don't need to follow anyone," the professor said, returning to the map on the now rumpled bed. "The diary is a valuable historical artifact, and I must get it back. But"—he closed his eyes briefly—"the information you need for your treasure hunt is already in my head."

"Oh, thank goodness." People like him and my sister amazed me.

"And on this map." He unrolled it and used the keystones to weigh the stubborn edges down. "The third capstan is in a hidden entrance to the caves inside the lighthouse. There," he added, pointing to the topographical map.

It pictured a cave entrance on the hill where the lighthouse stood. The underground maze branched off into several dead ends. "It requires my keystone, and this is the route the diary showed."

"I've got it," Duranja said, committing it to memory. I did the same.

Meanwhile, Dr. Fielding placed a sheet of paper over the map and traced a rough but accurate version of the direct route we'd need to take. "I believe the third capstan is at the start of the caves, and the last one is hidden deep inside." He glanced to us. "I will be the one turning both keystones and retrieving them afterward."

Duranja nodded. "I'll man the board with you. Verity will catch the doubloons and keep a lookout."

Dr. Fielding ran a hand under his chin. "The trick now is getting into that lighthouse."

"In that case, I think we have you covered," I said.

"The code is in the parrot," Duranja said as if he couldn't quite believe the words coming out of his mouth. "Luckily for us, Verity hasn't been able to part with the dumb bird."

I froze. *Oh no.*

No, no, no. My heart sank, and my brain went blank. "I had it on the trail. Before the rock fell."

"And?" Duranja demanded.

I patted myself down, even though I hadn't felt it bang around my hip for a while. And it never would have made it here on my shoulder or clipped to my belt. "I don't remember seeing it since the chaos on the cliff."

"A bright red parrot. You lost a bright red parrot?" Duranja barked.

"Oh, now you want me carrying it," I shot back. "He thought Pearl was ridiculous," I said to the professor.

"Still do," Duranja said. "Do you remember Pearl's birthday?"

"March! Something. Not with you pressuring me like that." And from the look on his face, I'd have to say Duranja was also drawing a blank. "Do you know?" I asked the professor, who looked at us like we were a wagon short of a wheel.

"The history books don't exactly cover bird birthdays."

Well, then they needed to be more thorough. "We can always try to have Frankie go look at the Post-it."

Although it hadn't gone very well the last time.

"Oh, yeah." Duranja tossed his hands up. "A ghost will fix everything."

"I wish." I had to get the bird back or those pirates were going to haunt me forever. Trouble was, Frankie was probably hanging out with them. They'd be on my case the second I wandered near that bar by the lighthouse.

At least we'd catch a break with the code. "Melody will know," I insisted.

"She'd better," the professor cautioned, rolling up the map, "because someone else may very well have our directions, our diary, and the keycode to the lighthouse."

He didn't need to spell out the consequences.

We hurried across the hall to find Melody on the floor with a cup pressed to her ear, and Ellis sitting next to her with his arms folded over his chest.

"She's as relentless as you are," he said to me the second I crossed the threshold to our room.

"Shhh!" Melody propped herself up on her good elbow.

"She says eavesdropping will distract her from the pain," Ellis said dryly.

"Is it working?" I asked, joining them on the floor.

"No," my sister said, sitting up with a groan. "But Rick and his wife are down in the library, discussing how they can get a look at the map you took a few minutes ago without looking suspicious."

I gaped at her. "They said they'd stay back and keep an eye on the twins."

"Which would be helpful, unless Rick and his wife are the ones causing the trouble," Ellis said soberly.

"Let's all watch our backs." I hated to think of the doctor and the author as shady characters, but if I'd learned one thing on this island, it was that I could only truly trust the people I'd come with.

Duranja and I filled the team in on the professor's missing diary and where we were headed next. "We need the door code for the lighthouse if we're going to get down to the caves."

"This sounds dangerous," Ellis warned.

"03051774," Melody said, without missing a beat. "Pearl was born on March 5, 1774."

Dr. Fielding smacked his leg. "Melody, you are a treasure."

I gave her a gentle hug. "I knew I could count on you."

"Always." She smiled.

Ellis grabbed the side of the bed and levered himself up. "It kills me that I can't go with you," he said when I moved to help him.

"I'll be careful," I assured him.

He nodded. "I know you're smart and cautious. But whoever is setting these traps obviously doesn't care if someone gets killed." He looked past me to his friend. "Promise me you'll take care of each other."

"Um..." I began.

"What?" Duranja asked.

"Swear on it. That you'll stick together. Work as a team," Ellis said, holding us to the fire.

Melody struggled up into a one-handed sitting position. "We won't be around to keep you from sniping at each other, and bickering could get you killed."

"All right," I said before she got preachier.

"I swear," Duranja said, holding up a hand and dropping it quickly. He looked to me. "We should go."

"I know you're a sweetheart," Melody said when he bent down to kiss her goodbye. "Now prove it to my sister."

"I'm just sweet on you," he replied, giving her an extra kiss on the head.

"You see what I have to put up with?" I asked Ellis, giving him a tender yet subtle goodbye kiss.

My handsome boyfriend pulled me in for an extra smooch and a nuzzle on the ear. Then, while his lips were pressed up against me, he whispered, "There's no one out there on this island you can trust except for Alec. Promise me you will."

I noticed he watched the professor as he said it.

"I will," I promised. "I'll be careful."

"It'll be fine," Dr. Fielding assured him. "I have the next keystone we need." His hands went to his jacket, fingering the lump in his pocket. "And Alec has the final one."

"That someone might hurt you to get," Ellis warned.

"We know what to do. Piece of cake," the professor said as if he were trying to talk himself into it.

Ellis nodded. "Let's hope so."

And hope the saboteur wasn't waiting for us.

Chapter Twenty

We crept along the upstairs hall to make our way out of the hotel. I kept my steps light and my mind focused. If we could make it away from the hotel unseen, we'd have an advantage. "Whoever took the diary is probably the one sabotaging the game."

"It has to be the twins," the professor muttered, "trying to secure the final victory."

Or someone else, who might be after a bigger prize.

Duranja led the way through Founders Landing. "Let's just stay alert and focus on getting this capstan opened."

"And the next one," the professor added.

The lobby lay blessedly quiet. All the same, we snuck around to the exit at the back of the stairs. No sense attracting any attention from Rick and Mindy if they were still in the library. Or Bill if he had any interest in where we were headed without any direction from him or the "game."

"Let's avoid the official paths," Duranja said, keeping up a strong, steady pace. We traversed the uneven ground north of where we'd originally ventured.

I wouldn't have been surprised if the twins had done the same. They might very well be ahead of us with the diary in hand.

"It'll be a longer route if we avoid the haunted bridge to the south," I said to Duranja's back. Not that I'd miss a trip across the crumbling rock catastrophe, but at this point every second counted.

"Oh, I'm not risking a bridge with chunks missing," Dr. Fielding insisted, catching up to me. "Remember? We said we'd do this safely."

"And I'm not about to tell Melody I let you fall off a bridge," Duranja said in a way that made it sound irritating. Probably because I'd proven time and time again that I could take care of myself. "And no way I'm taking you near any one of your supposed ghosts," he couldn't resist adding.

"Those supposed ghosts are the only reason we've done as well as we have," I pointed out. Frankie had rattled Ellis and me out of bed in time to confront the twins coming up off the beach, and the runaway bride had shown us where the capstan lay hidden on the cliffside.

Although speaking of the gangster, I hadn't seen Frankie since this morning. That probably meant he was getting into loads of fun trouble with the pirate ghosts. I hoped he hadn't gambled himself into oblivion or, worse, tried to nick their boat.

With any luck, he was keeping them busy. Because I really didn't want to run into those ghosts at the lighthouse, not when they'd insisted I keep an eye on their precious Pearl and I had no idea where she was.

To be fair, I'd done a great job...for almost twenty-four hours.

The afternoon sun hung low. Seabirds circled overhead, screaming what sounded like a warning as we pressed up the steep hill toward the lighthouse in the distance.

I adjusted the bag on my shoulder and felt Frankie's urn clank against my side. Technically, I didn't need to have it with me. My ghost had the run of the property wherever his urn was, and that included the entire island. But Frankie had a soft spot for his final resting place, and if I did run into trouble with the ghosts, it would be easier for the gangster to find me if I had his urn nearby.

Besides, the urn was vaguely Pearl sized and shaped. Telling the pirates she was safe in my bag was better than telling them she might have drifted out with the tide. Hopefully, they wouldn't ask to see her.

"Look," the professor said, pointing down toward the beach.

Rick and Mindy knelt at the edge of the cliff where the rock had nearly fallen on Melody. Perhaps they truly were dedicated to investigating the accidents. Still, it would be best to keep moving before they spotted us.

"Is anyone else having trouble trusting...anyone?" Dr. Fielding asked as we crested the hill and reached the long, flat expanse leading to the lighthouse.

It left no room to hide—for us or for anyone else.

"Yes," Duranja and I said in unison.

And unlike everybody else, I'd had plenty of contact with untrustworthy folks on the other side as well.

I gasped aloud when I saw what lay ahead. A trio of pirate ghosts stood drinking and smoking outside the ramshackle image of a building that glowed gray in the golden light of the waning sun. Shouts and laugher erupted from inside.

We didn't have time for pirates.

Worse, the rambling wooden shack extended straight into the lighthouse. There was no way around. I'd have to go through.

I clutched my bag tight. And here I'd been hoping to avoid the crew of the *Fortune's Revenge*. It would have been nice if they'd chosen someplace else to haunt this afternoon.

"Come on, Verity," Dr. Fielding urged, already several yards in front of me, with Duranja way ahead of him. "Why are you stopped?"

I hadn't realized I'd halted. At the same time, I wasn't overly eager to get going again.

"Cripes." Duranja turned to face me. "Are you getting squirrelly?"

I couldn't walk into the haunted pirate lair after I'd broken my promise to them. But there was no way around it if I wanted to go inside the lighthouse and find the third capstan.

"Frankie?" I called. He could turn my power off.

If he bothered to answer me.

"Frankie!" I urged.

"This isn't the time," Duranja warned. "Seriously. You know we need to get in there and do this."

I did.

It would also be a lot nicer without Frankie's power.

"Come on, Frankie, I don't want to see any pirates."

I sighed when he didn't answer. I mean, why couldn't he at least show up when I asked? "It's like talking to thin air."

"Yes," Duranja hissed. "It is!"

I forced my feet to move. "I really don't have the patience for you right now," I said, passing Robocop.

He didn't have to deal with a finicky gangster. Or face down any angry ghosts. All he had to worry about was the treasure hunt. And a potential attempted murderer on our tail.

Okay, this was bad on both sides. But still...

I braced myself. Maybe running into a gang of pirate ghosts wasn't as big a deal as I thought. Maybe they'd be in a better mood today. I hadn't messed up on purpose. Surely, I could explain it in a way they'd understand. They were bloodthirsty outlaws, but they'd had a few centuries to mellow out.

Or get worse.

We drew closer.

I heard a fiddle and a flute pick up a jaunty tune.

Maybe they wouldn't harass me if I kept my head down. Sometimes it took a while for the dead to notice me—or anybody living—if I didn't interact with them first.

Of course, messing with their hidden capstan might attract their attention.

Duranja picked up the pace and passed straight through the side of the pirate lair.

I slowed and watched Dr. Fielding walk through a broken, discarded barrel and an unlit lantern slug over a hook in the wall. The pirate music didn't even pause when he entered.

Lucky duck.

While I held Frankie's power, objects on the other side were as real to me as those in my own realm. I'd have to use the door. Which would be painful and awkward.

Touching ghostly objects gave me a mighty shock. It would also clue in any observant spirits that I could see the other side.

I kept my pace up and my steps light as I approached the door.

Nothing to see here.

I whipped a few fingers under the handle and braced for the cold, wet shock of the dead.

Steady.

The touch of the door handle chilled me to the core. It was like being invaded and exposed all at the same time. It stung down to my bones, a deluge of frigid, soaking death.

I yanked the heavy, ghostly door open with barely enough room to squeeze through, and hurried inside, making sure not to touch any part of the doorframe.

I brought a hand to my mouth at the smell of sweat, rum, and brine. Inside, a sea of unwashed, uncouth outlaws packed the dark, shadowy bar. Lanterns hung low from the ceiling. Barefoot sailors laughed and drank and carried on at rough, low tables, their loose, baggy trousers cut off below the knee, their billowy linen shirts more stained than white.

I scanned the room for Frankie. It wasn't too late for him to cut my power.

But he was nowhere in sight.

"Darn it, Frankie," I muttered under my breath. I mean, where was he if he wasn't gambling or drinking?

"Verity." Duranja stood with his hands on his hips, right in the middle of a table of men tossing coins and yelling out bets. Beside them, the pock-faced pirate made a great show of shaking a pair of dice over a pile of chicken bones. "Dr. Fielding is already in the lighthouse. I don't want to leave him alone in there."

I fought to keep my focus on my live companion instead of

the highly animated dead who surrounded us.

"Coming, Alec," I said, earning a frown from him.

"What's wrong?" he demanded, staring me down.

I never called him Alec. But I was nervous, on edge.

Pasting on a smile, I breezed way too close to a snaggle-toothed buccaneer who'd upended his chair in order to dance a merry jig.

Duranja's eyes narrowed at my chipper spirit, but there was no way I was letting him or anyone in this bar know that I saw anything but a snarly Robocop in a hurry.

Truly, there was no time to waste—in securing the coin from the third capstan, and in getting through this pirate bar in one piece.

"Verity, would you just get over here? We don't have time for this," Duranja stared me down as I worked my way around tables and elbows and drunk buccaneers.

He should try walking a straight line through a dead pirate party.

One packed with every crook on the island save for the one crook who could help me out of this mess.

A swarthy pirate reached through Duranja to grab a bottle of rum off the table. He drank it down, right from the bottle, while Robocop sighed and turned to walk ahead of me.

Honestly, it was a relief. I'd rather avoid Duranja's attention and anyone else's. And as we drew closer to the lighthouse, I resisted the urge to hum along to the quickening beat of the music. We might just pull this off.

I glanced at the fiddle player propped up on an old gunpowder crate in the corner. He grinned and winked at me.

Whoa, boy.

My time was up.

One of the large, roughened pirates I'd met earlier stepped directly in my path. His scraggly hair hung down over his shoulders, woven with beads and bits of bone. "Looking for a spot of ale, lassie?"

My heart caught in my throat. I dodged left and prayed he was talking to somebody else.

Pock Face blocked my way. "We told ye to guard the captain's bird."

No, no, no. "Ha," I hedged, feeling as trapped as a skunk under the porch. "No worries, she's quite safe." My voice cracked. I scurried sideways, desperate to see if I could locate Frankie.

"Where?" Pock Face snarled, displaying a mouthful of rotting teeth.

"Here in my bag," I said, patting the urn, trying to keep my voice even and my mood chipper.

The pirate brought a hand down to the revolver tucked under his belt. "Show me," he ordered.

I swallowed hard.

Duranja threw up his hands when he saw me standing paralyzed. "Shoot me now!"

He wasn't the one in danger of getting shot.

"I'm keeping her very safe," I insisted, voice shaky. Or at least I had. "Frankie..."

Now would be an especially great time for Frankie to turn my power off. I reached down into my bag to give his urn a rub, then a tap. Then a shake. "Good bird," I managed, although I doubted I was fooling anybody.

"*Well?*" Pock Face demanded as Eye Patch drew up behind him.

Maybe I could buy a few seconds. I cleared my throat. "I'm not allowed to show you on order of the captain."

"Liar," Bony Beads snarled. "Nobody's seen the captain."

"He's indisposed," Eye Patch said.

"Having his wedding night," Pock Face added with a randy chuckle. "We wouldn't dare disturb him."

Oh, my word. They didn't know something terrible had happened to both their captain and his bride-to-be. "She's not with the captain. I saw her this afternoon, trapped on a rock bridge south of here."

The pirate's eyes narrowed. "We don't take kindly to liars," Bony Beads growled.

Duranja stood behind him, waving his hand through Bony Beads's head. "Get a grip. There's nothing here. Air. The seabirds and the breeze."

"She's trying to distract us from Pearl." Pock Face closed in on me. "We ordered you to never let her out of your sight."

"To make sure there's nary a feather out of place," Eye Patch snarled.

Pock Face towered over me. "If you've got our precious Pearl in that bag, you'd better show us. Now."

"I'm telling you the truth," I vowed. Only I was a terrible liar. A bead of sweat trickled down my back. What was it with the pirates and that frigging bird? "And if the captain isn't around, what's the worry?"

I felt an awful chill as a scraggly-haired pirate bent down and shoved his entire head into my bag. "She don't have Pearl at all," he declared.

"You betrayed the crew," Bony Beads snarled.

"Pearl is safe," I said. "She's...having a spa day back at the hotel." His brows furrowed, and I quickly added, "A bath! I wanted to keep her clean."

That confused him long enough for me to call out a quick, "Frankie!"

"Verity," Duranja gritted out.

"Leave me," I said.

"I can't," he snapped. "Melody would kill me." He paced to the middle of the pirate bar, unaware when a scallywag slammed a beer down through his utterly thick head. "Why do you care about the bird you lost? We're after *real pirate gold*."

The fiddle ground to a halt. The flute player blew off key before his instrument clattered to the ground. Ale mugs banged down, and I turned to see the entire bar full of pirates glaring at me.

He might as well have lit Pearl on fire.

Bony Beads grabbed a bottle from the table next to me and smashed it on the floor.

Pock Face hissed and drew way too close, chilling me to the core. "Come to steal Pearl and rob us too?"

Hardly. "We're not positive about the gold."

"We'll get it if it's there," Duranja said confidently.

And he'd accused *me* of talking too much to the wrong people?

"I know where Pearl is," I said to the pirates. And I did...in the larger sense. After all, she had to be somewhere on the island.

"Pearl's long gone," Duranja said, exasperated. "The damned bird probably fell off the cliff and got washed into the ocean."

"Can you pipe down?" I pleaded with Robocop.

"Can you get moving?" he countered.

"No," I gasped.

One by one, the pirates at the tables surrounding us began to stand.

"She lied to us!" said one.

"She's a traitor," grumbled another.

"That's it." Duranja threw up his hands. "I'm going to check on Dr. Fielding."

I retreated from the pirates' frigid bodies and angry stares. "Your gold is safe." We hoped. "And Pearl can't have gone far, I promise." Even if I'd dropped her when Melody and Ellis fell on the cliffs, she could still be there. It wasn't as if she could fly away. "She's my top priority." Right after we unlocked Captain Bill's capstans and perhaps reunited him with his lost love.

And maybe unearthed a treasure.

But first I had to make it to the lighthouse.

Pock Face growled low in his throat. He glared at me, piercing eyes under bushy brows. "I challenge you to a traitor's duel."

I had no idea what that was, but it sounded unpleasant. "No, thank you," I managed.

The corner of his mouth ticked up, displaying a set of rotting teeth. "Wasn't asking."

He drew a sword from the sheath at his belt. "McGee—" he snarled.

Eye Patch whipped a steel blade from his belt and held it out to me. "A weapon for the lady," he rasped, with exaggerated sincerity.

"I don't like swords or knives," I said, polite as I could. My hands had gone sweaty and my knees weak. "Unless it's maybe to cut fruit." The ghostly weapon would be cold and wet and awful —and it would disappear in a minute or two.

Worse, I could get fatally stabbed by a pirate. Correction. I most definitely would. The last time I'd dueled had been in Lauralee's backyard with a pair of plastic lightsabers with her eight-year-old.

He'd cleaned my clock.

"How about I go find the bird right now?" Anything to keep from fighting men who did it for a living.

Pock Face snatched the sword from his crewmate and thrust it at me. "Take the sword, or I'll stab you with it myself."

I flung my hands out to the sides. "I invoke the pirate rule of parlay. You have to bring me in front of the captain to negotiate before any justice is served." I said it like I knew what I was talking about. And that I hadn't seen it in a movie.

The scar that went from his eye to his chin wrinkled when he frowned. "Like McGee said, the captain is indisposed." The man behind him made a sign of the cross. "And too bad for you, our ship don't honor parlay. Now take it." He shoved it into my right hand, and the icy metal seared my skin.

It was shockingly cold, and I lost all feeling straight up to the elbow.

"What are the rules?" I demanded. How could I get out of this with the least amount of damage? Because I didn't think the rest of the crew would take it kindly if I stabbed a pirate, no matter if it was in self-defense. Assuming I managed to get the sword close to him at all.

Bony Beads chuckled. He knew he had me trapped. "The rules are there are no rules. It's a fight to the death."

Only they couldn't die, and I could.

My extremities tingled. My breath came in pants.

Duranja stepped straight through the pirate. "Verity, we got into the lighthouse. The professor found the trapdoor. Now's the time to move."

Pock Face lunged and took a swipe at me with his sword.

I shrieked and retreated. "Could you give me a break, Duranja? I'm fighting a duel!"

"We don't have time for you to play ghost right now," Duranja barked.

"I don't want to play either," I cried, dodging the scarred pirate ghost, who laughed as he took another swing at me.

"Look," Duranja said as I slammed into him in my rush to escape. He grabbed my arm, and I twisted out of his grip. "Verity, listen! We're not the only ones up here. The lighthouse door was tampered with."

"Leave me alone!" I fell on one knee to evade another blow from the ghost.

Duranja stood his ground. "And explain that to Melody? No."

Pock Face turned for a fraction of a second to share a laugh with Bony Beads, giving me the opening I'd been waiting for. Only Duranja stood in my way.

"Move it or lose it." I leaped to my feet and shoved past him.

"What the hell are you doing?" he demanded.

"I told you, dueling!" I said, going for the pirate's forearm because that was the nearest thing, and I thought maybe he'd drop his sword if I hit him right.

Pock Face swung around and sliced at me before I could even get close.

My cheek stung, and I felt blood trickle down.

"What the hell?" Duranja sputtered. "Verity, why is your cheek bleeding?"

The fiddle player picked up the pace as I took off running from the laughing Pock Face.

"What just happened?" Duranja barked, hightailing it next to me. "You're bleeding out of nowhere!"

"Ghost pirates!" I skirted the long bar at the back, dodging barrels of ale, looking for a way out. "I told you I was dueling. Who did you think I was dueling with?"

"Hey, get out of there," the bartender hollered.

But he wasn't my biggest problem.

Pock Face leaped up onto the bar, scattering pirates and mugs. He reached down and slammed someone's abandoned tankard of ale. "Don't you love it when the wenches put up a fight?!"

His buddies guffawed and shouted.

But I saw what I'd been searching for—a door at the back of the bar. I ran for it, hoping the pirates were grounded to their bar and maybe they couldn't make it into the lighthouse. I hadn't seen the crew anywhere else on the island, and really, it was my only hope.

I shoved through the stinging, searing chill of the ghostly door, expecting to enter the lighthouse. Instead, I found myself in a dingy back room.

Pirates crowded a single long table, and at the head sat Frankie in a fancy chair. He'd traded his white Panama hat for a tricorn slung low to cover the bullet hole in his forehead that had killed him.

The gangster held up a hand, and the pirates quieted. "What I'm saying is if you want to recover the cursed gold at high tide, you need a diving bell with an air pump. The technology is really simple, see. What you do is...Verity! What are you doing here?"

"Frankie!" The pirates noticed me right about the time Pock Face burst through the door behind me. "Turn off my power, Frankie."

The pirates looked back at him.

Frankie hesitated. The corner of his mouth ticked up before he wiped his expression blank. "Do I know you?"

"Franklin Rudolph Winkelmann!" I shouted, scurrying around the table toward him, keeping an eye on Pock Face, who'd halted from surprise. "Turn off my power and do it *now*."

The gangster's jaw dropped, and he gave an uncomfortable chuckle. "Don't tell me what to do in front of my pirate mateys."

I worked my way around in order to put Frankie between me and old Pock Face. "They're making me duel to the death, and I don't want to kill anybody."

"Oh, you can't kill him," Frankie pointed out. "He's a much better swordsman than you."

"Thanks for the vote of confidence. Now turn off your power before anybody has to die." Including *me*.

Frankie looked down at the hand I couldn't feel anymore. "Verity, your sword is disappearing."

"Frankie! Just *help me*," I ground out, ready to stab him with the nub of whatever remained.

"Put down your sword," he ordered Pock Face. The pirate looked to the dreadlocked ghost next to Frankie, who gave a single, stiff nod.

Pock Face let out a low growl and sheathed his sword.

I breathed a sigh of relief while Frankie pulled a cigarette out from behind his ear. "Why do I always have to solve your problems?" he grumbled, gesturing with the unlit smoke. "Do you ever think of my needs? I have a pirate gang to run."

"He's brilliant," the one in charge said as Frankie lit up.

"Cutting edge," another agreed.

Frankie nodded and angled closer to me as he inhaled. "Don't ruin this for me."

Pock Face drew back his shoulders. "I was only fighting for Pearl. This girl failed to protect her. She lost Pearl and then lied about it. She's also after our gold."

"Witness," Bony Beads said behind him.

"Witness," Eye Patch agreed.

"Well, then"—old Dreadlocks leaned back in his chair—"by all means, kill her."

Chapter Twenty-One

I was cornered. The pirate ghosts had me trapped like a rat on a sinking ship.

"Frankie!" I cried. "Cut off your power now!"

It was the only way I had a chance of walking out alive.

My sword had disintegrated. I had no way to defend myself. Not like I could hold my own against a pirate crew used to fighting and brawling and dueling.

Pock Face closed in on me. I could see he enjoyed my fear.

Frankie took a sharp drag on his smoke. "You're putting me in a tough spot here, Verity."

He was in a tough spot? "They are going to kill me!" Pock Face leveled his sword at my throat. One slice would end me. I'd bleed out on the dirt floor of the bar.

Stumbling, I retreated as far as I could.

Three more pirates blocked my escape.

Frankie grimaced. "Okay, look. If you're going down into the caves where the lighthouse sits, you're going to want to see...everything, if you catch my drift. Otherwise, you're toast." He took a hard drag on his cigarette. "I mean, no other mortal has made it without...you know." He made a slashing motion at his throat.

"Yeah, well, I won't make it as far as the caves if you don't turn my power *off*!"

He shrugged. "I'll do you one better," he said, tipping the cigarette onto his lower lip and reaching into his suit pocket. "Now don't say I don't do you no favors."

He drew out a revolver and shot Pock Face through the heart.

The pirate crumpled to the ground, dead...again. For the moment.

"There," Frankie said, satisfied. He unhitched his cigarette and wet his lips. "You have about an hour to find Pearl before he wakes up and kills you."

"That's not fair," Bony Beads shouted. The rest of the pirates at the table leaped to their feet.

"Of course it's not fair." Frankie grabbed his mug of ale. "We're pirates, ain't we?"

There was a heartbeat of silence, followed by a roar of cheers. The rage on Bony Beads's face wobbled, then even he joined in.

Frankie raised his glass. "To trickery, deceit, and our dear Captain Bill...may he always shoot to kill." The pirates let out another whoop as Frankie turned to me. "Why are you still here? Go! I give you five minutes, ten tops, before they wise up and go after you."

My hands shook, and my brain had gone numb. "Thanks. I think."

I spotted a wooden door at the back. My way lay clear. The pirates behind me had moved to the table to toast. I gritted my teeth and yanked the door open and stepped straight into the lighthouse.

The round, stone space held absolutely no ghostly glow, which was such a relief. Just a musty smell and a fuming Duranja.

My fear morphed into anger. "Thanks for running your mouth and almost getting me killed." I was starting to sound like Frankie, but darn it, Robocop had it coming. "I was in real danger there," I said, flinging an arm behind me.

He didn't speak for a second. "You're still bleeding."

I swiped at my cheek, and my hand came away red.

"None of this can be real," Robocop insisted. "I saw it. Nothing touched you."

I held up my bloody hand. "Okay, then what's your explanation for this?"

He shook his head and let it drop.

A discarded parrot lay on the floor beside a ruined set of stairs leading up into the lighthouse. "Pearl!" I rushed to retrieve her. Her feathers were mussed. I smoothed them down. Next time the pirates asked for her, I'd have her well in hand.

"Take a look at this." He ushered me behind the stairs. "Melody's code worked. Only we weren't the first ones here." A trapdoor lay open on the stone floor of the lighthouse. "Dr. Fielding and I pried this open," he said, glancing at me. A set of spiral stone stairs led downward. "He said he'd wait, but you obviously took too long."

"Sorry, in the future I'll try to escape certain death a little quicker," I said, slipping Pearl into my bag.

Duranja closed and locked the lighthouse door behind us. "It's an old entrance to the network of caves underneath this part of the island. According to the professor, they used to pull rum and ale up through the caves to a bar that once stood on this very spot."

"Actually, it's right over there." I pointed toward where I'd almost gotten stabbed.

He raised a brow but didn't argue. For once.

I reached into my bag and dug past the urn for my Maglite. Duranja clicked his flashlight on and let me go first down the spiral stairs.

The stone gave way to rough island rock held in place with sandy mortar and pebbled with fossilized shells.

My light cut through the pitch black.

"Dr. Fielding?" I called. "He has a flashlight, doesn't he?"

"Yes." Duranja stiffened. "Maybe you'd better let me go first."

"It's fine. The steps are too narrow for you to squeeze past me." I hurried down another twist in the stairs, the air chilling as we went deeper.

We were almost there. We had to be. Then my light landed on the uneven stone floor of the chamber, and on the body of the professor sprawled at the bottom.

Chapter Twenty-Two

"Dr. Fielding!" I cried, leaping down the last few steps.

Blood, thick and dark, pooled around his head, spreading in a wide circle.

I stopped cold. "Did he trip?"

"Maybe." Duranja didn't sound convinced.

When his light joined mine, the whole scene looked worse. There was so much blood. And too many shadows.

"Go get the doctor," Duranja ordered, taking my shoulder and pointing me in the direction of the stairs.

"I think he's dead," I said, stumbling to catch the first step up. It must have just happened. I didn't even see a death spot yet.

"I think so, too, but we have to help if we can," he said, moving toward the body.

"Wait." I halted. "I can't go back through that pirate gauntlet." I was kind of shocked I'd survived the first time. "You go get the doctor."

"What? No. I can't leave you alone. It's obviously not safe here."

"I'll be fine," I assured him. "I know you don't believe this, but you'd be putting me in more danger by making me go through that pirate lair again." I swiped at the blood dribbling down my cheek. "If I get killed by a ghost on this trip, Melody will never forgive you."

"Damn it!" He raced up the stairs hard.

I turned back to the professor, not caring about the tightness in my throat or the shock of finding the professor crumpled and bloody.

With shaking fingers, I reached out to take his pulse.

I tried to remember the first-aid class I took in high school. They'd told us where to press.

Nothing.

I'd been fearing for my life while he'd been losing his.

All he'd wanted to do was preserve the artifacts and do a little good in the world.

Moments later, Duranja charged down the stairs to where the professor lay. Mindy and Rick followed on his heels.

"My God," Rick said under his breath while Mindy rushed to help.

The professor's entire head lay funny, and Mindy didn't have to examine him too closely before stepping back. "He's dead," she said solemnly.

"What happened?" Rick asked quietly.

Duranja had lit a series of lanterns hanging from the walls in the small, round alcove. It gave the room more light, while also making it feel like an interrogation cellar.

"Verity was having an...episode," he began.

"I was talking to ghosts," I corrected.

"So I stayed back with her and kept an eye on the lighthouse," he continued. "Dr. Fielding must have decided to go on ahead instead of waiting. Nobody else went in." He scanned our startled faces. "I think somebody was already inside when Dr. Fielding ventured down here. It looks like there's a killer on the island."

"He could have tripped," Rick said, giving the body a wide berth as he examined the situation.

"I don't think so," Duranja said, quick and efficient as he

patted down the professor's pockets. "His keystone is missing. He was carrying it, and now it's gone."

We'd feared someone would kill for the keystone, and now those fears had been realized.

"You touch the body?" Robocop glanced up at me.

"Of course not." It wasn't like me to disturb a potential crime scene. "Well, I did check for a pulse, but..."

I looked again and saw no disturbance in the blood other than where Mindy had stood. Duranja had somehow avoided leaving a trace.

Robocop shone his light on a small alcove cut in the rock. Just beyond it, at the entrance to an open chamber, stood the third capstan.

"The professor's keystone has been inserted," he said dully. "The capstan has been turned."

Mindy wrinkled her nose. "Somebody did all this for the third coin?"

"Not exactly," Duranja said as the truth settled over me.

"It doesn't make sense," Rick said, backing off from the body. "Why kill over a game?"

"Your team can't win anymore," Mindy said to me. "We can't win. The twins are serious competitors, but they're not going to murder an academic over a weekend treasure hunt."

Mindy had it right. It wasn't about the game. Our killer was after something much bigger. This was about turning all four capstans to find the pirate treasure.

"Bill had all four keystones all along," I said. But he'd still needed us to play the game. "He must not know where the fourth capstan is."

"Go get help," Duranja said to Rick. "Don't talk to Bill. Don't talk to anybody. Get to a landline in the hotel and call the police. Then get Ellis out here somehow and have him guard the body until they arrive."

Rick nodded and headed for the stairs.

"You too," Duranja added to Mindy. "Then lock yourselves in your room and remain there."

Mindy hesitated. "And you'll stay here in the meantime?"

"Of course," Duranja said, watching Rick go.

When the lighthouse door closed behind them, Duranja looked at the dead professor, then at me. "I'm done playing games." He reached inside his jacket and handed me the final keystone wrapped in cloth. "I'm going after a killer."

"Not without me," I told him, securing the keystone in my bag. I didn't know what was in those caves, but according to Frankie, I needed to be able to see the ghostly side if we hoped to make it out alive.

"Verity—" He held up a hand.

"I'm not going to explain." He wouldn't believe me anyway. "But I'm coming."

"If there's someone in the caves who would kill for that keystone, you'll be bringing it straight to them."

"That's true," I agreed. But I wasn't about to hand it to anyone besides Melody or Ellis, and they weren't around to take it. "But if they need it, it might come in handy for us as well," I said, patting the stone in my bag.

Duranja swore under his breath. "I'm not going to get rid of you, am I?"

"I thought that was my line," I told him.

He closed his eyes briefly. "Fine." He glanced into the darkened alcove that led to the caves. "Stick close. Follow my orders. And Verity," he added as if it pained him, "no more trouble with ghosts."

Bless his heart.

We'd have to agree to disagree.

Chapter Twenty-Three

We eased past the capstan. Dr. Fielding's killer had left the professor's cloudy pink keystone inserted in the slot.

"Stay with me," Duranja ordered, shining his light into the gloom beyond.

I nodded. We'd be better off investigating as a team, even if that meant putting aside our differences. For now.

Gravel crunched under our feet, all but announcing our arrival. This part of the basement appeared less finished until we stepped onto a stone floor once more.

My light caught on a long wooden shelf stretching back into the darkness. Then another. And another. "What is this place?"

"Looks like some kind of storage area." Duranja's beam lit upon a white stone wall. A wooden sign propped up against it read:

Dig for pirate gold!
Two dollars per shovel per day
Keep what you dig!

"I wonder how much gold they found," I murmured, my light catching advertisements for penny candy, "real" souvenir pirate chests, and séances that called upon dead pirates to give up their loot.

"Probably as much as we have," Duranja mused.

The shelves held dusty old models of wooden frigates, rusting ship bells, and moldering knots of rope.

Then, wedged against the edge of the shelving a few aisles down, we saw a capstan. Only this one was different from the others.

Duranja swore as we rushed to see.

For one thing, it stood too close to the shelves to turn. For another, instead of centuries-old stone and mortar, this capstan appeared to be made of chicken wire and plaster. And quite shoddily at that.

"No way that's real," I said, shining my flashlight in an arc around the room to make sure nobody took advantage of our distraction.

"It proves our theory about Bill," Duranja said. "He never found the fourth capstan."

One swift kick from Duranja sent the upper half of it toppling over. A silver coin clattered out and rolled across the floor.

But Dr. Fielding's killer was no longer playing games, and neither were we.

"Listen," Duranja whispered, and I could almost hear a faint shuffle in the dark. He glanced around us as if he could see what lay beyond our lights.

"Where?" I mouthed.

He shook his head. He didn't know, either.

This cellar appeared to be a dead end. The killer hadn't come back up the lighthouse stairs, so they had to be trapped. With us.

Then I caught a glow toward the back of the room.

My breath hitched. It could be a spirit—or a haunted object.

"Verity," Duranja warned, his voice low as I ventured deeper into the darkness without him. "What did you hear? I didn't hear anything."

"It's not what I hear, it's what I see."

"This had better not be a ghost. I said no ghosts."

"No offense, but it isn't really your choice. Or mine."

Ghosts and the objects they controlled tended to glow. Then again, so did individuals covering up light sources. So it could be a spirit, or it could be our killer.

I halted, glad for once to feel the weight of Duranja's presence beside me.

How much of a pickle were we in when I was relieved to have Duranja along for a ghost hunt?

We'd have to be extra careful with this one. If it was our killer, well, Duranja and I would take the person down. If it was a ghost, then maybe I could talk to it and see if it could tell us what had happened to the professor.

Or at the very least, what living souls had passed this way.

My flashlight danced over the uneven stone floor, the shelves stacked with wooden boxes to my right and left, and then onto a wooden shelf along the back wall. The shelving appeared real, but the plates, cups, and serving ware upon it glowed a vibrant, ghostly green.

I stopped short.

"It's ghostly serving ware," I whispered, not caring if he believed me.

I scanned for the spirit who haunted this room.

"It's Depression glass," Duranja countered, training his light over purple, green, amber, and pink glass items lining the shelf. "The glow is from the uranium in them."

"Really?" I asked, more relieved than anything. I didn't want to meet a ghost who made things glow in multiple fancy colors.

"Didn't your grandma have any?" he asked incredulously. "Mine still has a bunch. Look." He cast his light up to a faint, glowing purple bulb. "Somebody turned on a black light bulb behind the shelves."

"It could have been left on from...whenever someone else was down here," I suggested, looking at all possibilities.

"More likely the killer came this way," Duranja offered, saying what I was really thinking. "Probably searching for any light they could find. Or a way out." He scanned his beam over the solid wall at the back.

But it didn't track. "If it's Bill, he'd know those things."

Duranja nodded grimly. "If they're still here, let's not let them know where we are." He killed his light.

I stiffened and cut my light as well. "I didn't hear anyone leave." And the gravel just past the real capstan would have made noise.

"Exactly," he murmured.

We were hunting a killer in an enclosed space where there was a lot of room to hide.

If they hadn't attempted to flee, they wanted something in this room. Or they wanted something we had.

"Stick close. I'm going to get the jump on them," Duranja said against my ear.

That sounded like a terrible idea. But I wasn't about to wander away in the dark. I followed the faint hiss of his breath as he led me up an aisle we hadn't tried yet.

My own breath came hard but as silent as I could make it as we crept through the darkened storage area.

Duranja stepped over the remains of the ruined plaster capstan with eerie precision, and we veered left to search the next aisle.

We kept alert for the slightest sigh or shuffle that would give away the killer. Every nerve tingled.

When I wasn't sure I could take it a second longer, we reached the final aisle where the killer might be, the last place to hide.

And then I saw...it.

A faint silver glow emanated from the stone near the far right corner. It formed the outline of a door.

I tugged on Duranja's shirt and pointed.

He looked, then batted me away when I tried again. He turned to go the other way.

Because he can't see.

I drew closer to the glow of the door.

He tapped my side lightly to direct me with him.

This time, I swatted him away.

The killer could be behind the door. I knew that. Or maybe, like Duranja, they hadn't seen it at all. Either way, I had to know what it was.

An old barrel of ale stood in the way. "We need to get behind this," I whispered. "Trust me."

"You're nuts," he muttered. When I didn't budge, he shoved his flashlight into my hands and rolled the barrel out from the wall, both of us cringing as it creaked over the floor.

"Look." Duranja took his light back and flicked it on. He watered down the beam with his shirt and quickly scanned the white stone wall. "Nothing."

"Not nothing." My heart sped up.

A lever stuck out from the wall, glowing gray. I wasn't sure if it was from the light beyond the wall, or if the pedal itself was not of this world. "Now do you see?" I asked, shining my light on it.

"How in the world?" Duranja uttered. It was the closest I'd ever seen to him speechless.

Either way, I'd take it.

"I told you. I'm tuned in," I said, stepping down on the cold, metal lever.

A thundering creak echoed throughout the chamber as the hidden door opened inward.

"They'll know where we are now," Duranja said, flipping his light back on and running it behind us.

"It's the pirate cave," I said on an exhale. "I think we're about to find the fourth capstan."

A long chamber ran straight from the door we'd opened and tilted down into the darkness.

"I'll go first," I insisted.

"That's my line," Duranja said, guarding our rear.

I shone my light inside. Drilled into the ceiling with rusted chains hung a rotting wooden sign. There wasn't much left of the earthly version, but the ghostly one glowed clear and bright, complete with a crude skull and crossbones etched at the top.

Go back!
No soul can escape the depths of the caves within

"Look," I said, stepping inside. A heavy iron gate on chains had recently been dragged away from the entrance to the caves, leaving a trail of rust in its wake.

Duranja let out a low whistle.

"I think this is what we might have been moving as we turned those capstans," I said low, under my breath.

"Not us turning," Duranja muttered, running his fingers along a pully mechanism near the top. "We never got to use a capstan. But if you're right, there'll be three more gates like this one."

"And a spot for our final keystone," I murmured. I cast my light down the dark cave passageway.

Duranja glanced behind us. "Yeah, well, forget the treasure. At this point, my job is to find a killer."

"It's all tied up together." I ventured farther in. "Think about it. The keystones are real. The capstans—save for the plaster one —they're real. Someone killed the professor to get whatever is at the end of this hunt."

"Get back here," he hissed as I reached a break in the passage. A corridor split off to the left. I ducked inside to see how far it went.

"Verity!" Duranja's harsh whisper echoed down the chamber.

A set of ghostly numbers glowed gray, painted on the rock.

1722

"Look! It's the same year I saw on the anchor of the *Fortune's Revenge*." It had to mean...something.

"Verity," Duranja hissed, his footsteps scraping on the floor of the passage, "I said I'd stick with you, and I will, but not down some crazy side passage and—hey, that's the year the *Fortune's Revenge* set sail."

"You can see it?"

"It's painted on the rock."

"Still think I'm crazy?" I asked, glad to note the numerals existed in the real world as well. It was sometimes hard to tell with the ghostly glow on top.

Laughter echoed from deep inside the cave.

"Did you hear that?" I asked softly.

Duranja paused a beat. "Hear what?"

A shout echoed from the same place.

"That."

It came from the direction of the main passage. "This way." I scrambled past Duranja, eager to hear more.

It could be our fugitive from justice, but I doubted it. From the noise the hidden door had made, we'd have heard them enter. Besides, we never would have found this place without the ghostly glow from the pirate warning. I was pretty sure nobody else had that going for them.

"Verity—"

"Shh...Let me listen." I was rewarded with the murmur of voices. I could have sworn I heard the word "Bill."

"Come on," I said, leading Duranja down the main passage.

"What? No," he hissed, keeping pace behind me. "I said we need to go out. You're going in. Hold up!"

The cave split again, and I jagged right.

"You're going to get us lost." He scrambled to keep up. "The killer is probably behind us. We have to go back."

I was finding answers. "Look." I pointed to a rusted iron gate up ahead, open on its hinges.

He barked out a laugh before closing his mouth, horrified at the sound he'd just made. "I don't believe it."

"I'm telling you, it's all connected." The treasure hunt for the medallion, the use of the real artifacts, the accidents, the murder, it all led to something.

Duranja frowned, but he didn't argue. "I don't know how Ellis puts up with this."

"You wouldn't," I said because there was no man better than Ellis Wydell.

"The problem with you is that you don't see trouble coming until—" The echo of metal gears grinding drowned him out.

"The door!" He scrambled back the way we'd come.

Ohmygosh. I dashed after him down the corridor, up the chamber, flying for the exit as we watched the stone door slam closed.

"No!" Duranja beat on it, searching for a handle or a lever.

There had to be a way to get it open. I scoured it with my light.

Duranja grappled with the edges. "The seal is tight."

"There's no lever on this side," I warned. No handle. No foot pedal.

No way out.

"Oh, my heavens." I stepped back, heaving.

Duranja stood eerily still. "Nobody knows we're here."

Nobody but the killer.

Chapter Twenty-Four

Okay. *Think.* "There's still a great deal of cavern we haven't explored yet," I said. "Maybe we'll find a back door." Plus, Frankie had said there was something I needed to see.

"There'd better be a way out, or we're in real trouble," Duranja uttered.

My flashlight beam danced over the walls of the narrow passage, up to the rotting pirate sign warning of death to all who dared enter.

Fat lot of good that did us now.

First things first. "How much air do you think we have?" I asked, my breath going shallow.

Duranja ran a hand over the back of his neck. "I'm not worried about air. We have plenty of air. But do you realize nobody is going to find us in here?"

I gripped my flashlight tighter. "They might."

I couldn't imagine how frantic Ellis would be if I went missing. Melody, too. "Melody and Ellis at least knew where we were going. Eventually, they'll find us."

I just hoped they didn't ask the wrong person too many questions, or they could be in danger too.

He dropped his hand. "I never would have found this place without you, and now you're stuck in here with me."

It was the first time Duranja gave me credit for any aspect of my ghost hunting, and now I didn't want it.

"Alec, the killer is going to have to come back. I mean, there's something big down here." It had been hidden for centuries, and now that we'd discovered the way in, they wouldn't just abandon the place.

He gritted his jaw. "They can wait a month. Or a year. Or however long it takes for us to die of dehydration or starvation."

We had to think positively. "You forget, we have Frankie," I said, working it out in my head. "He can...well, he can't tell anyone where we are. But he's friendly with the pirates, and they might know a way out." I didn't care if it made sense to Duranja or not. He'd see soon enough. "Frankie!" I called. "Frankie." I dug past the cloth-wrapped keystone in my bag to the urn at the bottom. "Come on, Frankie," I coaxed, giving it a little rub.

Duranja slapped a hand over his eyes. "I said no ghosts."

I drew the urn out of my bag. "I don't know why he's not answering."

"I admit you might have some kind of intuition, and that's probably how you found this place," Robocop said flatly, planting his back against the door. "And maybe you cut your cheek with the power of thought the way some people can make themselves sick by thinking about it. I don't know. But what I do know is that every time you've called that name, you've come up short."

"My gangster *is* notoriously unreliable," I admitted.

"Like, maybe you should go home and read tarot cards instead of talking to ghosts," Duranja suggested.

"I'll keep that in mind," I said absently, running my fingers over the dented brass urn, over the green stones glued to the rim. "Come on, Frankie." He had to know this was urgent. He'd just shot a fellow outlaw for me.

"He's probably busy managing the pirate horde," I said, refusing to give up as I tucked the urn back into my bag. I just hoped the poor gangster hadn't gotten shot or stabbed for the way he'd defended me in the bar. Not only would it knock him out for a while, but it would also most definitely put a kink in his budding pirate empire.

I grabbed my light and trailed it over the white rock wall stretching out a few feet on both sides of the door. I just wished Frankie could tell Ellis or Melody or any live person that we were in here.

As long as I was wishing for that, I might as well wish for an open door. And a remorseful killer who would turn themselves in.

Failing that, we'd have to keep trying. "Think back," I said, training my light down the passageway behind us. "There was a cave map in Captain Bill's diary."

"That someone stole."

"Okay, but it also means he made it through the caves and back out."

"He was also probably smart enough to leave the door open."

I'd about had enough of this negative Nelly. Nevertheless, I kept my voice sweet. "As I said, maybe there's a different way out." It was certainly worth investigating. "Let's see where the passage leads."

Duranja pushed himself off the wall. "We could get lost and never found again."

I couldn't tell if he was being sarcastic or not. "So your solution is to stand here and die of dehydration with your back planted against a locked door that nobody we love will ever find or open."

He frowned. "Survival 101. Always stay put when you're lost."

"That only works when someone is coming to find you."

His lips twisted in satisfaction. "So you admit—"

"Shh..." I tossed a hand up. "The voices are back."

"Oh, good."

They echoed up from the cave, but I couldn't make out words.

"Something's happening down there. I need to check it out." It beat debating with mister doom and gloom. "I wasn't kidding about the ghosts possibly knowing of another way out."

Duranja looked at me like I'd told him I wanted to dance naked and consult a crystal ball. "You let a killer escape. You trapped us in a hole. And now you say you hear voices and want to go looking for ghosts?"

Because standing around, waiting for a rescue team that didn't exist, was a better solution.

"The only way out is through," I prompted, and when he didn't move, I went ahead and left without him.

"Verity," he called after me.

"The ghosts can't even hurt *you*," I called over my shoulder. I was done dealing with him. I'd been trapped in dark holes before, and I knew hanging around and waiting to die was no way out of them. Robocop might be good at his job, but I was also very good at mine.

My flashlight cut through the pitch black ahead. I avoided the passage we'd already taken to the left, focusing on the murmur of noise coming from deep underground.

Frankie had said I'd need his ghostly powers to get out of the caves. I was ready to test that.

I cut right into the tunnel we'd explored earlier and passed the open gate.

So far, so good.

I ventured deeper, ducking under a low ceiling.

A tinny laugh drifted up from farther down the passage. *Yes.* I was going the right way.

"Verity." Duranja's loud whisper drowned out the sound.

"Shhh," I urged as Robocop invaded my tunnel. His light blinded me, and his boots crunched up a storm. He needed to simmer down, or I wasn't going to know which way to go.

He took up the entire passage behind me, breathing hard. "Melody would kill me if I left you in a cave."

And here I thought I was the one who'd left him. I pushed forward, seeing spots from the light he'd aimed at my head. I shook off the cobwebs and listened for the voice.

Bill.

The voice echoed low and deep.

It came from an offshoot to my right. I followed it into a small cavern. Stalactites dripped from the ceiling. Water trickled over the rocks jutting out from the walls. "It's beautiful," I whispered.

"It's a landmark," Duranja observed. "And a cautionary tale." He shone his light down to the cave floor across from the water running down the rock, to where a skeleton lay half-crumbled against the wall.

"It's not a pirate." It wore the remnants of tan pants, suspenders, and a raggedy shirt tied around his head.

"Poor soul," Duranja said low under his breath.

"I know, right?" He'd most likely died scared and alone. I hoped he'd moved on to a better place.

Duranja withdrew his light from the grisly scene, and so did I.

"Let's keep moving," I said, pressing on.

"I know you don't know where you're going," he said matter-of-factly. But I heard him crunching behind me.

We walked for several silent minutes.

My light danced off the cave walls. "I know you want to marry my sister."

I heard him stumble. "I figured she'd tell you," he said, recovering. "I hoped it would make you nicer to me," he added, almost as an afterthought.

"Please." I ducked under a low section in the passage. "I'm nice to everyone."

"You never liked me. You don't even try to hide it," he said, grunting as he tried to make himself smaller. "You like skunks and bunnies and squirrely old ladies, but you don't like me."

"Why should I like you? You think I'm crazy, and you treat me accordingly," I said, glad when the passage opened up again.

"Well, you have to admit, you don't always look like you know what you're doing."

That was because a lot of the time, I didn't. There was something to be said for winging it. Especially in my line of work.

Goodness, I was starting to sound like Frankie.

"What are you thinking?" he asked as we took a hard corner.

I leaned my back against the wall and looked at him. "I'm thinking we got off on the wrong foot."

"And stayed there," he agreed. The watery light cast shadows over his face.

"You're not completely terrible," I admitted. "You have good morals, and you love my sister."

"Thanks, I think?" He sort of chuckled. "I mean, you're not so bad yourself. You try hard and care about people." He shrugged a shoulder. "And you might have some weird connection to the deceased that I don't understand."

"Might?" I asked, tempted to turn my flashlight into an interrogation light.

He held up a hand in mock self-defense. "I'm trying, I really am."

Was he? "Does this mean you'll give me the benefit of the doubt?"

"I'll try," he pledged.

Well, how do you like that?

I directed my beam forward and began walking again.

But I should have known it wasn't over. Not with Duranja. "Does this mean I won't keep catching you in places you don't belong?"

Talk about a tall order. "I'll try," I promised as we came upon a small cavern. "Does this mean you won't automatically accuse me of murder every time I end up around a dead person?"

"There are protocols," he said as if I were the unreasonable one. "And how many more dead bodies do you intend to find?"

Bill...

The voice echoed clearly, closer this time.

I counted four different passageways off this main room. "That's the one." I pointed to a small hole directly above a mound of rock. It appeared large enough for one person to fit through it at a time.

"You're going to get us lost," Duranja warned.

"Or found." I avoided stalactites as I scrambled up onto the mound of rock. "I know it makes no sense. I know it goes against everything you think and feel, but I'm serious." I sat and dangled my feet down into the opening. "You're going to have to trust me," I said over my shoulder. At his frown, I added, "When we left, the last thing Ellis said to me was to trust you. Please. Trust me." I jumped down into the next passageway. A narrower one this time. It offered two choices, right or left.

Duranja's light bounced through the opening I'd just vacated.

"It's difficult to trust someone so...unconventional," he insisted, hoisting his legs through the opening.

"That's the nicest word you could come up with?" I asked, waiting for him on the other side.

"I mean, do you realize what it all sounds like?" he asked, jumping down. He landed hard next to me. "Do you have any clue what it's like to deal with you?"

"All I know is that if you want a future with Melody at all, we have to stop debating every little thing and start giving each other the benefit of the doubt." Or we'd all be miserable.

He ran a hand down the side of his face. "Problem is, I don't know where to begin."

Then I would. "I know you have my back because you promised Melody and Ellis. Also, you are a man of your word, and my sister loves you. Both of them trust me and my ghost-hunting skills. Can you please let that be enough to trust me for now?"

"I followed you this far, didn't I?" he asked as if he couldn't quite believe it himself.

"That you did," I admitted.

"And for the record, I'll always do my best to keep you out of trouble because it's the right thing to do," he said pragmatically.

That was debatable. "Okay, well, give me a bit, and I'll get us out of these caves."

For once, he didn't argue.

Bill.

"This way," I told him.

I led us down the passageway to the right, ducked under the low ceiling, and hung another right toward the cavern. Duranja stuck close through every turn.

Bill.

I hurried down the corridor. My light bounced off a steady stream of water that ran from a cupped rock into a small pool. My stomach sank. We'd seen this place before.

"We're going in circles," Duranja groaned.

I halted as a ghost with a lantern appeared down the corridor. "Where am I?" she wailed. "Where am I?" She glowed gray, wearing a simple collared day dress and holding a lantern. "Where am I?" She passed into the cavern wall and disappeared before I could recover from my shock to speak.

"We may be a little turned around," I admitted, "but we're following a voice that will lead us to Captain Bill, or at least someone who knows about him."

"You mean dead Bill," he said flatly.

"The ghost," I agreed.

Why else would they be calling his name?

Bill.

Duranja ran a few fingers along the bridge of his nose but didn't argue.

"This way," I said, choosing the left of three passageways.

"We chose that one before," Duranja warned.

"Not at this intersection," I corrected.

"Yes, at this intersection," he said behind me.

I had a sinking feeling he might be right.

~

An hour later, my light bounced off a steady stream of water that ran from a cupped rock into a small pool. The skeleton in the tan pants lay across from it. Tears burned the backs of my eyes.

"This way looked different," Duranja protested.

The darkness around us made the passages feel endless, right up until a rock or a wall loomed up out of nowhere. I kept a hand on the cold wall to my left, if only to try to orient myself.

It wasn't helping.

I'd called for Frankie.

He wasn't responding.

I'd let Duranja lead the way for the last several twists and turns because I wasn't getting any closer to the ghosts, and he'd insisted we try his way. A better approach.

To the same place.

I touched a toe to the muddy trickle. "At least we have water." We might be down here for a while.

"Don't you dare drink that," Duranja said like a scandalized schoolmarm. "For all we know, that's what killed him." He gestured to the skeleton.

I planted my back against the rock wall next to the poor man's waterfall and closed my eyes, trying to think of what to do.

The air in the chamber chilled my damp skin. The frantic search had begun to feel awful, but standing still felt worse.

"You'd better not die and leave my urn down here," Frankie warned.

My eyes shot open. There he stood, a stalactite jutting through his head, in all his gangster glory. Well, save for the tricorn hat. "How did you find me?" I gasped.

"Don't get delirious on me now, kid," Duranja answered half-heartedly, giving in to his exhaustion as he leaned against the wall.

Meanwhile, Frankie wrinkled his nose, offended by my isolated desperation. "I know where my urn is at all times."

"We're trapped down here with the person who killed the

professor," I said. "I thought I could follow the voices to Bill, but I don't hear them anymore."

"You're tracking Bill?" The gangster blocked my way. "You think he's just going to let you take his stuff?"

"I don't want treasure anymore," I confessed. "I just want to get out of here."

"He's in some kind of honeymoon lair," Frankie said, dragging a hand along the back of his neck. "Nobody's allowed in, not the crew, nobody. Captain Bill's orders. He needs time with his new bride."

"His bride is on the bridge," I insisted.

"Maybe she needed some air." Frankie waved away my concern. "There's no way I'm letting you barge in there, screw up any chance of me getting my hands on some wedding loot, and give the captain reason to kick me out of the gang."

He was being ridiculous. "You're not in this gang, and it's not even a gang. It's a crew. A ship's crew. Do you even know how to sail? And besides, you live in a shed in my backyard, not on a haunted pirate island."

"When did you get so mean?" The ghost balked. "I'd make a great pirate. Time at sea changes a man," he said, lowering his hat to cover the bullet hole in his forehead.

The ferry ride over here had taken twenty minutes, tops.

"Show me the way out, and then we can decide what to do," I said, launching myself off the wall.

"You don't think I'm trying?" Duranja tossed his hands up.

Frankie hedged. "What makes you think I know how to get back out?"

"Frankie!" He'd better be joking.

He glanced at the walls, uneasy, as if just realizing our predicament. "I was following my urn, and now that I found my urn—"

"You didn't mark a trail or anything?" I demanded.

"Did you?" he shot back. He whipped off his tricorn hat and wiped the sweat from his forehead before planting it back down over the bullet hole between his eyes. "Captain Bill is the only one who knows the way through. I mean, he made a rudimentary map, but it doesn't have any of these winding passages on it."

"Then we have to find Bill," I insisted.

The gangster dug a finger under his collar. "His honeymoon suite is hidden for a reason."

Bill. Once more, the voice echoed from the passage ahead.

"You hear that?" I challenged the gangster. "I've been following that voice for hours, and I'm not getting anywhere. This is an emergency."

"Oh boy," the gangster said, beginning to panic. "If we fail, I'll have to haunt these caves forever. With you two."

This was no time for him to lose his cool. "Frankie, you need to be a leader." Not the getaway driver or the conman or the hired gun like he'd always been. "You've scoped out the territory. Now go haunt the bar; get the gang behind you. Tell them I have Pearl and make them help us get out of here."

He nodded a few too many times. "I can haunt a bar."

"Yes, you can." He'd haunted many bars. More than that, he was a ghost, and he could go anywhere on this island as long as he fixed the place in his mind. "Go, Frankie."

And with that, he disappeared.

"He can do it," I murmured to myself.

He had to.

If Frankie had taken command of his life when he was alive, he never would have gotten shot in the first place. Well, at least not when he did.

I had to take charge as well.

Duranja leaned against the wall a few feet away, staring at nothing. He wasn't even making fun of me anymore.

"We can't keep doing this," I told him. We were wearing ourselves out and going nowhere.

"I can keep at it until I drop," he insisted. "I just need a minute to think of what to do next."

I ran a hand along the cold, wet rock wall, to the place where two passages met and broke off into a half-dozen more. I swore we'd tried them all.

"Maybe we need to mark them better," Duranja said, coming up behind me.

We'd tried stacking rock piles, but it was hard to tell which were ours. Little stacks littered the passageways, markers left by other doomed souls.

Maybe we just had to try harder.

Or...my fingers touched a jagged groove on the top of a flat piece of rock jutting out from the wall. As I examined it closer, I could see the faint outline of a perfect circle around it.

"Look at this," I said, digging a fingernail around the circle.

Duranja's beam illuminated the marks. "It looks like a set of claw marks."

"Up on the wall?" I asked. "It's not from a bat." The prints were way too big. "More like a—"

"Bird," Duranja finished. "But they're too clean to be real."

I gasped and reached for my bag.

"What?" he demanded.

"Captain Bill's cave," I said, digging past Frankie's urn. "Captain Bill's bird."

"That's not what I meant," he countered, but he didn't argue when I pulled Pearl from my sack. She was posed in a curious manner, her head slightly crooked compared to her feet. And wouldn't you know it, her little wooden feet lined up pretty well with those claw marks.

"Holy smokes." Duranja exhaled when Pearl's wooden parrot feet fit perfectly. "What the hell does it mean?"

Righty tighty, lefty loosey.

I held Pearl in place and gently twisted to the left. Her little metal-reinforced feet dug in as the stone disk turned.

"Look," I said, "she's pointing to the opening we first came through."

"That does us no good. That's how we got in here."

And so I tried the right.

The circle moved, and Pearl's slightly crooked head looked straight toward a narrow gap half hidden behind a pillar of rock.

"That must be the way," I said past the lump in my throat as I met Duranja's wide-eyed stare. For once, he didn't have anything smart to say.

His jaw tightened as he blew out a breath. "I can't believe it. But you might be right."

Chapter Twenty-Five

"Good job, Pearl!" I gave her a little hug and a stroke on the head.

If she were alive, I'd give her a treat.

Duranja opened his mouth and then closed it. "The bird's dead. She can't hear you."

I clipped her to my shoulder. "She's not dead. She's pining for the fjords," I quipped. The prospect of finding a way out made it easier to joke.

Duranja lost it.

My word. I'd never seen the man laugh before. I felt myself joining in.

Duranja fought to keep a straight face. "She's bleeding demised. She has ceased to be. She's an ex-parrot." We doubled over again laughing, relieved and happy, and apparently, we'd finally found something we had in common.

"*You* like Monty Python?" I mean, truly. I couldn't believe Robocop had a sense of humor.

He wiped a tear out of his eye. Oh, my goodness. Had he ever laughed so hard he cried? Add that one to the list.

"Hey," he said, "if Melody ever forces us into a double-date movie night, at least we know what we're watching."

"You got it," I told him.

He grinned back at me. "Now let's go see where this bird wants us to go," he said, leading the way down the corridor where Pearl had pointed. "She's not haunting you, is she?" he asked over his shoulder.

"Unfortunately not," I said. How cool would that be?

We walked a little farther.

"Animals don't have to stick around as ghosts unless they want to," I said, "and if they do, they're never bound to any one place or person."

"They're free to live as they wish?" Duranja mused as if considering the possibility. "I like that."

So did I.

We reached another fork in the path. "There," he said, pointing to a patch of rock between the two passageways, where another print had been etched in the stone. He stepped back to let me and Pearl check it out.

It was crudely carved, yet a perfect fit.

Beautiful.

"If these are everywhere, we're not lost anymore." I tested it again. "Look at this. If you twist her to the left, she points the way out," which was the way we'd just come. "If you twist her to the right, she points the way in."

"How did you know to keep the bird?" Duranja marveled.

"The ghosts told me," I said simply.

This time, he didn't argue.

My excitement built as I settled Pearl's feet into the rock. One gentle twist and she pointed the way.

"Have you stopped to think where she's leading us?" Duranja asked, aiming his light down the low-ceilinged, narrower passage.

That was the million-dollar question because we definitely wouldn't have picked this tunnel on our own.

Oh, Bill...

Lookie here.

"I don't know where we're headed," I admitted, "but the

voices are getting louder." I gave Pearl a quick kiss on the head. "Good bird." Sweet bird.

"She's still dead," Duranja teased, bending over to explore the new passageway.

"But leading the way," I said, on his heels.

"Yes, but..." He stopped, and suddenly his stance loosened. "I have to say something to you," he tossed over his shoulder. "I think, after what you've shown me, there might be something to all of this. Don't—" He held up a hand before I could respond. "Don't say anything. I'm not ready to talk about any of this." He shook his head and eased past a jutting rock. "I don't understand it, but please keep doing it."

"Yay," I said to Pearl, unable to resist giving her little wooden foot a high five.

The voices grew louder on the next turn and the one after that. And that was when I realized we might have stepped into more trouble than we'd left behind.

Have a spot of ale? A gravelly voice echoed through the dark up ahead.

A gruff laugh. *Bet Bill wants one.*

Can you hear us, Bill? another taunted. *Or are you dead to the world?*

I tugged on the back of Duranja's shirt. "I don't like what I'm hearing from up ahead. We have to prepare for the possibility that Captain Bill won't be able to help us. I think he's been captured." At his narrowed eyes, I added, "Someone's taunting him." Bill wasn't responding at all, at least so far as I could hear. Maybe he couldn't.

Duranja gave a curt nod, his light dancing over the tight walls.

The gang above had no clue. If Frankie managed to get them down here, they'd be in for a shock.

Robocop halted as the corridor began to open up. "Back against the wall," he ordered. "Cut your light."

I did.

Spots clouded my vision as my eyes adjusted to the sudden, all-consuming darkness. I felt like I'd been swallowed up whole.

"What's happening?" I rasped.

I felt his shoulder touch mine as he leaned in close to whisper barely above a breath. "I heard something. Up ahead."

"Bat?" I mouthed as quietly as I could. Although come to think of it, we hadn't encountered any critters save for Pearl. And we'd brought her in with us.

"Not a bat."

I braced myself against the wall, my heart doing a brisk pitter-patter. I'd prepared for the possibility of angry ghost pirates this far back in the caves, but not for the living.

We'd discovered the secret door. We'd entered alone. Did someone else find another way in?

But we'd left the door open behind us for a while, and we'd spent a good amount of time wandering in the caverns. Someone could easily have entered behind us and snuck ahead while we were lost.

Duranja scooted forward. I did the same. Inch by inch.

After what seemed like an eternity, he stopped. "Give it a sec."

What did he mean? I couldn't see a thing.

We sat in the dark, listening.

You want your precious bird? a salty voice taunted.

I unclipped Pearl from my shoulder and held her tight.

Footsteps gritted against the floor of the cave. Duranja stiffened next to me. The sounds must be coming from our world. At times, I found it hard to tell.

Then came the faint rip of Velcro and the soft tinkle of metal as Duranja retrieved a pair of handcuffs from his cargo pants and secured them behind his belt.

A watery flashlight beam found us, and we shrank back. Yet some of the light remained, filtering dimly through a narrow break in the rock ahead.

Duranja and I hovered at the edge of an underground cavern, waiting for them to move on.

When they did, we crept inside, moving as slowly and silently as we could.

"They're in the next room," Duranja mouthed against my ear.

I wanted to jump them and to curl up into a ball, all at the same time. "Any idea who?"

"No."

"They must have the cave map."

"They might be our killer."

The cave was pitch black and hard to navigate in the dark, but turning on our flashlights would give away our position immediately. Duranja gripped my arm, and I wrapped it around his. I stuffed my flashlight in my belt and held my free hand out in front of me, wincing at every slight crunch our feet made on the floor of the cave.

A reflected beam of light traced past a hand-sized slit in a rock that looked like a candle melting from the ceiling.

We went that way until we reached it, stuffing our bodies against the rippled pillars.

A figure moved past us down the corridor. Duranja touched my arm to still me as the light slowly faded.

My mouth had gone dry. I counted to at least ten before Duranja's light flicked on under his shirt. I couldn't see the edges of the cavern from where we stood.

Duranja tugged at my sleeve and pointed to a break in the rock about a yard from where we stood. I hurried that way and, with his light behind me, spotted scratch marks in the rock at about shoulder height, the same as before.

I wedged Pearl's feet inside and turned. She pointed us to the right, where the light had disappeared down the corridor.

Duranja nodded, and I secured Pearl in my bag. I needed her close if things got dicey.

He kept his light shielded, barely visible as we stepped into the corridor. This one soared tall enough that the inky dark swallowed our feeble light in every direction save for a few feet in front of us.

A muddy string lay on the cave floor at our feet. I tugged at Duranja's sleeve and pointed. Our visitor had come into the cave prepared. The lead string ran behind us into the darkness, and up ahead, to where our visitor had retreated.

Duranja drew his gun. "Stay here," he mouthed against my ear. "Trust me."

I nodded, not that he could see it.

He was going to use the lead string to track down our potential killer.

Only that left me here alone. Not quite lost. Not quite found.

He cut his light and faded into the darkness, following the string. The occasional click of his footsteps evaporated as he moved down the passage.

For the first time in my life, I worried about him.

There was no reason for anyone but the murderer to be down here. I had no doubt that the person ahead of us had followed us from the storage room into the caves. They'd gotten in front of us, so they'd probably know which way to go, most likely because they had the map from the diary. And they'd proven that they would kill in order to possess whatever treasure lay buried in these caves.

A light flicked on in the passageway where Duranja had disappeared.

He'd never betray his location, which meant someone else must have found him first.

Sweet heaven. I felt my way backward. I frantically tried to remember how many steps we'd taken, how far we'd come before reaching this exposed hallway and the string and the killer.

My mouth went dry, and my fingers shook. I wasn't armed. Not unless you counted an urn and a bird. And as I'd proved in the pirate bar, I wasn't a fighter.

I felt a void in the wall behind me and ducked inside a cavern as a light blasted through the hole near the rock pillars that had hidden us before. I rushed to see out, and about fell over when I saw a figure crouched at the rock wall, a few feet from where I'd stood.

His head whipped toward the right, and he quickly stood. And when the echo of Duranja's footsteps sounded down the passage, he fled.

"Verity," Duranja whispered when he found no sign of me.

I risked my light under my shirt in order to make it back out into the hall. "It's me," I announced to the armed officer.

"I lost him in the cave," he said low, slightly out of breath. "It splits off too many ways." He ventured a light down toward where the intruder had disappeared. "He heard me coming after him. He dropped the string. Now we're running blind. I'd give anything for that diary."

Not necessarily blind. "We have Pearl." I drew the parrot from my bag.

"We do," he agreed, the corner of his mouth ticking up.

"The pirates told me to keep Pearl close. They ordered me to keep her secret. They said she was precious. Maybe they meant she could lead someone to Captain Bill's treasure."

"She could be a key as well as a map," he said, finishing my thought and pointing to a now familiar etched circle on the wall above me.

Captain Bill had cherished the bird. He'd made her the key to navigating his hideout of caves. "It can't be a coincidence," I said, locating an etching on the wall and inserting her little wooden feet.

I sure hoped it wasn't a coincidence.

I saw no door. Nothing to indicate we could go this way. But if our intruder had the map from the diary and he was using it to search this particular wall... "This has to be the way to *something* Captain Bill wanted to hide." Hopefully the final capstan.

Did our host back at the hotel know where this was headed all along?

I tried to turn Pearl to the right.

Or was our weekend host the one who was following us now in the caves, hoping we'd lead him to the pirate treasure?

We had the last keystone. Pearl knew the way.

I felt something give and turned the bird harder to the right. The turncap rumbled under my hand and wrenched the bird out of my grip.

"Did you see that?" I hissed, fighting the impulse to shout. Giving in to the urge to jump up and down.

Duranja swore as Pearl began to turn with it, around and around.

"Look, look, look!" I triumphed.

A door in the rock rumbled open on rusty hinges.

"I see," Duranja gritted out.

"You need to work on your happy face," I said breathlessly.

A light illuminated the passage to our left.

"What do you want to bet our murderer heard that loud and clear?" Duranja murmured, gun at the ready.

There was nothing to do about it now as the door yawned open on a cavern glowing with dead sailors and the spoils of their plunder.

Chapter Twenty-Six

I snatched Pearl out of the lock and tucked her under my arm.

The cavern was as big as the hotel lobby and laden with wood barrels and chests, bolts of fabric, and even a full-sized cannon right inside the door. No telling how they got that down here. Discarded rum bottles littered the floor. Immense, rusting iron candelabras as tall as me dotted the space. The remains of ropy balls of tobacco spilled from canvas bags amid a sea of eighteenth-century sailors, who smoked and lounged on large stacks of hemp-bagged rice, sugar, and dried fish.

"This is a trip," Duranja marveled, going straight for the cannon.

"Yeah, I was expecting...gold. All the movies have pirates sitting on a big stack of coins, not fabric." My flashlight beam caught a pile of fish bones intertwined with a centuries-old bolt of flowered silk.

A second later, I wished I hadn't said that, as every dead guy in the room turned to look directly at me.

I whipped Pearl behind my back.

"You look like you've seen a ghost," Duranja said.

Now was not the time.

"Don't be ridiculous," I said, braving the room. These had to be the men I'd heard taunting Captain Bill.

I discreetly clipped Pearl to the back of my belt, thought twice about that, and untucked my shirt to cover her. I wasn't crazy about the feel of centuries-old bird feathers on my back, but it was better than attracting the wrong kind of attention. I sidestepped around a ghostly stack of crated candles, pretending not to notice.

Duranja ran his light over the inside wall. "Is there a way to close the door behind us? Maybe at least try to be sneaky about this?"

"Do you really want to block our only exit?" I had mostly, sort of, almost full faith in Frankie and his pirate friends leading us out of here, but our odds went down if we were trapped in a cavern. Not to mention, if the ghosts noticed me, I wanted a clear door to run through.

"Good point." Duranja lit a rusted-out candelabra. "Can you believe it? Nobody's laid eyes on all this booty in hundreds of years."

"Nobody found the cave." Until us. And now we were in serious danger if our intruder came back.

I should have known Duranja had already anticipated trouble. In an instant, he'd gone from historical ogling to defense. "Light the rest," he said, tossing a book of matches at me. "I've got the door." He took up position right inside, shielded by the opening in the cavern, and waited.

I ventured forward, lighting candelabras as I went. If Duranja was setting a trap for our killer, I'd help him get a clear shot—if it came to that.

In doing so, I passed by a small army of men in breeches and hose, with pistols stuffed in their belts and swords sheathed and at the ready. Several wore old navy jackets, their hair tied back neatly in ribbons.

I felt the eyes of one of them on me. He was roughly my age, his nails trim and neat, his face unscarred. Handsome, even.

"Don't ye bother with the living," a pirate with a short,

scruffy beard told him, finding a new position on a sack of sugar. "They'll get lost down here and die like the rest of us."

Another licked his lips, watching us. "I dunno, Filch. They got in; they could lead us out."

"We've had more than a few live souls down here over the centuries. Ain't none of them got out."

The portly third of the trio huffed. "Nobody's going anywhere." He wore so many pistols in his belt, he'd never be able to sit. "You pledged loyalty for life and beyond."

"Maybe they left a trail." Scruffy Beard's sword rattled as he stood and made a move for the door.

"Leave the room and I'll shoot you," Mister Handsome said, cocking his pistol. "Orders are to stay here and guard Bill."

I scanned the room for Bill, hoping he looked like his portrait. The pen and ink drawing hadn't been very detailed, but I'd know a captive when I saw one.

The guy with the armory in his belt rapped on the back wall of the cavern. "Wakey, wakey, pirate prince."

I ran my light over the back wall and saw what appeared to be solid rock. It glowed gray and ghostly. Solid on their side as well.

Curious. Because I sure didn't see any captives in the cavern where we stood.

I chewed my lip. I was missing something.

"What's going on?" Duranja asked, from his position at the door. "What do you see?"

"Nothing," I said, skirting my light away from the rock, glad he'd caught me before the sailors figured out I was eavesdropping on their conversation.

At least I could be thankful this time that Duranja was entirely too observant.

A sailor on the other side of the room struck a match against the cave wall and lit the pipe jutting from the corner of his mouth. "I don't see any of us getting out soon," he said, taking a deep inhale and shaking out the match. "The commander still has to get married, and who knows how long that'll take."

"Centuries," guffawed a bald man lounging on a crate with his back against the wall.

I made a studious observation of a moldering sack of sugar.

Wasn't Bill the one who was supposed to get married?

Mister Handsome stalked up to the smart aleck and planted his gun against the man's temple. His victim's face went slack as he cocked the trigger. "The lieutenant hears you laughing and he'll do worse than shoot you."

The man began to shake. "Didn't mean nothing by it, Harry," his voice quivered.

Their boss had to be the one tormenting the poor girl on the bridge. Bill was being held captive down here. Bill's crew was none the wiser.

Only I didn't see Bill.

"Stay away from the cage!" Scruffy Beard stood and pointed as his shaking friend retreated from Mr. Handsome's pistol straight toward a rusting iron parrot cage resting atop a stack of wooden tea crates.

"The bird is in the ether," his buddy said, waving his pipe. "Ain't nobody tell me an attack bird is coming back from the in-between over an old cage."

"I don't know about that," I muttered, unable to resist running my light over the rusting iron. "Sounded to me like Pearl would attack anybody who touched her special spot. Bill's own crew seemed downright afraid of her." And she had a reputation for being fierce in battle.

Part of me would sure love to see it.

Handsome turned and locked eyes with me.

Whoops.

"Duranja," I called, my voice an octave higher than it should have been.

He was guarding the door, watching for the killer, but if I didn't fix this, I was about to have twenty pirates in this cave making my previous duel up in the bar look like child's play. Especially considering how many crew were sporting ghostly pistols. And this time, Frankie wasn't here to call them off.

Duranja kept his eyes on the door.

Think. I was about to have a real problem, and I didn't see any way out.

Other than distraction.

"Duranja, look!" I called, knowing he'd yell at me. Hoping the pirates would notice or care or *something.* Anything to give me five seconds to at least find a weapon. "Fire!" I hollered, remembering my mother's advice on getting attention in an emergency.

"Where?" Duranja turned away from the door, lowering his gun with military precision to assess the new threat.

Just that moment, a gun emerged from the shadowy cave entrance, held by a steady hand.

The murderer had found us.

The handsome pirate slapped his leg and chuckled. "Now this —I like this!"

In horror, I watched the killer step into the room behind Alec, expecting Rick or Pirate Bill.

Then I saw the bloodstains on the shoulders of his jacket.

It couldn't be. It wasn't possible.

I screamed as Dr. Fielding stepped inside the room behind Duranja.

"Drop your weapon," the professor stated coolly, his own pistol aimed at the back of Duranja's head.

Duranja winced and did as ordered.

I ducked behind a stack of crates.

"Too late, Verity," the professor added, kicking Duranja's pistol under a mess of rotting fabric.

"Is that who I think it is?" Duranja gritted out, unable to turn.

"He was supposed to be dead," I said, stepping away from the stack of crates, trying to process the sudden appearance of the professor. "The doctor said so. Why would she lie?"

Duranja's shoulders stiffened. "Because she's in on it too."

"Mindy and I are starting a new life," the professor said, keeping his gun trained on Duranja's head. "With a little pirates' gold to ease the way."

"Good luck with that," Duranja muttered.

Wait. "How?" I stammered. Mindy and the professor? The professor and Mindy?

"She's into real history," he said, "unlike her showoff husband. We met last year at a collectors' event, and it was magic."

"Is a divorce too old-fashioned for you?" Duranja snarked.

The corner of his mouth tilted up. "With her prenup? Yes. Rick can keep his money, but I wouldn't dream of asking her to give up her lifestyle. I think I'd like a private yacht, too. A renovated museum. Self-sponsored digs." He adjusted his grip on the gun. "I hate that I have to shoot you. Nobody was supposed to die."

"They were just supposed to get hit in the head with a rock." I stepped past the seven-gunned pirate, wishing ghost bullets would work on Dr. Fielding.

I had a plan.

As long as the pirates didn't make their move first.

Luckily, we seemed to be entertaining Mister Handsome. Evidently, he liked drama. Still, he hadn't called in the guard. I had to be thankful for that. He leaned against the wall by the door, pistol cocked at his shoulder, watching us.

The professor had his attention fixed on Duranja, rightly seeing him as the real threat.

But maybe I could do something.

"I admit dropping the rock was a desperation move," Dr. Fielding said in a way that would have been self-deprecating if he hadn't been holding a gun. "But I couldn't let you follow me into the cave once you used your keystone."

"So you injured our friends," Duranja snapped.

"I was hoping to take your entire team out of the game," he admitted. "Failing that, the twins were on your heels. If they got the second and third coins, your team would give up as soon as you were eliminated. After all, this is just a birthday party for you. And with three coins, the twins would have no motivation to even kick over the fake fourth capstan."

"So you saw that," I said, wishing I had something heavy to toss at him.

He stiffened. "The diary was wrong. It showed a second trapdoor along the left-side wall, but it wasn't there."

"Should have done your own research," Duranja taunted.

Dr. Fielding shot me a steely-eyed glare. "I was planning to. But I didn't have the lighthouse code, and Verity wouldn't put down that stupid bird."

Until I'd lost it on the hillside.

"You took Pearl!" I exclaimed.

Scruffy Beard gasped at the mention of her name, and his buddy made a sign of the cross.

Dr. Fielding didn't flinch. "If you'd just stayed at the hotel like Mindy, you'd have been fine."

He'd tried to injure all kinds of people so that they'd stay at the hotel, including Rick and the twins. "Did you boobytrap all of the capstans?"

"I figured one of two things would happen. Either I'd use whatever keystones I could win and get through the traps fine because I knew they were there, or somebody else would unlock the capstan but get hurt or discouraged in a way that wouldn't let them follow me."

He was a real peach. "Did Bill know you were slimy?" Our host hadn't exactly been fond of Dr. Fielding.

Duranja took a sly step toward the professor while I spoke.

Dr. Fielding's eyes narrowed at Robocop. "Bill and I never got along. He wouldn't let me near the artifacts unless I played the game," he sneered. "Bill thinks it's all a game. He's a clueless idiot, followed around by pirate fanboys like Rick who only encourage him. And the twins—I can't believe Bill got a high-level team to play his silly game."

"So Bill isn't in on this at all," I said.

The professor snorted. "He doesn't even know he has a real treasure on his hands. I think he hopes it, but he's selling his own fantasy."

"And what was supposed to happen on the next hunt?" Duranja had taken another sly step toward the professor.

Dr. Fielding sneered. "There won't be another hunt. Bill put his last ten grand into this travesty, hoping to sell the next one. But once it gets out how unsafe this island is, Bill's hotel will be out of business. As we speak, the twins are back at the hotel puking their guts out. Seems the hotel water is to blame. Won't that look bad on social media? People injured. People sick. Why, it's dangerous to so much as stay at the hotel. I guarantee no one will want to come here after this weekend. Bill will be forced to close up shop and leave this place to me."

There would only be one capstan left to turn.

"And you have the last keystone," I said.

"Not to mention the other three," Duranja added.

The professor had amassed the other keystones to "preserve them." No doubt he'd made imprints or outright copies.

"Bill could never spot a fake." He grinned. "With the island abandoned, an official death certificate eliminating me from any suspicion—"

"Courtesy of Mindy," I gathered.

"And a private yacht at my disposal, I'd be free to take every piece of treasure out of this cave at my leisure."

"You just needed to find a way in," Duranja said dully.

"Clever of you to do that for me," the professor said. "I'm eternally grateful." Dr. Fielding tightened his grip on the pistol. "Take one more step near me and I'll shoot," he warned Duranja. "I meant it when I said I didn't want anyone to get killed. I've been trying to think of another solution, but I don't see any other way out with you two."

It wasn't like we could promise not to tell. Dr. Fielding would never believe us anyway.

Maybe we could prove ourselves useful. "Have you thought of how you're getting out of this cave?"

Duranja shot me a glance. "I studied the cave map in the diary," he said. "You got lost the same as we did because the side passages you took to get here weren't on the map."

Dr. Fielding's ears reddened. "I laid a path to lead me out. Mindy sidelined Rick before he ever got a chance to go for help. She's waiting at the door right now, and she'll only open it for me."

Duranja cocked his head. "Well, you might have a little trouble getting there if you kill us because I cut off the lead string to your last several passages while I was out looking for you."

Dr. Fielding's cheeks reddened. "You're bluffing," he insisted.

He had to be bluffing.

Unless that meant Duranja trusted Pearl to lead us out of here.

Duranja held a hand out, then slowly reached for his pocket.

"I'm warning you." Dr. Fielding aimed the pistol at Duranja's chest as Robocop delved into his pocket and drew out a length of string.

Dr. Fielding cussed. Duranja grinned. And I wouldn't have been surprised if the professor had pulled the trigger right then and there.

"You idiot!" Dr. Fielding kept his gun trained on Duranja while inching backward toward the hall. His chin jutted, and his gun hand shook. "You deserve to die down here, not me." He dragged the flashlight out of his belt, flicking it on. "You'd better be lying about that lead string," he threatened before whipping the light into the hallway behind him. "Son of a—"

Duranja launched himself at the professor, who fired his gun. The shot zinged past me, and the boom of the gun echoed through the cavern.

In a flash, the pock-faced pirate who had dueled me in the bar appeared in front of me. My heart dropped, then soared as I realized Frankie and his reinforcements were here.

Chapter Twenty-Seven

"Told you we'd find them here!" Frankie crowed, sword in hand as he led the crew. "Let's make 'em pay!"

The pirate horde let out a mighty yell as they descended on the sailors, realizing they'd found their captain's kidnappers.

The professor fired off another shot. I covered my ears and raced for Duranja's gun. Pock Face swooped down on me when I bent down to grab it. "You still owe me a duel!" he shouted, pointing at me. "You think your friend killing me can get you out of it?"

I'd been hoping.

"I challenge you to a duel to the death," he hissed.

"Please, not now," I protested. Not ever again.

"Focus." Frankie floated above him. "Stay with your battle buddy. We fight in teams. They've got Captain Bill. Let's free the captain!"

The pirates rushed the cavern guards, fighting with precision as ordered. Since when was Frankie a military expert? But Pock Face only had eyes for me.

He unsheathed the short blade from his belt and swung it at me while I dove for Duranja's gun at his feet. The ghostly blade was an instant from slicing my neck when a pair of frigid, wet hands grabbed my ankles and yanked me backward across the floor, nearly paralyzing me to the bone with cold and death but also saving my life.

"Argh!" Frankie yelled, dropping me.

"Thank you, Frankie! You're my hero!" I stumbled to my feet.

Meanwhile, the handsome sailor had Pock Face in a headlock.

"I'm a huge hero!" Frankie gushed. "Look at me," he shouted, retrieving his sword. "I lead troops. I save lives! I—"

I screamed in shock as the bearded guardsman from the cave stabbed Frankie through the gut with a longsword. I felt the echo of the deadly blade as a hard, sick shock of energy that made my head buzz and my fingers go numb.

"Frankie!"

He collapsed facedown onto the floor. It had happened in an instant.

"No." I rushed for him. "Don't die!"

He clutched his abdomen and coughed. "I'm not dead yet."

Thank heavens. "Hold on, Frank!" I hollered as Pock Face broke free and lunged at me with his dagger.

"Don't call me Frank," the gangster choked out.

I had no weapon. No way to stop Pock Face even if I were crazy enough to try to knife fight him. He chortled, displaying a mouthful of rotten teeth.

I turned and ran toward the wall, leaping over a dead (again) sailor and making a desperate dash for the rusting cage stacked on tea crates. I felt Pock Face's cold breath on my back, the stench of death, as I banged a hand against the glowing, rusted cage, glad my fingers were numb, as it sent an icy shock through the rest of my body that made me dizzy. I kept going, dropping to my knees by the cave wall.

Squawwwk!

The vicious, angry, put-upon ghost of Pearl appeared in a whirl of wings and feathers as she streaked out of her cage and straight for Pock Face.

The pirate shrieked as the eclectus parrot dug her claws into his nose.

"Argh!" He swung his blade in a wide arc, stumbling backward. Pearl refused to let go. The pirate stumbled over Frankie into the thick of the battle, where Mr. Handsome shot him in the back before being tackled by Dreadlocks.

Only when Pock Face fell on his face did Pearl let go of his nose. She perched on his head, ruffling her feathers while the ghost bled out.

That would teach him.

"Okay," I said, voice shaking as I climbed to my feet. "Don't mess with Pearl, right?"

Squawwwk!

She took off like a shot. I flinched, ready for an attack. But she launched herself straight up through the roof of the cave and was gone.

Meanwhile, Frankie lay writhing on the floor.

I scrambled back to him. Thank goodness he was still with us.

"Frankie!" I dropped to my knees and turned him over as gently as I could, not caring about the sting or the wet or the invasive cold. "What can I do?"

The battle raged all around us.

He'd lost his tricorn hat. The bullet hole in his forehead glowed dully in the light from the candelabras. Blood trickled from the corner of his mouth. "You can stop touching me and let me enjoy this." He coughed again and grinned.

He was delirious.

"Frankie, you're dying!" I wailed. Yes, he'd done it before, but never for me, and I couldn't help but be touched and grateful. I felt the sting of tears.

The corner of his mouth cocked up. "Isn't it great?"

"It's awful," I protested, wishing I could get him out of the line of fire.

"Do not weep for me to die, but be glad that I lived," he sputtered in a most un-Frankie-like way.

"Excuse me?" He'd grown deathly pale. He really had lost it.

"I always wanted a slow, dramatic death," he squeaked, coughed gently, and then he died.

I didn't see how this was better than being shot in the forehead. I knelt, frozen, unable to look away from his bleeding body on the ground.

He'd died—again—saving me.

Frankie, the gangster.

My friend. Sure, he'd be back in an hour or two, but he never sacrificed anything for anybody.

Maybe he really was becoming a better man.

And now that he'd done it, I realized with sick horror that I was stuck with his powers.

"Where's Captain Bill?" Frankie's dreadlocked friend shouted at me. He fired a shot at the bearded guardsman who'd stabbed Frankie, taking him down.

"I don't know!" I pleaded, reality surging back in an instant as he took a shot in the arm from the seven-gunned sailor.

I dove out of the way of the second shot. And the third. I rolled sideways, petrified when a blade slammed into the place I'd vacated a breath before. The handsome guardsman snarled down at me. "Well, hello, my little spy."

"I'm not a spy," I insisted, scrambling to my feet. "I'm alive."

"Very clever technique," he said, taking a swipe at me.

I backed up fast. I didn't have a sword. I didn't know how to fight.

I turned and ran, leaping over the professor and Duranja as they grappled for a gun on the floor. I wasn't sure whose. Dr. Fielding got an arm free and reached for the weapon. I doubled back and stomped his hand. He let out a yowl as Duranja flipped him over. I grabbed the gun as he punched Duranja hard with a knee and snatched the other revolver.

"Freeze!" I ordered, aiming the gun at the professor.

He raised his weapon, and I dove behind a crate full of crystal just as he fired in my direction.

Glass shattered. The professor shouted, and I popped my head up in time to see Duranja clock him in the kidneys with a lit candelabra.

I would have cheered, but Eye Patch appeared before me, whipping his sword in fury. I scrambled backward and hit the cold stone wall of the cave.

"Let this be a lesson," he taunted. "Never mess with pirates."

He raised his sword, enjoying my terror.

I searched frantically for a knife, a gun, a spare goblet, anything. This room had been filled with sailors for centuries, somebody had to have dropped a weapon along the way. But there was nothing. I was unarmed.

"Duranja!" I screamed. He sat on Dr. Fielding's back, cuffing him.

He'd never get close in time to help, and if by chance he did, he couldn't save me from a ghost. He couldn't even see the danger.

Eye Patch chuckled, enjoying my terror.

"Please," I begged him. If I died, my sister would never forgive herself for taking us on this weekend.

And who would take care of my skunk? I scrambled sideways to escape.

He blocked me.

Lucy needed me. Lauralee's kids might be great babysitters now, but what about when they got older? What if they lost interest?

Did they even know what her favorite toys were? She had more than just her banana. I didn't tell them everything before I left.

I thought I'd be back.

"Let this be a warning to anybody else who neglects Pearl," he snarled, bringing the sword down. I braced for the sharp, cold sting of the blade that would end my life, but it never came.

Instead, a shot rang out, and Eye Patch fell down dead.

Bony Beads held the smoking revolver.

"What?" he said to his shocked comrades. "Frankie the Fierce said he'd show us how to make moonshine if we keep this kid alive."

"Ahh!" His buddies raised their swords.

"It's as smooth as lighter fluid," I promised, voice shaking as I climbed to my feet. Seemed Frankie had been sharing his flask. And looking out for me.

Meanwhile, Duranja had Dr. Fielding cuffed on the floor and stood reading him his rights, oblivious to the raging battle on the ghostly plane.

All this fuss and death over a bunch of old, rotting trade goods.

Frankie lay dead, as did Pock Face. Mr. Handsome lay crumpled over Seven Guns. Dreadlocks grinned at me as he strode through the remains of the battle. His side had won. The guardians of the cavern would stay dead for at least an hour, giving Captain Bill's crew plenty of time to free their leader and grab a few extra bottles of rum—if there were any left to drink.

And then I saw something painfully familiar on the wall at the very back of the cavern, to the right of a rusting candelabra that stood unlit. I hadn't made it back that far.

A hole about shoulder high had been carved into the rock in the exact shape of a keystone.

Chapter Twenty-Eight

Hands shaking, I reached into my bag for the remaining keystone. With fingers still numb from the touch of the ghost, I unwrapped it gently from the cloth. The blue sea glass appeared smooth and lustrous, as beautiful as any precious stone.

Throat tight, I placed it into the wall.

It locked in with a thud and a click.

A perfect fit.

I waited for a moment, unsure what to do next. There was no capstan for me to turn, only slight indentations in the wall where Pearl would fit perfectly.

I glanced back to my ghostly friend on the floor, dead again because of me. Frankie was the guy who'd once refused to ride across town to help me unless I did something for him in return. And tonight, he'd taken a sword blow meant for me. He'd bribed a pirate to watch out for me. He'd come a long way, and so had I.

"This is for you, Frankie." I gripped the stone and turned.

Metal clanked. Gears ground. A circular section of the wall that held the keystone retreated as a hidden door rattled open an inch, then two.

"Verity, wait for me," Duranja called, struggling to keep the cuffed professor from bolting. If Dr. Fielding fled and got lost in the cave, Robocop would feel honor bound to track him down and get him out safely, when all I wanted was to get out of this warren of caves and spend the rest of my life above ground.

"I've got it," I assured him, hoping I was right.

At least someone knew where I was this time in case the door slammed closed behind me.

I didn't wait for it to grind open all the way. I glimpsed enough through the opening to realize what I'd found. And what I saw made me gasp out loud.

Here was the real treasure room, grander than any I'd ever imagined.

A staggeringly tall pile of gold bars lay stacked next to an enormous carved wooden throne big enough for three men and topped with a massive red silk cushion. The seat of power was rotting in the real world, but glorious on the ghostly side of the veil. It stood in the center of the room on an elaborate rug, waiting for the king of the castle. Or the captain of the ship, as the case may be.

This had to be Captain Bill's private getaway.

A rich banquet table stood nearby. In real life, a thick coat of dust and grime coated the serving ware. In the ghostly realm, an ornately stacked pillar of apples, pears, and oranges dominated a table loaded down with roasted turkey, roasted potatoes, bread, cheese, and nuts. Wine waited, uncorked, next to a pair of crystal glasses.

An enormous bed with sumptuous covers dominated the far wall.

I'd heard the pirates outside taunting him, but I saw no sign of the ghost.

"Captain Bill," I called, my voice sounding louder in the smaller cavern. When I received no response, I pressed deeper into the room. "Sorry to intrude, but my name is Verity Long, and it's very important that I speak with you." I ventured past the throne, resisting the urge to touch it. Maybe he'd learned to ignore the living. Or all people, considering the taunting he must have endured. Well, he'd best get ready for some kindness and consideration because I was here to free him, and even better—to help reunite him with his bride.

A ghostly figure lay crumpled behind the throne.

"Bill?" I rushed to see, hoping it was him and that he wasn't hurt too badly.

The muscular bear of a man lay unmoving. A scar cut across his brow, giving him a rough look despite his high cheekbones and slack jaw. He sort of resembled the ink drawing in the library. Nothing like our host Bill. He wore his beard scruffy, his hair long, and he kind of reminded me of Jason Momoa.

"What do we have here?" A striking ghost shimmered into existence, wineglass in hand, feet resting on the banquet table. He wore his hair tied back in a silk ribbon, his white linen shirt unbuttoned to the chest like a romance novel hero. The rings on his fingers glittered with jewels as he sipped from his cup, watching me.

"I'm here for Captain Bill," I said standing my ground.

His gaze traveled down the length of me before he dismissed me with the flick of a hand. "Leave me, foul temptress."

"Oh, I'm not a foul temptress. I'm from Sugarland, Tennessee," I assured him.

"You're also alive," he observed with new interest.

"I am," I said, leaving the next move up to him.

"For now," he said.

That didn't go well. "Whatever you're doing in here with Captain Bill is done," I stated, hoping I was right. At his raised brow, I added, "I'm helping his men find him. They're in the room right next door, so you'd better not try anything." At that same moment, it occurred to me that I didn't know any of their names. "There's Pock Face and Bony Beads. Wait. His real name is Red Jack. Oh, and the dreadlock guy."

His eyes widened in surprise. "Diabolito."

"He kind of does look like a Diabolito," I conceded.

I jumped as the door to the chamber ground closed.

"Verity!" Duranja hollered from the other side before the thick rock between us snuffed all sound from the main chamber.

I stared at the ghost. "You did that." I tried not to let my panic show as my heart sped up.

He smirked and popped a grape into his mouth. "It's a security feature. You can thank Bill for that. Oh, wait. He's not alive to hear you."

This was bad. "Bill's crew can still get in here," I insisted. The fancy schmancy ghost might have me trapped, but he was stuck in here as well.

He ran his fingers over the silver derringer tucked in his belt. "I assume, since we're having this lovely conversation, that you are in our world, not your own. Does that mean this will work on you?" he asked, pointing the pistol at my heart.

I flinched.

"Good to know." He pressed his lips together, suppressing a triumphant grin. "You call Bill's crew, and I kill you. Make you like Bill here. Get you on a schedule. You'll find I'm a very patient man."

"Excuse me?" I didn't understand. "Who *are* you?"

He kicked his feet off the table and stood, wineglass in hand. It was then that I saw blood soaking the left side of his shirt, and suddenly I knew. Legend had it he'd been stabbed in the heart. But legends were often wrong. I was in the presence of Captain Bill's vengeful brother.

"Ethan Brown," he said, giving a practiced, courtly bow. He joined me to stand over Bill. "My brother here thought he could marry my betrothed." He raised a glass to the throne, the gold. "He kidnapped her to his pirate island. But I hired men to rescue her. I sailed to find her. And I killed him on this very spot," he said, looking down at the body. "Damned fool won't leave," he added, nudging one of his brother's muscled arms with the toe of his polished boot.

I'd heard of ghosts haunting their death spots, but they were always awake and functioning. "Has he been dead this entire time?" I'd never seen anything like it.

"I wish," Ethan said, fingers whitening as he gripped his glass. "He keeps waking up. He wants to 'rescue' my betrothed," he ground out. "So I kill him again. And again." His features hardened, and he stared down at his brother with contempt.

"For how long?" I gasped.

"Every hour since September 21, 1736," he said ruefully.

Poor Bill! "And after he's dead, you drink his wine and eat his wedding feast." Again and again.

"My wedding feast!" He flung his glass onto the floor. "Catherine was betrothed to *me* by her father. She's my bride. Mine!"

Spilled wine seeped into Bill's hair. A glass shard glittered on Bill's cheek.

Ethan wiped the corners of his mouth with the tip of a finger. "Now look what you made me do."

"You realize you're dead, too. You could move on at any time. End this." Who wanted to spend eternity seeking revenge?

"I won't leave without Catherine." He touched his bloody side. "She belongs to me. The wedding contract was finalized by both of our fathers. She's docile and perfect. An ideal lady in every respect. Bill kidnapped her to this wretched island and stabbed me before I was able to kill him for it. He lay dead, just like that"—he grinned—"and I ran for her. I found her on the bridge. I told her it was over and Bill was dead. She could stop pining after a pirate and accept her good fortune as my bride!"

His face fell.

"She jumped, didn't she?"

"She was distraught. I said it wrong." Blood seeped between the fingers he held to his side. "Women are sensitive creatures. I should have been more careful with my words. I wasn't thinking. I was bleeding out. It was a horrific sight. If I could explain it to her correctly, she'd know I'm the one she belongs with."

"She's terrified of you." No wonder poor Catherine had been

paralyzed with fear on the bridge! We'd rushed her like a motley gang of outlaws.

"She's not!" He raised a hand to strike me. Before I had a chance to flinch, he yanked his hand back. "I died right in front of her. I shouldn't have done that. Any lady would have been distraught at such a sight."

"You were stabbed," I said quietly, not willing to provoke him again.

"Bill became a pirate to help run supplies to the colony. Taxes were outrageous, and we were barely making it some years. But he enjoyed it too much and nearly sullied our family's good name beyond repair. He couldn't possibly be a proper husband for such a fine lady. He only proved it by sneaking her out of her father's house in the dead of night like a brigand. Her father was furious. I swore to him I would make things right and, in return, marry Catherine myself. She'd have her honor and a proper place at my side forever." He checked his watch. "He'll be waking up soon," he said, drawing his revolver.

No. "You've got to stop killing him. End this."

He wrapped a finger around the trigger. "He'll never win. I win." He pressed the gun to Bill's back. "Catherine will come to her senses. I get an hour to visit her every time Bill dies. I explain to her that she is mine. One of these days, she'll stop jumping."

I very much doubted that. "You need to let her go. You need to let this end."

His face twisted with hate. "Bill stabbed me. He killed me when all I wanted was Catherine." His finger whitened on the trigger. "This is his fault, not mine!"

I could have sworn I saw Bill's finger move.

Ethan stared at his back, itching to pull the trigger.

"Don't you worry, my dear. I won't leave you down here with a dead man. I've got more than one bullet in this gun."

Chapter Twenty-Nine

I grabbed a gold brick, letting the ghostly metal singe me to the bone as I whipped around and clocked Ethan in the back of the head.

He fired his gun.

The bullet ricocheted off the floor and whizzed past my ear as I stumbled sideways to avoid passing straight through Bill.

Ethan crumpled to the floor. I landed next to the golden throne just as Bill rolled over, drew his sword, and stabbed his brother in the stomach.

Ethan gasped and gurgled before dying. Again.

Bill staggered to his feet, sword at the ready.

"I'm a friend!" I said, holding my hands up. "I hit Ethan with a gold bar so he wouldn't kill you again," I added, pointing to the discarded metal brick. "Catherine is waiting for you on one of the rock bridges." The only one left—in my world, at least. "She's upset. You need to go to her."

Captain Bill stared at me with piercing eyes. "Who *are* you?"

"I'm Verity Long from Sugarland."

"Sugarland?" His brows knit. "Is that an island?"

"Unto itself. Now go. I'll watch your brother." And kill Ethan again if I had to.

He shook as he looked down on his tormentor. "I will not turn my back and let him double-cross me again."

I understood stress and how it made it hard to grasp the obvious. But if he could allow himself to trust me, it would all become clear. "I can see—"

"Spirits," he finished. "I know I'm dead. My brother, Ethan, shot me in the back. He poisoned the ale in the bar and killed my men. Or so he's bragged for the last several centuries. He will not leave me in peace until he marries the woman I love."

"He said as much to me," I admitted.

"Catherine loved me from childhood," Bill gritted out. "We were always promised to each other. Killing me didn't change that, and it never will."

"She's waiting for you," I reminded him.

"I won't appear at the same time he always did," he vowed to me and himself. "I won't sully our reunion like that. The bridge is our place," he said gently.

"I'm sorry." I wished I could make it better for him. Then I remembered. "I have something for you."

I'd nearly forgotten. Although in my defense, I was a little distracted by the very tall, very handsome pirate. A little thrown by the stabbing and the attempted shooting. Not to mention the handling of one too many ghostly objects. I reached behind me and unclipped Pearl from my belt and extracted her from under my shirt.

Shock slacked his features. "Is that...?"

"Pearl," I said, gently presenting her to her owner. "She helped us find you."

"My precious Pearl," he cooed, his ghostly fingers passing straight through her.

"I think the real Pearl is in the ether. That's an in-between place."

"I know. I could feel her waiting for me." His eyes misted. "I'd have loved to call her back to scratch their eyes out, but I'd never risk her like that. I'd never call her back to suffer." He straightened and cleared his throat. "Pearl!" he called in a loud, booming voice. "Pearl, my darling!"

Squawk!

The ghostly bird shot through the closed door, a flurry of feathers and birdy joy as she dove for his outstretched arm. She shrieked, dancing up and down his arm, puffing up her feathers, shaking them out, and then puffing them up all over again.

"There's my princess," Bill cooed, giving her air kisses while she bobbed and cried and nudged him with her beak. "It's all right now. It's safe for you. You've missed me? I've missed you, sweetheart."

She splayed out her tail like a fan and waggled it. Then she touched her beak to his nose, and he smiled.

I felt the corners of my mouth tug up. "Your men are terrified of her."

"As they should be," he baby-talked to his bird.

"Even the guards outside were afraid of touching her cage."

"My brother's hired scum," he said flatly, letting Pearl climb up onto his shoulder. "They taunted me day and night, or so Ethan told me. They never knew when I'd be awake, so they kept at it."

"It helped lead me here," I said, hoping that would be a small consolation.

He glared toward the cavern that had held his tormentors. "No doubt my brother promised them the riches that should have gone to the colony."

"This was all for the colony?" I asked, gesturing to the wealth scattered around me. It seemed a bit much. Especially the gold bars.

"Well..." The corner of his mouth tilted up. "Not *all* for the colony. What the King's Navy overcharged in taxes, I took back with interest." He shrugged a shoulder. "I mean, I *am* a pirate."

I could see why Frankie liked these guys.

"Verity!" Duranja's muffled voice sounded from the other side of the wall.

"That's my friend," I told the pirate. "I used your keystone to get in here, but the door closed on me."

"Then let's get you out," he said, stroking Pearl's tail.

Captain Bill waved a hand, and the door creaked open on its hinges.

"I did it!" Duranja announced, stumbling in.

I'd let him think so. "I'm over here," I called.

"Are you all right—holy hell," he said, marveling at a table just inside the door that was laden with jewels, necklaces, and even a diamond tiara.

How had I missed that?

"I found Captain Bill," I said, taking the pirate to meet Duranja.

"You did more than that," Bill said, smiling down at me.

"This is my friend Alec," I said to the captain. "He can't see you, but he helped me bring your crew down here." In a way. If he hadn't exposed me back in the pirate bar, we might not have gotten Bill's crew fired up enough to follow me.

"Pleased to meet you, Alec," he said to the stunned Duranja, who couldn't take his eyes off the stack of gold next to the antique throne.

"I owe you both a great debt," Bill said, stroking the bird on his shoulder. Pearl preened his long hair with her beak. "Take whatever you like in payment. Consider it a pirate's reward."

"Thanks, that's very kind." I turned to Duranja. "He said we can have anything we'd like."

"Anything we'd like?" He was going to have to close his mouth and take his eyes off that stack of gold eventually.

And then I spotted the perfect reward.

The nearby table laden with jewels held something special.

"Look," I said, pointing out a gorgeous, sparkling, antique diamond ring. "Melody would adore this."

Duranja lit up in a whole new way. "She would, wouldn't she?"

I caught the pirate's eye. "It's for his love," I explained. "He's been saving for a ring so he can propose."

Bill glided to the table and touched the ring. "Then I am honored to be of assistance."

Duranja's eyes widened as the diamond ring wobbled and slid forward an inch, then two, before tipping off the edge.

I caught it and placed it neatly into Duranja's open palm.

He stared at it for a long moment. "Did that just—" He shook his head. "No," he decided.

While Duranja inspected the table, trying to figure out what kind of tilt it could possibly have that would make a ring suddenly slide and fall after two hundred years, the dreadlocked pirate inched through the door, blade at the ready.

"Captain," he uttered, his eyes going wide at the sight of Bill.

"Diabolito!" Bill greeted him with a booming voice and a slap on the shoulder. "Guard my brother, who lies dead on the floor. Remove him from this place. And kill him again as necessary."

"With pleasure," Diabolito promised.

"And what about your reward?" Bill asked, noticing Duranja admiring his ring.

"I'm fine," I insisted. It all seemed a bit overwhelming.

"How about this?" he prodded, leading me to the table where a small golden parrot with ruby red eyes perched next to a monster of a dinner knife. "To remember us?"

"It's perfect," I said, picking it up and tilting it, watching the eyes glitter. "Thank you."

"Now I must see to Catherine." Bill began to fade. "Thank you again, Verity." He tilted his head toward the stuffed bird I held. "Turn left when you leave the cavern outside this one. Pearl will show you a back way down to the beach."

"It was my honor to help." I said it with all sincerity. Because it was. "Take care."

"Come, dear one," he said to his bird, "let's go find my darling bride."

I sighed with pleasure.

"We did a good job here," I said to Duranja once Bill had gone.

"I think we did," Duranja said, giving up on the science behind sliding rings. He stood and surveyed the pirate's secret lair. "Now what about the rest of this loot?"

That was the trick. "If word gets out about this treasure, Captain Bill, Catherine, and Pearl will never have peace." They'd suffered too much already. Constant fortune hunting would ruin this place.

Duranja nodded. "Very wise, Verity."

"I do my best." It was all any of us could do, really.

Besides, I had everything I needed. A loving sister. A boyfriend I adored. And a chance to turn something right that had been wrong for centuries. Plus, my own little Pearl.

Duranja held the sparkling diamond up to the light before pocketing the ring.

"I'm trusting you not to screw this up," I added.

"I'll do my best." Duranja grinned.

We slipped out the door, and Duranja eased it shut. I took hold of the keystone and turned it until I heard the locking mechanism slide into place.

"What did you find?" Dr. Fielding demanded, hands cuffed behind his back, a knot the size of Cleveland on his forehead. His legs flailed all wonky as he attempted to clamber across the cavern floor toward us.

"Nothing but a pile of old bones." Duranja shrugged.

The professor's shock and disappointment would have been comical if he hadn't hurt so many people in his desperation to seize the treasure we'd chosen to conceal.

Right now, all we had would be the professor's word if he decided to talk. And the professor's greed if he was determined to try to unlock the inner sanctum.

I eased the keystone out of the hidden door. "Quite a shame you went through all that trouble to trick everyone," I mused.

"You didn't search hard enough," he said haughtily. "With my guidance, you could have found a treasure beyond your imagination. We could have split it and gone our separate ways. You don't understand—"

The more he complained, the more my grip loosened on the relic. Finally, it slipped through my fingers and shattered on the floor.

The professor went silent.

"Oops." I shrugged.

Chapter Thirty

"So what happened to Dr. Fielding?" Melody asked.

Duranja tilted his head. "You mean after he ran smack-dab into some old rum barrels and knocked himself out while trying to get away from me?" He went for the dramatic pause.

He'd earned it.

"I arrested him," Duranja said simply.

Melody laughed and kissed him on the shoulder.

"I mean, when does that kind of stunt ever work?" Duranja shook his head.

We'd checked in with our significant others soon after Pearl led us out of the cave. We'd taken the pirate crew out with us—including Ethan and his men—since Captain Bill was the only one who knew how to make it out of the caves on his own. And after being released from a few centuries in captivity, I had a feeling he'd be busy with Catherine in his private love nest for quite some time.

And so, we wound our way out of the caverns, trusting Pearl to lead us. And she did.

Bill's crew was overjoyed when Dreadlocks related the news of Bill's release. They decided to wait for him at the hideout by the lighthouse for as long as it took him to return, celebrating Bill's actual reunion with his one true love. That was where we'd left them and their temporarily re-deceased brethren.

Frankie too, although it hurt to give him up to the care of pirates.

They insisted it was only right, him being an important leader. He was the one who'd led them back to their captain and made the gang whole again.

I had a feeling Frankie was going to enjoy the attention once he recovered.

As soon as Ethan's men met the free air for the first time in centuries, they disappeared, leaving Ethan alone with the crew of the *Fortune's Revenge*.

I didn't see that going well for him.

Afterward, Duranja carried Melody downstairs for a group meeting in the library, and then he helped Ellis, too—despite my boyfriend's protests that he could indeed walk with a twisted knee. Spoiler alert: he couldn't.

The others deserved to know what was going on. Duranja sat on the couch next to Melody, holding her good hand while she propped her ankle up on a pillow.

I shared the overstuffed chair by the fireplace with Ellis. He'd insisted. Even with his knee propped up on a pillow.

"We found a landline back in Bill's office and called the local police to come pick up Dr. Fielding for attempted murder. They might not be able to make that stick, but at least he'll probably have to answer for reckless endangerment for pushing the rock down on us," I explained to the group.

"Charges will depend on the DA," Duranja added. "We'll need to go down and give statements. They'll call us when they're ready." He glanced to the group. "They'll want to talk to the rest of you as well."

Our small band of treasure hunters was down to seven—the police had detained Mindy for questioning while she waited outside the cave door for Dr. Fielding.

According to the police, she'd blamed everything on the professor the moment she saw a badge.

Rick braced a hand on the fireplace, his head bowed. "I never saw it coming."

"Me neither," Melody murmured, no doubt regretting her trust in the professor.

"We can't fault ourselves for being good, trusting people," I said. Mindy had appeared to be a good person. The professor as well. You had to give yourself a chance to get to know people before judging.

"I mean, I knew she wasn't happy," Rick added, gesturing helplessly. "And I didn't like the way he was always sniffing around. I just didn't think...this."

"I'm sorry," I said, wishing I could take away some of his pain.

He pressed his lips together. "Thanks."

"But everyone still had a fun weekend," Bill said, again in pirate garb, his delusion intact. "And since Dr. Fielding has been, ahem, disqualified, there will be no coin awarded on the third capstan. That means Zadie and Zara win the weekend with two coins!" he announced.

We responded with a smattering of applause as he gathered the twins near the hearth to accept the ten-thousand-dollar gold coin. They remained a bit pale from their health scare, but true to form, they'd bounced back well.

The twins paused for a photo with Bill and their prize, but it didn't seem their hearts were in it.

Even Bill caught the change in mood. "I'm afraid that aside from the contest, the island doesn't have much else to offer." He perked up. "Unless you'd like to see the collection of pirate sword hilts my grandfather dug up on the beach. No doubt they were used in real pirate battles."

I'd had enough of real pirate battles. "Bill," I said, "I'm excited to tell you that you have more than a few sword hilts." And whatever else his father and grandfather had dug up over the years.

Duranja's eyes glittered. "Down in the caves, we found a

cavern full of pirate loot. I'm talking silk, sugar, crystal wine goblets—all from the hold of the *Fortune's Revenge*."

Bill went red in the cheeks and gasped.

"What?" Rick choked.

"No way!" Zara said, pocketing the coin.

"We even found the parrot cage that belonged to Pearl," I added, stroking the stuffed bird on my shoulder. I hadn't quite been able to let her go yet.

"Wait." Zadie strode toward me. "How do you know it's from the pirate era?"

"Well, it has to be," Bill boomed, tickled beyond belief. "It's on Phantom Island!"

"Call in some archaeologists," I said. "I'm sure they can verify the find." After all, it was the real deal.

Bill brought a hand to his chest. "A new pirate find. On my island. How can I thank you?"

"By making this place a success," I said. He'd believed in this place when few had. "You deserve it."

"It is a pretty cool island," Zara conceded.

"Agreed," Zadie said, "the place is amazing." She began pacing near the hearth. "There's nothing else like it, and we had a blast here." She exchanged a glance with her sister. "But you need more than pirate loot to draw a real crowd."

"You haven't seen the loot yet," I pointed out.

Zara began her own pacing by the antique globe on the bearskin rug. "Yeah, but Zadie and I were talking. You've got the perfect place for an island adventure getaway. I mean, rock climbing on the north part of the island, rappelling down the cliffs to the beach—"

"Parasailing over the wreck of a pirate ship," Zadie added.

"Or you could dive the wreck!" Rick jumped in. "I'd love to do that."

"What about pirate cave ghost tours?" I asked, joining the fun.

"We'd get all kinds of free publicity, what with archaeologists documenting that pirate cavern you found." Bill slapped a hand on his chest. "The tours could watch the archaeologists in action."

"You'll need investors," Zadie stated.

"We've been looking to do something new," Zara said on her heels. "I mean, we've got ten thousand dollars burning a hole in my pocket."

"Plus the *Treasure Race* money," her twin added.

"We could put it back into the island. Bill could handle the hotel and the history, and we could spearhead the outdoor adventure attractions."

"You'd do that?" Bill asked, shaking Zadie's hand, then Zara's. "That's a great idea. I could use some fresh blood around here."

"As long as you can keep up with us," Zadie teased.

"My one demand is that we bring up Pearl's cage and display it here in the library," Bill insisted, stalking to a sunny spot near the window. "Right here. We'll place stuffed Pearl inside, where she can overlook Pirate's Bay."

"Be careful with that," I warned. "Pearl attacks anyone who touches her cage. Be prepared for a nosebleed if you start messing with it."

He raised a finger. "We'll add a warning sign. *Beware ye who touch the cage of Pearl the Pirate, lest ye be cursed for all eternity.*"

Or assaulted by a ghost bird. But seeing as none of the tourists would notice... "That should work."

Ellis slipped his hand into mine as I explained the real story of Captain Bill and the crew of the *Fortune's Revenge* to a rapt pirate Bill and the others.

Afterward, Bill took Zara and Zadie into the bar to toast their new business venture. Rick followed to console himself with some scotch.

There was one part that bothered me, though. "How much did Ethan hate his poor brother that he was willing to kill him over and over again for centuries? I mean, how could he think what he was doing to Catherine was right?"

"Love and hate both can make people do some crazy things," Melody reasoned.

And bad feelings could be dangerous when they festered.

I glanced to Duranja, content with my sister.

It was easy to make assumptions about people based on feelings. Heck, on more than feelings—on actions, on experiences. But we couldn't know everything going on inside them.

Maybe sometimes it was okay to give a person another chance.

"I believe Verity really did meet Captain Bill," Duranja said out of blue.

"For real?" Melody said, proud and excited and not half as happy as I was.

He shrugged. "I'm starting to think so." He looked to me. "How else can I explain some of the things that happened in those caves?"

"And in Sugarland," I added.

"Don't push it," he warned.

Later, he accompanied me to the rock bridge. For protection, he'd insisted, much to Melody's delight.

"You just want proof there's a ghost," I teased.

"Like it or not, I'm your partner in crime," he said, shrugging a shoulder. In his hand, he held the journal my sister had given him.

"Melody handed mine to me after dinner," I said, patting the journal in my bag. "She says we're behind."

"I'll see if I can get us an extension," he said, flipping the book in his hand. "I can be quite persuasive."

"I don't even want to know."

As we neared the bridge, I saw a pair of ghostly figures gathered close at the center. It was Captain Bill, standing hand-in-hand with Catherine. She appeared radiant in her wedding jewelry and gown, and blissfully happy.

Even the bridge itself appeared more solid. Maybe it was the angle or the lighting. Or maybe together, Bill and Catherine wouldn't let it fall.

She'd waited more than two centuries for her one true love, and he was her reward.

He leaned down to give her a long, lingering kiss that went on and on and on.

Perhaps for another century? Because now they had all the time in the world, together.

"Our job here is done," I said to Duranja.

"Not quite," Robocop countered, eyeing his journal. "Haven't we been through enough this weekend?"

Did he mean the falling boulder, the ghost who wanted to kill me, or the attack parrot?

He held the book of questions aloft and strode for the cliff.

"What are you—" I began.

He wouldn't.

I chased after him, clutching my bag. "We *shouldn't*!" Oh my word. "Is that why you wanted to come out here with me?"

"It is a side benefit," he said, holding his journal over the cliff. "I will if you will."

I stood, shocked. "Why, Alec Duranja, you are such a rule breaker."

I never in a million years would have thought he'd be willing to do that. Or that I would want to so bad.

He grinned. "I'm a reasonable man."

"And I'm willing to do what I must in a crisis," I said as I drew the journal out of my bag and held it over the drop-off.

Were we really going to do it?

The wind buffeted the cover, and the pages flapped in the breeze.

And then we both let go.

He laughed and so did I as the dreaded journals spun and fell and landed who-knew-where.

"You know, I don't even think Melody's going to mind," he said on the way back.

"She wanted us to get along." We just happened to bond over tossing our journals over the side of a cliff.

"Plus, Melody being Melody, you realize she has backup copies," Duranja said.

"And backups of the backups," I added.

Then I recognized a pirate I hadn't seen since we first set foot on the island.

He sat a short distance away with a fish and a knife, on the edge of a jutting rock overlook, watching the sea.

"Give me a second," I said to Duranja.

The ghost turned as I approached. It was him, the lone sailor who'd warned me about the curse.

"Did I make it better?" I asked as he stared out into the ocean.

He paused his knife. "You did. Now this island can be a true haven, no longer under the shadow of its past. We can all live free." Smiling, he gestured out to sea. "Isn't she a beaut?"

"Is that...?" Holy heck. He was pointing to a pirate ship. A full-blown tall ship with rippling sails and a Jolly Roger, sailing out of the hidden harbor below the cliffs.

"Do you see it?" I asked Duranja.

Robocop squinted. "The foggy, ripply...maybe?"

The living were more likely to experience ghosts if they believed.

At least Duranja was trying now.

"I sailed it," the pirate crowed, happily slicing into his fish.

"You were the first mate?" How wonderful.

He chucked a bit of fish guts off his knife and off the cliff. "I was the cook. And the only one who didn't drink the poisoned ale. I was too busy fixing dinner."

"Well, wasn't that a stroke of luck?" I marveled.

"It was that day." He dug back into the fish. "I saw old Ethan tell the poor lass that our captain was dead. He showed Pearl's body as proof." He shook his head. "The captain would have to be dead before he'd let go o' his Pearl." He ripped out a fish bone and tossed it over. "I ran back to warn the crew, but they were all dead." He dug around and retrieved another bit of bone, tossing it. "Ethan used Pearl to get out but left his crew lost in the caves."

"Ethan drove Catherine off the cliff," I said, putting it together.

"Then he died," the cook said, setting aside the fish. Another whole one materialized in his hand. "I saw the entire thing. Nobody ever notices the cook. Nobody ever thanked me, either."

"My mother could probably relate," I told him.

"Well," he dug the knife into the fish's belly, "I buried Pearl. Used an iron ammunition box as a coffin. Figured the ship was mine at that point. But, nah. You ever tried sailing a pirate ship by yourself?" He pointed his bloody knife toward the bay. "I wrecked it into those rocks yonder. Had to swim back." He dug deep into the fish. "Alas, the *Fortune's Revenge* was no more."

"Well, what did you do?" Poor man. Stuck alone on Phantom Island.

He shrugged. "Well, if I couldn't have the boat, I'd take the island. Buried the crew. Kept their gold. Built a house out yonder."

That sounded like a desolate existence. "You just...stayed?"

He scratched his cheek with a fishy finger. "Oh, I visited the mainland from time to time, caught rides on the traders. Found myself a wife. My descendants still live here."

"Bill," I guessed. "Who would have thought?"

"That he's descended from a pirate? Diabolito would have laughed his butt off. But I can't complain. I kept all the stuff."

"And spread the story of Captain Bill and his bride."

"Not my fault it changed with the telling." He ripped the bones from the fish.

"Thanks for talking to me. Is there anything I can help you with before I go?" I asked.

"You brought peace to this place. I think I'm going to enjoy that very much."

I smiled and looked at Duranja, who had remained respectful during my entire ghostly encounter.

"I think I might have seen a whale in the fog," he offered.

It was a start.

"Let's walk around," I prompted, steering him away from the bridge.

"So we're headed for the pirate bar," he said, playing along.

"Where else?"

But to my surprise, he was a good sport. He let me open the door for him. And then he stood and accepted pats on the back from the various outlaws, half-drunk already, celebrating their win with good wine they'd ferried from the honeymoon suite.

"It got chilly all of a sudden," he said, shivering.

There was no party like a ghost pirate party. And now Duranja could say he'd been to one—if he ever chose to admit they existed.

"You!" Pock Face shoved aside his laughing, drinking compatriots to get to me.

Oh no. "Frankie!" I frantically scanned the bar.

Please be awake.

"You can guard our precious Pearl anytime!" he boomed, raising a mug of wine to toast.

"She's one heck of a bird." I smiled. "Thanks for trusting me with her."

He lost the grin for a second. "I never trusted you. But I did enjoy threatening you," he admitted before tipping his head back and howling with laughter.

"Hey, I'm looking for Frankie," I said, worried I hadn't spotted him yet.

The gangster was usually hard to miss.

Pock Face pointed his mug toward the back room.

I found Frankie seated near the head of the table, next to Diabolito, whom I'd learned was second-in-command.

"Frankie!" I said, thrilled to see him. "I'd hug you if I could."

"You already gushed enough," he said, pleased as punch. "It

was nice to finally get a good death scene." He turned to Diabolito. "This girl cried over me."

Diabolito guffawed. "A girl at home, a girl in port. You really are a pirate."

No way. Absolutely not. "That could not have been fun for you." He'd been stabbed, bleeding out. It had been awful.

"It was no picnic," Frankie admitted, "but you gotta admit, my last words were killer."

"Your last moments were," I agreed. He'd sacrificed himself to save me. That took internal fortitude. And growth. Although I didn't think Frankie would want to hear about it.

"I'll give you a minute with your live girl, Silver Tongue," the second-in-command said, slapping him on the shoulder before striding out, leaving us alone.

"You got a nickname?" I asked like a proud mamma.

"Yeah." Frankie grinned. "I like that it has money in it. And speaking of money." The gangster rubbed his hands together. "I hear the captain offered you all the loot you wanted. This is it. The mother lode. We're rich!"

"Um," I began.

But his eyes were wide with greed and excitement. "Did you go for the gold bars or the jewels? Or both?" He paced, thinking. "Gold bars are fun to stack but hard to move. I'll grant you that. But you had the whole crew at your disposal, seeing as you saved the captain *and* were their only way out. Gotta hold that power high over their heads, or they'll walk all over you. So yeah, gold and then jewels just for the wow factor and—" He saw the look on my face and halted.

"What did you do?" he demanded.

"I saved Captain Bill," I said, "from centuries of torture."

"And?" Little splotches appeared on his forehead.

"He rescued his bride," I said happily.

"*And?*" Frankie's hands formed fists.

"And I was so grateful you rescued me at great peril to yourself." Not just saving me from a beheading, but he'd voluntarily touched me for the first time since...ever.

"You were right. I'm a leader. I'm a respected member of the crew, so I stepped up," he gritted out.

"You don't seem as happy as you should be about that," I hedged.

"You didn't take the money, did you?" he asked, throwing up his hands.

"I took a lovely little parrot, just like Pearl. But I'd never sell it." It was a memento.

"And?" Frankie prodded.

"Well, I helped Duranja pick out a ring for Melody," I added.

The gangster swayed on his feet. "You don't even like him!"

"He's not so bad." We would be at odds again if he caught me snooping around somewhere I shouldn't once we returned to Sugarland, but what were the chances of that? "We're working it out," I assured him.

"Working it out?" He spun a circle. "I saved you so that you could grab the loot! Anything I steal goes back, but you could have kept it all. I admit, it's fun to take stuff temporarily, but we had a shot at permanent loot, and you messed it up. I could have had gold walls in my shed! A stack of ingots in the shape of Frisky Pete!"

"I thought you were past all of this. Don't you want to change and be free someday?" If his best shot to be ungrounded from my property had to do with shedding ties to his ashes and his life of crime, he had a long way to go.

"I am getting better," he said earnestly. He looked to the ground, then back at me. "I always wanted to be a leader. I just didn't think I could be."

"And now you are," I said, understanding. "You're right, that's a big step." It might not be the growth I'd envisioned. Then again, when did Frankie ever do what I expected?

"I almost wish I could stay," he added quietly.

"I'm sorry," I said. He was still tied to my property whether we wanted it or not.

"Nah," he said, waving me off. "I like my place. And I couldn't give Molly up. Not for anything." He removed the tricorn hat and tossed it onto the table. He thought twice and picked it up again. "But I did learn a few new tricks," he said, planting the hat back on his head again, sliding it down so that it covered the bullet hole in his forehead. "You ever heard of the dead man's scramble?"

"Never," I vowed. And I'd probably be sorry later that the mere thought of it made him grin.

"How about the short ship pickup?" he asked, pouring a drink.

"I'm going to regret this trip, aren't I?" I asked as he turned his back on me and began gathering books and papers. "They said I could take these. Well, maybe not all of them," he said, making a stack. "But they'll have to catch me if they want them back. How long until our ferry leaves?"

"Not soon enough," I told him, eager to get home and happy that he'd found a missing part of himself.

And grateful that I'd managed the same.

Epilogue

Six months later, I was telling the story to Lauralee's neighbor. She'd caught me out in the backyard, babysitting Lauralee's kids, and had been talking over the fence, trying to talk me into entering Lucy into a pet costume contest with her Maltese, Bernie. He had a great bee outfit, and Lucy could be a bird.

"Wait," she said, halfway through my tale of ghosts and pirate gold. She dashed into the house with Bernie barking and chasing after her, only to return with a glossy brochure. "My niece sent me this. She thought she recognized you."

The front featured a photo of a parrot swooping over a pirate map and read *Phantom Island Adventure Awaits!*

I cracked it open to find glossy photos of our weekend adventure. I saw the twins ringing the bell to win the treasure box quest. Ellis and me enjoying a glass of wine in the library, and Rick holding up his antique mug. And there was more, so much more.

Families digging for "buried treasure" in the sand, divers exploring the wreck of the pirate ship in the bay, cave tours featuring the excavation of the "pirate booty," kids hugging stuffed plush versions of Pearl.

"This is the way it should be." I smiled, running my fingers over a photo of Bill posing in full pirate gear next to Pearl's cage, which held a place of honor in the lobby of the hotel near the anchor of the *Fortune's Revenge*. The door of the cage stood open in front of a tray where visitors left coins and tokens for the taxidermied bird inside. A caption explained that Bill always left the cage door open because nothing could contain Pearl.

There was even a quote from me beside a photo of the restored rock bridge. "This is where the ghost bride waited for her lost love and reunited with him at last." –Verity Long, professional ghost hunter.

There was a photo of a couple on the restored rock bridge at sunset. Bill and the twins had taken care of Catherine and Captain Bill's special place, installing new handrails on both sides and clearing the slippery pebbles from the path.

And upon reading the caption, I learned it was a place to honor love.

Couples married there. Others would toss a pearl off the bridge to remember Catherine and for luck in finding their own true love.

Their memory would be honored, cherished, and remembered. Always.

"Melody picked a nice place for her birthday weekend," Meredith said, admiring the place the island had become.

"She did," I agreed. And I was thankful for it.

Note from Angie Fox

Thanks so much for running around on this crazy pirate adventure with me. I've always loved pirate legends, spooky caves, and hidden treasure puzzles. Dropping the gang into the middle of it all was too much fun to resist. Plus, we all know we'd never get to know Duranja a little better unless he could go a hot second without being able to threaten Verity with arrest. Working together instead of at odds is always better, right?

The next book brings us back to Sugarland and straight into the heart of the isolated, abandoned part of town near Maisie's house—the one you all keep asking me about. Yes, there's a reason why nobody goes there anymore and of course, it involves juicy secrets, 1950s ghosts, and Elvis. Death at the Drive-In releases on March 19, 2024!

If you'd like an email when each new book releases, visit my website to sign up for new release updates. I don't email often, but when I do, it's always something good.

Thanks for reading!

Angie

**Don't miss the next
Southern Ghost Hunter mystery
Death at the Drive-In**

Verity's quest to save her friend takes her to a long-abandoned
part of Sugarland where rockabilly ghosts rule.

Coming March 19, 2024!

About the Author

New York Times and *USA Today* best-selling author Angie Fox writes sweet, fun, action-packed mysteries. Her characters are clever and fearless, but in real life, Angie is afraid of basements, bees, and going up stairs when it's dark behind her. Let's face it: Angie wouldn't last five minutes in one of her books.

Angie earned a journalism degree from the University of Missouri. During that time, she also skipped class for an entire week so she could read Anne Rice's vampire series straight through. Angie has always loved books and is shocked, honored and tickled pink that she now gets to write books for a living. Although, she did skip writing for a week this past fall so she could read Victoria Laurie's Abby Cooper psychic eye mysteries straight through.

Angie makes her home in St. Louis, Missouri with a football-addicted husband, two kids, and Moxie the dog.

If you are interested in receiving an email each time Angie releases a new book, you can sign up for new release updates on her website.

Connect with Angie Fox online:
www.angiefox.com
angie@angiefox.com